Praise for
BRET LOTT
and
THE MAN WHO OWNED VERMONT

"Engrossing…one of the most interesting stories of the sadness of American men." — *Los Angeles Times*

"A vivid example of mind and spirit grappling with oppressive fates." *Time*, Recommended Fiction

"Beautifully written, quietly thrilling, exemplary in its compassion…a stunning debut." —Phillip Lopate, author of *The Rug Merchant*

"Bret Lott is a superb writer. *The Man Who Owned Vermont* has a deep and truthful message." —Barry Hannah, author of *Airships* and *Hey Jack!*

"An extraordinary book…full of surprises. Bret Lott is a talent to be reckoned with." —Josephine Humphreys, author of *Dreams of Sleep* and *Rich In Love*

"Bret Lott is an unnerving writer in that this story is so clean and apparently so familiar. But the surface is thin ice.…He tempts us onto that surface and lets us crash into the icy water of our not yet ruined hope. May many more books follow this one!" —James Baldwin

"Lott has given us in sparse and poetic prose, a tale about the power and intricacy of that thing called love. This novel, his first, leaves us waiting and eager for another." —*Atlantic Constitution-Journal*

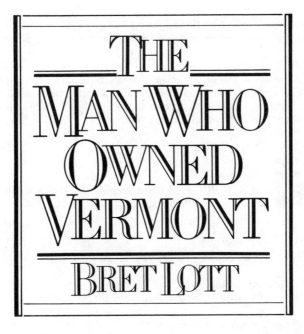

THE MAN WHO OWNED VERMONT

BRET LOTT

WASHINGTON SQUARE PRESS
PUBLISHED BY POCKET BOOKS
New York   London   Toronto   Sydney   Tokyo

PUTTERHAM

PBK

3 1712 01329 3637

Portions of this novel first appeared, in slightly different form, in the *Iowa Review, Writer's Forum, Ohio Journal,* and the *Yale Review.*

This novel is a work of fiction. Names, characters, places and incidents are either the product of the author's imagination or are used fictitiously. Any resemblance to actual events or locales or persons, living or dead, is entirely coincidental.

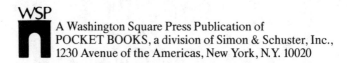

WSP

A Washington Square Press Publication of
POCKET BOOKS, a division of Simon & Schuster, Inc.,
1230 Avenue of the Americas, New York, N.Y. 10020

Published by arrangement with Viking Penguin Inc.
Library of Congress Catalog Card Number: 86-40427

ISBN: 0-671-64587-0

First Washington Square Press trade paperback printing May, 1988

10 9 8 7 6 5 4 3 2 1

WASHINGTON SQUARE PRESS and WSP colophon are registered trademarks of Simon & Schuster, Inc.

Printed in the U.S.A.

For Melanie Kai Lott

I was dumb and silent,
  I refrained even from good;
And my sorrow grew worse.

—Psalm 39

ONE

I liked this plumber. He had come to the front door and knocked solidly three times, then three times more before I could answer. I liked that, liked the sound six square knocks made through the apartment. I was there alone. I had things to sort out.

I opened the door, and the plumber stuck out his hand. "Lonny Thompson," he said. "Landlord sent me up. You've got a leak somewhere in your bathroom."

"Rick," I said. We shook hands. He knew how to shake hands; grasped my hand just past the knuckles, then squeezed hard and shook. I judged he was fifty, fifty-five years old.

He said, "Glad to meet you. Now where's this damned leak?"

He led me to the bathroom, as if he'd been here plenty of times, though I'd never seen him around the building before. We walked through the front room into the kitchen, then into the bathroom, the plumber turning his head, looking everything over. There wasn't much left in the apartment; my wife had taken most everything. Only the sofa bed and the black-and-white portable were left in the living room, one of those small rented refrigerators in the kitchen. Even the hamper in the bathroom was gone. "Moving in?" he asked once we were in the bathroom. He didn't look at me.

I said, "Well, not really." I didn't want to get into it.

He set the toolbox on the toilet lid. "Oh," he said, and started unbuttoning the gray down vest he wore over a red and black plaid wool shirt. He took off the vest, then the shirt, and dropped them both on the floor. Under the wool shirt he wore a gray workshirt, the same color as his pants, *Lonny* stitched in red thread above the shirt pocket. He had on old-fashioned plastic-framed glasses, the kind of frames that started out thick across the top and thinned down to wire along the bottom edge of the lenses. He went right to business, got down on his hands and knees and opened the cabinet beneath the sink.

I said, "Cold outside?"

"Where have you been?" he said, his head under the sink. "Thirty-five degrees and dropping. Supposed to get the first snow tonight. Believe it? Snow already."

I said, "I guess I haven't been paying much attention." I squatted down next to him to see if I could tell what he was doing, if I could learn something.

"Bet you haven't been paying much attention to any leaks then, neither." He laughed. "Your landlord called me this morning. Five feet square of ceiling in the apartment below came right down on the breakfast table." He pulled his head out from under the sink and looked at me. "How'd you like that for breakfast?" We both laughed. He went back under.

I said, "I know. He called me and told me the whole thing. That's a funny story." I stood up slowly, pushing on my knees, then picked up his shirt and vest from the floor. They both smelled of cigarettes—years of cigarettes burning down to the filter, I imagined, while he drained sink traps and tightened pipes; and they smelled of burnt wood. I imagined this plumber standing beside a campfire at dawn, a rifle crooked in his arms. I folded the shirt and vest and put them on the toilet tank.

I went to the bedroom and looked out the window. There had been a good blow several days before. Most every leaf had been stripped off the trees, and I saw things I hadn't been able to see in the summer, things like the Ford dealership sign on the main street in town, the charcoal-colored hills, chimneys. The sky was an even ash gray all the way across. He was right about the snow coming.

All these things looked strange under that gray sky, but what seemed most strange was that the grass down in the yard was still green. That green next to all those bare gray trees and the gray sky and the hills looked odd.

I went back into the bathroom, and I don't think he even knew I had left. I said, "Do you know what the problem is? Do you know what's wrong?" I sat on the edge of the tub.

"Tell you the truth, I don't." He pulled out from under the sink, closed the cabinet, and sat Indian-style on the floor. "All those pipes look fine. No loose fittings, no water marks, no nothing. But you better believe there's a leak somewhere." He motioned toward me. "I want to look at the tub next."

I got up quickly and pulled back the curtain.

The plumber kneeled against the tub and ran his fingers along the edge where the walls and the tub met. "This caulking along here can go," he said, "and then every damn time you're standing in the shower, water'll seep down through these joints and collect beneath the tub. I seen that happen before." He came to a small crack on the lip of the tub, stopped and examined it a moment, then went on. "I seen it happen once where all the water collected underneath the floor beneath the tub. This was a bathroom on the first floor of a house, and they didn't have their basement heated. Know what happened?" He grinned up at me. "All this water's been collecting, and then a big freeze came along and the water froze, broke right through the bottom of the tub, put a half-inch crack three feet long right down the center. I seen that."

I said "No," and crossed my arms.

He finished checking the seal around the tub. "Your caulking's not shot, that's for sure. Not the greatest, but not shot to hell." He then started feeling the floor along the tub, pressing down every few inches with the palm of his hand. "Pull your curtain closed," he said.

I leaned over him and pulled it along the rod, stepping over him still kneeling and feeling the floor. I said, "What do you think?"

"You do keep the bottom of the shower curtain inside the tub when you shower, don't you?" he said.

I said, "Of course," and laughed.

"You'd be surprised," he said without looking up.

He checked either end of the tub where the curtain touched the walls. "You know sometimes water sprays out of these edges. Sometimes people don't get these curtains completely closed." He flipped the ends of the curtain back and forth to see where they fell. "Do you have a glass?" he asked, very matter-of-fact, as though the question were the next logical thing to say. "And fill it with water," he added. He was still flipping the curtain back and forth.

I got the red plastic cup from the toothbrush holder and filled it. I handed it to him, expecting him to drink it.

"Sometimes along the floor, water can seep in, too," he said. "This is a good test." He then poured the cup of water on the floor along the edge of the tub. "How about another?" he said. I filled it again, and he emptied it on the floor. "If it seeps down and disappears, why then we've found our leak."

But the water did nothing, only sat in a puddle along the entire edge of the tub. We watched that water for a good three minutes, but nothing happened. "Well," the plumber finally said, "that's not your problem, either. I was afraid of this." He stood and dusted off his hands, though I was sure they weren't dirty. "We better mop this up." He waved at the floor.

I got the last clean towel from the closet and dropped it on the water, pushed it along the tub with my foot.

He said, "I'll bet it's your toilet. If it's your toilet, we've got troubles. Your landlord's got troubles."

I dropped the wet towel in the tub.

He took his tool chest from the toilet lid, set it on the floor, then lifted the lid and flushed the toilet. "Toilets I hate," he said. "That's why I always wait until last for them. Some plumbers don't mind them, some love them. Me, I hate them. Too much water swirling up around everywhere." He stood over the bowl, looking at it as though it would say something to him. After a moment he closed the lid, and saw his folded shirt and vest on the tank. I picked them up, felt to make sure the radiator was cold, then set the shirt and vest there.

"Thanks, buddy," he said.

He set the tank lid on the toilet seat, then flushed the toilet again and played with the bulb, flicking it up and down. He reached his hand down into the rising water and opened and closed the round hatch at the bottom. The inside walls of the tank were all brown and rusted, making the outside of the tank look that much whiter. He put the lid back on, then got down on his hands and knees again. He started feeling the floor around the base of the toilet, just as he had along the tub, pressing the palm of his hand down every few inches to test it.

I assumed he was going to ask for another cup of water, so I filled the red plastic cup. I stood with the cup of water and said, "You need some water?"

He had already worked halfway around the toilet; his head was back under the tank. He stopped feeling the floor. "Christ, is that all you do?" he said over his shoulder. "Ask questions?" He forced a laugh, but I knew he meant what he said. He went back to testing the floor. "There's enough water in this damn toilet already. If there's a leak, I'll find it with the water that's already here, thank you."

I dumped the water into the sink. "Sorry," I said. I stepped over him and started out the door.

"Hey," he said. I turned around. From where I stood I could see his face under the toilet tank. He was smiling, and said, "Hey, it's these damn toilets I hate. Sorry."

"That's okay," I said. I squatted and watched while he tinkered with a knob on a pipe leading from the tank to the floor.

A few minutes later he was finished. He got up and again dusted off his hands.

He said, "I'll be damned if I can find what's your problem. I can't find no leak anywhere, so it must be somewhere down in the floor, down below here. I've seen some strange things before, some strange plumbing problems, so nothing I find'll be a surprise." He flushed the toilet again. "You can never tell what's going on when it comes to plumbing," he said, staring at the bowl. "Maybe there's a leak in the roof and when it rains the water pours down between these walls and collected in the ceiling of that apartment below. I've seen that happen before, too. I've seen the ceiling of a first-floor apartment fall in because there was a leak in the roof three floors up." He looked at me, then at his shirt and vest on the radiator. "But I'll be damned if I can find a leak here in this bathroom."

He reached for his shirt, but I picked it up first, unfolded it and handed it to him. He sort of smiled as he put it on and buttoned it up. Then I handed him the vest.

He said, "So did you say you were moving in or moving out?"

I put my hands in my pockets. I figured I would have to say it to someone sometime, and I liked this plumber. "Neither, actually," I said. "I guess my wife was the one who moved out." I waited for some reaction. I waited for him to say something.

But he only finished buttoning up the vest, then picked up his toolbox and led me out of the bathroom, through the kitchen and back into the front room. He glanced around the room again.

"One thing's for sure, though," he said.

I said, "Oh?"

"Yeah," he said, "your landlord's going to have to spring for a new toilet sometime soon. That one in there's about shot." He stood at the door, his hand on the knob. "I'd say that one in there's at least fifteen years old, and it's not a very good one. He's going to have to get a new one, and I don't envy him having to pay for it."

"How much do they cost?" I said. I wanted to listen to this plumber talk about things he knew.

"Really depends," he said. He seemed to enjoy talking about it, and took his hand off the knob. "You can buy a good one for, oh, about a hundred fifty, hundred seventy-five. Last you a good twenty years. But then on the other hand you could buy a cheap one, seventy-five to a hundred, have it last fifteen years, and have to flush it three times just to make sure everything goes down." He pushed an imaginary lever on an imaginary toilet several times to show me what he meant.

He turned and opened the door, and I could smell the cigarettes and burnt wood. I didn't want this plumber to leave. I wanted him to stay and tell me more about plumbing, more stories. I said, "I guess you know a lot. About plumbing, I mean."

"Thirty years," he said, and pointed to his head. He smiled. "Thirty years." He walked out into the hall, turned and said, "I'll be seeing you whenever that landlord of yours decides to spring for that toilet. So long."

I said, "See you." I started to close the door, then stepped out into the hall.

"Lonny," I said. "Hey, Lonny."

He was already a few steps down the stairs, but stopped and turned around. He looked surprised. He stared at me a few seconds, then put his hand on the back of his neck.

"Jesus, buddy. Jesus, Rick," he said. He seemed to look past me. "Don't ask me," he said. "Don't ask me a goddamn thing about anything other than plumbing. I'm just the plumber."

I stood there a moment. He looked away. I said, "You hunt, right?"

"Yeah, I hunt," he said. He was quiet a moment, then said, "I'll call you sometime when we go hunting. When we go deer hunting. You can go with us. I know where you live." He waved and disappeared down the stairs.

"All right," I called down. "I'll be here."

Back in the apartment I could still smell his shirt and vest. I looked out the window at the odd green against the gray, and smelled the cigarettes and burnt wood. I knew he would call me.

I stood at the window a few minutes, looking down at the lawn, and then Lonny came from inside onto the steps, walked across the grass. He was carrying his toolbox. He crossed the street, the collar of his shirt turned up and covering his ears. His pickup was parked at the curb across the street, a dull red Dodge with LONNY'S PLUMBING AND HEATING painted across the rear panel of the bed. He climbed in, started the engine. A blue cloud of smoke and steam poured out the tailpipe. He drove off.

That was Saturday morning. I looked at my watch, saw it was only eleven forty. I had the rest of the day to do whatever it was I had to do. Sort things out.

I flipped on the set, sat on the sofa and watched a pregame show. I watched the game that followed, and the one after that. It wasn't until the third quarter of that second game that I looked out the window and saw the snow coming down. Snow had already collected a half-inch on the bottom edge of the window pane. It was a fine powder, not heavy, but constant, and I knew we'd have a long snow.

I turned back to the set. One of the teams had just scored a touchdown, a black player standing in the end zone, his arms above his head, his knees buckling beneath him in a slow dance.

It snowed the rest of the afternoon and into the night; by the time the apartment was dark except for the bright black-and-white images from the set the snowflakes had become larger, heavier, more like pieces of cinder falling in the dark. Near nine I unfolded the sofa bed, made and ate a sandwich, and then went to bed.

The set played all night, and I remember waking up now and then to some old movie, and to the black snow falling outside the window. That is how I dealt with the situation that first weekend. That is how I began to sort things out.

Paige had left the Wednesday before. It wasn't as if I hadn't known a thing about it, either. I had known. I had known there would be one day, one moment, one instant when I would see she was actually going to do it. That instant came Tuesday night, when I came home from work, set the keys on the television set, and heard her crying. I went back to the bedroom where I found her sitting on the floor, her back against the wall, her legs up against her chest. She hugged her legs, and cried without looking at me. This was the moment I knew she was gone.

The next morning a man I'd never seen before, a young guy with a droopy mustache, pulled up outside in a U-Haul truck. He got out. He held a piece of paper in his hand, looked at it, then up toward our window. I was watching all this from the front room. He entered the building.

"Don't worry," Paige said from somewhere behind me. I didn't turn around. "He's no one. No one you should worry about." She was quiet, then said, "He's just a kid from U-Haul. I hired him to give me a hand. He's no one."

I turned around, my arms crossed. Paige stood in the doorway between the kitchen and front room. She was wearing an old green and red plaid flannel shirt and gray sweat pants, her hair just brushed through. She wore no makeup, her eyes no less red and puffy than they had been last night. She would think herself ugly like this, I knew, but she wasn't.

I looked down at the floor. "So who should I?" I said. "Who should I worry about?" Before I even let out the words I knew there was no need for me to say them. There was no one. She was leaving because of what was inside this apartment, not because of something she was headed for out there.

She laughed, put her hands on her hips. She looked down

and shook her head because we had been over this before, and because we both knew that what I had said just then was only something said. It meant nothing.

"What about work?" I said, and looked back to the window.

"I called and told them I'd be off today." She went back to the bedroom. "What about you?" she called out.

I heard her in the room, heard things moving around. She came back into the front room with our two suitcases and a garment bag.

The U-Haul boy knocked at the door. Neither of us moved. She stood with the bags, I stood with my arms crossed.

"Small day," I said. "I can write my orders from here, then head in later."

"You're not going to help here," she said. She set the bags down. The U-Haul boy knocked again.

"Fine," I said. I went to the door, opened it. The U-Haul boy stood there smiling, a set of multicolored papers in his hand. He had on jeans and a UMass sweatshirt.

"Mrs. Wheeler here?" he said.

I stepped to the side, pointed at my wife.

After a moment he quit smiling as, I figured, he pieced together what might be going on here this Wednesday morning.

I spent the rest of that morning watching my wife and my belongings move out while I sat on the sofa: here came the mattress and box spring, my wife and the young man struggling to clear the threshold and turn toward the stairs; next the dark oak footboard and headboard; the mirror from the dresser, then the dresser itself; the nightstand, the lamp, the hamper, the color TV, the bookshelves, the coffee table. Then the U-Haul boy brought up boxes from the truck, and the two of them stood in the kitchen folding and taping, folding and taping, neither saying a word. Things were placed in the boxes unwrapped and in no order. She put plates and food from the cupboards and refrigerator in the same box, then he carried the box out; she emptied clothes from the closet and pots and pans into another box, and so on.

The last thing they took out was the refrigerator. The U-Haul boy brought his hand truck upstairs. The refrigerator had been unplugged when they first took out the food. I could feel already the warmth building inside the box, so that when Paige and this boy finally opened up the refrigerator in its new home out would pour this musty, stale air, and that would be me, I thought, that would be me for her.

They fought with the box down the stairs. I heard each loud bump as that refrigerator fell from one step down to the next. When they'd finally made it to the bottom of the stairwell I heard the U-Haul boy's voice, and then heard Paige laugh.

She came back upstairs alone, walked to the middle of the room, stood there.

"Well?" I said. My voice was loud in the room. My voice banged off the walls.

"Well," she said.

I looked up at her, then to the light fixture above her head, then to the wall behind her.

"Last time," she said. "There's not another chance." She held her hands behind her back. "As it is I'm not going to come back in here if you spill everything here and now. I'm not moving everything back in here just because you tell me exactly why you're doing what you're doing."

But I wouldn't break. She knew why. She knew the whole thing. She wanted me to say out loud to her what I knew we'd both been thinking about the last six months. She waited for me, waited, and then she was gone, out the door and down to the truck where the U-Haul boy, seated on the passenger side, waited for her. I watched from the window as she climbed in and drove off.

So that this feeling of waiting was strong in me when I woke up Sunday morning, the television still on, the snow outside still coming down. I sat up in bed, and waited until I recognized the room.

I threw the sheets back, put my bare feet on the cold floor. I stood and went to the window. I no longer had the green against the gray to worry about: snow had covered everything, and hung thick on empty branches. The snowflakes were now big and wet and fell quickly; the air had already started to warm up. A car drove by, silent on the snow. The snowplows had not made it out yet. There was this, too, to wait for. All these things: the snowplows, the melting, that green beneath the white, Lonny. Paige.

Monday morning I was back at work. Wednesday I had done as I told Paige I would: I had filled out sales orders from the sofa, guessing the number of cases of RC, Diet Rite and Schweppes mixers my independents and package stores would need. It had not been difficult to do this. I knew my route well. Thursday and Friday morning I had called Glenn Mitchell, my supervisor, and told him I couldn't make it in. I had told him I had the flu.

My first stop was a Price Chopper on King Street. It was about six thirty. Most of the snow had melted Sunday so that now the parking lot was covered with brittle sheets of ice that shattered and cracked as I walked toward the store. I hadn't known how I would feel getting back to work. I still didn't.

I got to the front entrance of the place, and stopped. I had my route book, my pens; I had fact sheets on all our sales. I was wearing my light blue RC shirt and navy blue tie, my company-issue navy blue pants, my steel-toed black shoes. I had on my RC jacket. I had everything. I looked up into the blue-black sky, saw a few stars. My breath shot out of me in a cloud as I looked at that cold sky.

My route book under one arm, I turned to the Out door and pulled it open, walked in.

On top of one of the registers was a small radio, the check-stand microphone taped onto the radio's speaker. ZZ Top blasted across the market. Cardboard boxes were everywhere along the front aisle and down each grocery aisle. Stockers, dressed in old jeans and T-shirts, were kneeling, quickly cutting open more boxes, throwing stock onto shelves, facing cans, bottles, what have you.

I breathed in the warm air heavy with bakery smells. I listened to the loud, fast music, heard stockers singing as loud as they could as they worked. I had forgotten over the past few days that Thanksgiving was coming up, was next week. The last time I had been in here was a week ago, and since then they had put up Christmas decorations. Red and green tinsel garlands hung from the fluorescent lights, from the meat case at one end of the store to the bread aisle at the other. Cardboard reindeer hung from the ceiling by fishline. A huge stuffed Santa stood atop the courtesy booth.

I looked around. It felt good being in here.

I made my way through the checkstand and past the cardboard to the soda aisle. I'd usually run into the Coke or Pepsi salesman about this time, but no one was there. I checked my product, wrote down on the back of a Day-Glo carton stuffer how many cases of what I'd need to fill the shelf. There wasn't much I could put up. Coke owned the shelf in this part of the state: I had two facings of cans for RC, they had twelve for Coke. I had two for Diet Rite; they had eight each for Tab and Diet Coke.

It was with Schweppes that I made some money. My mixers were about even with Canada Dry facings. They outsold us at the holidays, but not by much. And this year we'd been told by our supervisors things were up at the main office, that they were working to change things this year. Schweppes, they told us, would outsell Canada Dry this year.

The mixer shelf was blown, and I wrote down how many cases I'd need from the back room: three tonic, four club soda, four ale, one bitter lemon, one diet tonic. I turned and headed down the aisle toward the rear of the store and the back room.

A voice came over the speaker. "Wheeler the RC man," it said. It was Cal, the assistant manager. "See me in the back room. The rest of you shits clear the cardboard. Opening in twenty minutes." The radio came back on, Van Halen.

I smiled, then laughed, and that feeling, the jump of my chest as I laughed, reminded me of how long it had been since I had. I had laughed when Lonny told me of the ceiling falling in below me. That was it. That was the last time. I went to the back room.

More cardboard was piled up in the back room. Three bag boys, all young and pimple-faced, were baling. One bag boy stood at the edge of the cardboard pile and threw cardboard into the mouth of the baler, another arranged the cardboard so that none hung out of the bin, and the third worked the controls, pushing the button that brought down the protective cage door and then started the steel slab down onto the trash, smashing it into a bale. When the slab had smashed as far as it could, the bag boy at the controls pushed another button. The slab rose, the cage door opened, the first bag boy threw in more trash.

The doors from the grocery floor banged open then, and Cal came in, yelling. "What the shit you assholes think you're doing? Three shits for a job one of you could do? What do you think?" He brushed my shoulder as he went at them. He hadn't looked at me. "You think I'm some kind of idiot I can't tell you're all jacking off back here? You don't think we're really opening in fifteen minutes? You don't think frozen, milk, and nine through sixteen haven't been cleared yet? And you shits still got to mop? Then bag some old lady's groceries soon as doors open?" His back was to me, one hand on his hip, the other in front of him in a fist. "Carl, get the hell off the buttons. You and John get over to frozen and start filling carts with trash, and Bob, you stay here and bale. Got it?" The three boys stood with their arms at their sides, nodded. Carl and John, the one who had arranged the trash after it had been thrown in, ran past me and out the double doors to the grocery floor. Bob continued throwing cardboard into the baler.

Cal turned to me. He was grinning, then shouted after the two bag boys, "And you shits want to be clerks."

I was smiling, too. Cal came up to me, slapped me on the shoulder. "How the hell are you, Wheeler?" he said. He was shorter than me, with red wavy hair that fell and curled just above his ears. He had a mustache more sandy than red, and he was a little overweight. He was wearing corduroys and workboots, a paint-stained sweatshirt. His arms were big, and his slaps on my shoulder always came harder than I expected.

"Same," I said. "Killing myself. Or trying to."

He turned, walked back toward the stairs up to the office. His turning and walking away was a sign for me to follow him.

"So," I said. "You called me back here just so I could stand there and watch you chew out your boys?"

"Hell yes," he said. We started up the wooden staircase, Cal two steps above me. "Nothing better for you. You don't sell enough RC shit in here to warrant your coming out to sell *me* stuff. Just thought I'd entertain you. Felt sorry for you is all."

"Thank you," I said.

We went into the office, a long, white room with large windows looking down onto the grocery floor. Desks sat under the windows. I could see the entire grocery area, from the front row of registers and the flower shop to the frozen aisle where two boys broke down cardboard boxes in slow motion.

"They don't seem to have learned much," I said.

Cal was taking off his sweatshirt, had it pulled up over his head. His T-shirt was pulled up around his chest, and I saw his pale, fat stomach. He finished pulling off the sweatshirt, then pulled down the T-shirt.

"Punks," he said. He dropped the sweatshirt on the floor, opened a desk drawer and pulled out a wadded-up white dress shirt. He pulled it on, buttoned the top collar button. He turned to the window and looked down at the two. "Those punks are worthless. But union says we have to give them thirty days. I'll tell you, it's only been six, and I can tell those two aren't going to make it. They won't. I should write notes to their mothers, pin them on their shirts so they won't lose them." He'd finished buttoning up the shirt, then shoved the tails into his pants. He opened one drawer, then another and another, then moved to another desk and opened another drawer before he found a clip-on tie. "That note'd read, 'Dear Mrs. Whose-its. Here's your shithead son. Please keep him at home until he can move faster than shit through a turtle.' " He laughed, put on the tie.

I smiled, turned from the window.

He took a lime-green vest from the coat rack behind the door, put it on. "Big news, eh? Going to be a big holiday for you."

"What?" I said.

"The big news from headquarters. From the big boys." He looked at me, his mouth straight, his head tilted. He straightened his vest.

"The shelf's blown, if that's what you mean. I'm filling it before I take off."

He buttoned the vest, then turned to a desk. He shuffled through loose sheets of paper on the desktop. He found one, pulled it out of the mess, then shook it in my face. It was one of our fact sheets, the one about Schweppes mixers for the holidays.

"This came down in the mail Saturday, along with a nice, sweet, mamby-pamby letter from the buyer explaining that from the Monday before Thanksgiving until the day after New Year's you've got an end display of Schweppes."

I said, "Great." I said, "Finally." I didn't say anything more.

"Are you all right?" he said. He put the paper on the desk. "I mean, you sick still?"

"Still getting over the flu," I said.

"The flu. That's what that punk substitute salesman of yours said on Thursday. A kid not much older and with not many less pimples than those two down there."

I looked back to the frozen food aisle, where the two bag boys were still dogging it. Cal sat on the edge of the desk. "But there's nothing I can do about them, except can them when the probation period is over. So what I've got to do is put up with it." He looked down at his feet, then at me. "You don't look sick to me," he said. "Maybe you're not feeling good, but I don't think it's because you're sick."

I turned to the window.

"Shit," he said. He stood and straightened his tie again, pulled the vest down to cover his belly as best he could. "What do I care? You're just the RC salesman. No, now you're the Schweppes salesman. Wheeler dealer the Schweppes man." He laughed. I gave a little laugh, too.

I followed him down the stairs to the back room and out onto the floor. He showed me the end he wanted the Schweppes on: a full end on the bread aisle. It was a good spot. Coke had a two-liter display there right now. I would have to have all their product repacked before we could start our own display. It was a big job, but the case sales would more than make up for the problems of building the thing. I started thinking of the extra money this would bring, extra money for Christmas, but then I thought, for whom? To spend on what?

I took down his case order, a number, he told me, that had also come down from the buyers. "Nothing's left to me any more," he said. "I can't even order my own stock any more." He ordered straight from the letter he held in his hand. "One hundred twenty-five cases to start, and then keep the back room stocked at twenty-five cases per for ale, club soda, tonic, ten cases per for bitter lemon and diet tonic."

By the time I'd stocked the shelves, filled out the order sheets, and straightened my area in the back room, the store was open. I went out onto the grocery floor. The bag boys still had three aisles left to clear. The floor still had to be mopped.

Cal stood at one end of an aisle, the two boys midway down and breaking up cardboard boxes a little faster than when I had seen them from the office. I came up behind Cal, heard him shout in a whisper, "You punks keep this pace up and those old bags who just walked in'll have your jobs. Those old women can bag faster than you shits. Can mop, too."

I stood next to him, said, "You've only got a couple weeks to put up with them. Think about that. Your problem's going to go away."

He looked at me. His face was red from the shouting, his

neck muscles taut. Then he laughed out loud, slapped my shoulder again. "Wheeler dealer the Schweppes man," he said. "You get over your being sick. It's just not worth it."

Outside the sun was about up, everything—my car, the market, the rows of empty grocery carts along the front window—bathed in a faint blue, almost violet. Ice still cracked under me as I made my way to the car, climbed in.

I was home by five. Though I'd had my biggest day since just before Labor Day, merchandising had been light. Most of the day had been spent filling out paperwork: display request forms, sales order sheets, my tally sheet, special product delivery for some stores. Some managers, like Cal, wanted the displays up as soon as possible, and I'd had at one point to call Mitchell at the office and ask exactly how many displays I could expect to have built the next day.

"Not enough," he'd said over the phone, then coughed his smoker's cough. "Funny thing. Lynn Andros did too good a job selling to the buyers. We've got too many displays coming in. Everyone wants them tomorrow. No chance."

"So how many?" I asked again. I was at a phone booth outside a D'Amour's Big Y. I wanted to know what I could promise before heading in and talking to someone.

"Hell, go ahead, Ricky. Promise them the whole goddamn world, you want to. Be a salesman. We'll take care of it. We'll cover you."

I'd known his "We'll cover you" meant he couldn't, and so I'd had to have all my cases after that post-delivered. More paperwork.

At the office all I'd done was turn in my orders, my display requests, post my sales on the board, then I took off. Some of the men who'd been filling in their sales on the board when I'd come in were still at it when I left, still marking in with a green pen on the room-length board all sales of items over projection, using a red pen for sales under. Everyone's Schweppes were in the green today. Everyone's. I'd overheard some of them talking about going over to the Rusty Nail to drink and celebrate, but I took off. I hadn't even checked in with Mitchell.

I went into the apartment, dropped the keys on the set like I had done every night I'd lived there. But now the set was a black-and-white portable, the old Zenith we'd had for a couple years before we bought the color one Paige took with her. I thought about that, about the TV set, about when the room had been filled with furniture and the walls hung with pictures and a candle set on the kitchen table. I sat down on the couch.

We had been fighting again. Probably about money, though I'm not sure. Money was something we fought a lot about then. Or maybe it was some guy I'd seen her talking with when I visited her at the department store the night before. Regardless, we were fighting again.

We'd been married a little over two years at that time. This was before I took a job as merchandiser at RC, back when I was a stock clerk at a Food King in Springfield, working midnight to nine, Paige working at a department store in Holyoke, back before she'd got on at the university. We were living in Springfield in an old brick apartment building behind the Motor Vehicle Registry.

She'd said, "Do you want a divorce? Do you want a divorce?" She pulled off her wedding rings and tossed them into the ring tray on the dresser. I followed her into the bathroom, where she started to brush her hair. Her teeth were clenched.

"Listen," I said. "Listen." But then I stopped. "You don't even understand," I said. I took off my ring then, too, and threw it in the bathroom trash. I looked down into the garbage, but couldn't see the ring among the Kleenex and Q-Tips.

I turned and went into the living room, took the car keys from the top of the TV, and slammed the door behind me.

That was how that battle finished. I won.

I got into the car and raced the engine as if the sound were some sort of victory cry. I knew she heard it, the apartment we were

living in back then only one floor up, the bathroom window facing
the parking area. And so, for greater effect, I shoved the car in
reverse, backed out, and did the best I could to make the tires
squeal as I took off. They didn't.

So maybe we'd married too young. So we hardly ever saw
each other, what with our schedules the way they were. I've
known lots of people who've made bigger mistakes. But those are
things that have been gone over time and again. It was this fight.
This fight in particular.

This fight in particular because I just took off, drove north
on the interstate, not knowing if or when I'd turn around and go
home to fish my ring out of the junk in the trash basket. Sometimes you need to be by yourself for a while, and north seemed
best. Neither of us had ever been north of Greenfield, never been
to Vermont or New Hampshire, not to mention Maine. We had
once made it to Albany, for what reason I can't remember, but
never north.

And so I headed that way. Paige had never been to Vermont.
Paige had never set foot in that state, and I had won the fight. I
would go and claim it for my own.

There was not much to be seen in the way of civilization
along the interstate between Springfield and Vermont. There was
the mill in Holyoke, some houses, billboards, etc., around Northampton, the Motel-6 in Deerfield, some more buildings near
Greenfield. Still, the closer I got to Vermont the more anxious I
became, until when I finally crossed the border I nearly laughed
out loud.

At that moment anything was possible. There was a car in
front of me, a girl driving. I thought, I can seduce that girl. I can
pull up next to her, roll down my window, ask her to coffee in
Brattleboro, and the rest would be easy. I own Vermont, I thought.
It belongs to me and Paige will never have it. I glanced at the girl
as I passed. She didn't even look at me. But then, why should
she have?

Like the drive up, Brattleboro, too, was nothing much to shout
about. At least what I saw of it. I drove down the main street off

the interstate, past a used-car dealer, a shopping center, convenience stores, bars, and whatever else you find in these small towns. I stopped the car at a package store and bought a single bottle of one of those expensive imported dark beers, then used the inside lip of the ashtray to open it up. Some of the beer spilled into the ashtray, but I didn't mind. I laughed a little.

I started home, there not being much gas left, maybe enough to get me back to the apartment, and Paige to work and back the next day, and I realized I was thinking about her and knew I would have to face her when I got home. As I crossed the border, I thought, I will have to walk up those stairs and open the door, set the keys back on the TV, and face Paige. I pictured her still brushing her hair, teeth still clenched, and her hand pulling the brush back through her hair with quick strokes like it was a knife. She tilted her head down and to one side, looked out the corners of her eyes to the reflection of her auburn hair, and stabbed me, stabbed me. If she felt like that, I thought, I would dig my ring out of the trash and drop it into the garbage disposal and turn it on. To hell with her.

I got home near nine and, it being one of Paige's nights off, found her sitting on the sofa watching television. She ignored me and stared at the set. I dropped the keys on the set and waved at her, the empty beer bottle in my hand. She did not blink. I just sort of laughed at her then and made a hissing sigh. Once I was in the kitchen, though, she spoke.

"Where have you been?" she said. "Wasting money, I suppose."

She couldn't break me. "Nowhere. Around." I looked for something to eat, opened the refrigerator and nosed around. I found some egg salad in a Tupperware dish and some bread and closed the door.

She said, "And drinking. Driving and drinking. Smart."

I set the dish and bread on the counter, opened the kitchen garbage can and dropped the beer bottle in, making sure to strike it on an empty jelly jar at the bottom. Both the bottle and jar broke. "Smart enough to know when to get away from you," I said. I was in rare form.

After I made my sandwich I heard her get up from the sofa. She turned the television off and came into the kitchen. I walked back into the bedroom and sat on the bed with my sandwich. I wanted her to follow me this time. I took a bite and noticed that her rings were no longer in the tray. "Where are your rings?" I called out. "In the garbage disposal?"

She came into the bedroom, crossed her arms and leaned against the closet door. The rings were back on her finger, and it looked like tears were in her eyes.

"Look," she said. "Look, stop it. Let's stop it. Let's stop fighting."

I set the sandwich down on the night stand and stood up, put my arms around her. "I'm sorry," I said. "I'm sorry we fight. You're right. We have to stop. Don't cry." She leaned against me. I felt her tears through my shirt. "Don't cry," I said again. I think I meant it, too.

"I can't help it," she said into my shoulder, then pulled away and wiped her eyes with the back of her hand.

"Here," I said, and held her face in my hands and wiped a tear with my thumb. "Let's go find my ring." I led her out of the bedroom and into the bathroom. I sat on the toilet and put the trash basket on my lap, started fishing through the garbage. Paige sat on the edge of the tub and wiped her nose with a Kleenex.

I poked around for a few minutes looking for that ring, and then I said it. Why, I do not know. Maybe because I wanted her to feel better. Maybe I just wanted to talk.

I said, "You know, I wasn't going to tell you this, but I own Vermont." I looked up from the garbage to Paige. She blinked a couple of times, her eyes still red.

"What?" she said.

I went back to the garbage. "I said I own Vermont. That's

where I went tonight. To Vermont. You've never been there before, so I claimed it for myself." I found the ring at the bottom of the basket and pulled it out. "Here it is," I said. I smiled and slipped the ring on my finger. "You know what I mean?"

She looked at me. "You shouldn't have told me," she said.

I said, "Why not?" but by that time I think I already understood. By that time I saw how far ahead of me she really was, how much more she could see than me.

"You told me," she said. "You told me, and you shouldn't have. Now I know."

She took it from me just like that.

She stood up and held her hand out to me, and I remember looking up at her and thinking, That close. That close, but I knew she was right, and that I had lost.

I woke up not remembering having fallen asleep. I jerked my head up, blinked. The room was dark except for the faint, deep blue from the window. From where I sat on the sofa I could see one or two stars, sharp-edged and white in the crisp air. The room was cold; I'd forgotten to turn the heat up when I came home. I opened my mouth. My ears felt hot, and I was hungry.

The phone rang. I stood, walked along the front of the sofa, my hand out in front of me in the dark. The phone rang again. I knelt down at the end of the sofa, felt around the floor for the phone. I found it, picked up the receiver. I put it to my head, and felt the cord end at my ear. I turned the receiver around, said, "Hello?" The plastic was cold against my head.

"Gene?" a woman said.

I was quiet a moment, then said, "Nope. No Gene."

"Sorry," she said, and hung up.

I knelt there, my knees on the hardwood floor, while the blue outside deepened and more stars came out. I got up, sat on the end of the sofa. I dialed information, my fingers counting over which square buttons to push on which row.

"What city?" the operator said. It was a man.

"Northampton," I said. "Maybe Amherst."

"Name?"

I held the receiver to my ear a few seconds before I hung up. Though I'd known him for two years now, ever since I'd taken the route, I didn't know Cal's last name.

I couldn't remember having sold more Schweppes since I'd started for the company. We had end and island displays in all Price Choppers, Stop & Shops, Food Kings, Big Ys, all the big chains. It had meant extra work for all of us; sometimes we didn't have enough display men to cover all the displays going up, and so Mitchell and the other supervisors had us build some of our own, smaller displays in the independents.

It didn't matter. I liked doing the extra work, liked having to plan out exactly how a display should stand, liked having to throw cans of tomato sauce or two-liters of Coke into grocery carts in order to clear an A-bin for the end. I folded cardboard trays, laid them out this way and then another, figuring the best and most sturdy way to stack product four, five, and six trays high. I enjoyed wheeling product out of the back room onto the floor, then opening the boxes and pricing the bottles. Older women would ask me where Tender Vittles were or where they could find deli dill pickles. In the past I'd pointed at the RC logo sewn to my shirt, said, "I don't work for the store, ma'am." But now I was stopping and helping, walking them a few aisles over to whatever it was they wanted, as though I were interested myself in knowing exactly where Chicken Rondelles could be found. Then I'd go back to my product, finish pricing, dust it and put it in the trays. I'd stack up the empty boxes on my hand truck, go back to the back room, toss the boxes into the baler, wheel out more product.

This was how I spent the rest of that week. Thursday, the day I called back on Cal's market, was Cal's day off. I'd made it a point when I'd come in that morning to ask one of the stockers what his last name was.

I came up to one of the stockers working the cookies/crackers aisle. I said, "Maybe you can tell me. What's Cal's last name?" I was embarrassed asking the question because I was Cal's salesman and should have known his last name a long time ago.

"Riley," he quickly answered without looking up. He didn't lose a beat as he threw boxes of Ritz crackers onto the shelf. The case empty, he tossed it aside, pulled a box cutter from his apron, then removed the top from another cardboard case with four quick strokes. He put up more product.

I worked as late as I could, got up as early as I could, so that by the weekend I'd nearly forgotten what the inside of this blank apartment looked like in daylight. One night I'd done the laundry; the towel I'd used to sop up the water Lonny had poured onto the floor had begun to mildew. Another night I did some shopping at a Waldbaum's near the house. I pushed the cart down the soda-pop aisle, then spent the next half hour straightening the shelf, wheeling product out of the back room. It was after nine, and no one working in the store even knew what I was doing.

Another night I decided to go out with the others after work. We ended up at the Hot L Warren in South Deerfield, a loud place that had been a hotel once, or so everyone said. We sat around tables drinking, talking about sales like we always did.

Tim Springer was there, and Ron LaReaux, Will Tremblay. Most everyone else, guys I'd built displays for, rode with, covered during vacations. And here I was, one of them. A salesman.

I looked at them in the dark of the bar, and in the noise of the band playing old rock-and-roll tunes, and in the air stiff with smoke. I watched Springer and how he cupped his hands around the tip of his cigarette each time he lit a new one, even though there was no breeze in here, and I watched LaReaux, so fat he could barely squeeze into the captain's chairs they had here, and how he chased every beer with a shot, his eyes shut tight with each jigger down. And I watched Jerry Landers, a short, bald-headed man with long, thick arms, who held his left hand in front of him, chest high, index finger pointing like a gun. I watched as he nervously jerked his hand down in a quick motion, again and again and again. Had the place been empty and quiet, you could have heard the knuckle crack each time. He drank and smoked and ate stick pretzels all with his right hand, as though he'd lost the left in a war.

I watched these salesmen, and I drank, and I laughed some, and I wondered about them all. I'd met them with their wives, girlfriends, children at company banquets and softball games and barbecues at Look Park. I'd seen them then and how they acted with their families, folks who weren't salespeople, and had seen how they had all tried their best to relax, by dancing with a woman, or by slugging a softball to left-center, or by laughing while flipping burgers with a long metal spatula.

But now they were different. We were different. All of us were sitting here doing our best to forget what we did for a living by talking about it, because that was all anyone ever talked about whenever we got together: sales.

Around eight thirty I stood up, said I had to go.

Springer clapped shut his lighter, drew dead air into his lungs. "Where you going so soon?" he said. "Paige riding your ass?"

Slowly he let out smoke. Landers shook down his finger, looked up at me and grinned.

I looked at my watch. I said, "You know it."

I made it through the weekend by watching ball games again: three in a row on Saturday, then two and a basketball game on Sunday.

I'd done some thinking, though, that weekend in front of the set. I thought about how I should have called her office at the university sometime during the week, should have taken some time from killing myself for the company and Schweppes and the holidays in order to talk to my wife. And then I thought of Paige, and I thought of her being my wife. I thought of that word, *wife*, and how Paige had been my wife. I wondered what she thought of the word *husband*, and wondered if I'd ever see her again, if she was still my wife or if she'd cut that idea out of her mind by that time. I wondered if the word *husband* had already died in her.

It was in January that we'd gone to the wedding. Snow lay thick and black on the roadside as we headed down the interstate. Though it wasn't snowing, I had the wipers going to keep the dirty spray from car and truck tires off the windshield. I kept using the wiper fluid, the blue juice spurting out and keeping things clear, until just past the Holyoke Mall, when the fluid ran out. I ran the wipers a little longer. Dirt streaked across the windshield in two wide bands.

I leaned forward, back, to either side, to see out the windshield.

We were headed for the Villa Napoli, a restaurant and banquet hall in West Springfield. A friend from Paige's office, Lora Mascotte, was getting married that day, at the banquet hall. I'd never been inside the place before, but had passed it a few times when I'd run relief routes a couple summers back. It was an ugly place: a large box of a building with white stucco walls and no windows, pillars in front holding up a red, green, and white plastic awning, statues of cherubs and Roman soldiers and women in flowing gowns holding urns.

"Just leave the wipers off," Paige said. "Let the spray build up until you've got enough to wipe off. That'll clean off the dirt." She straightened her dress, ran a hand across the material. She touched both ears, checking her earrings.

"You want to drive?" I said. "You don't have to sit here with this crap on your windshield so you can't see the car in front of you. You want to drive, you drive."

"Settle down," she said. "You just don't want to go."

"That's exactly right," I said. I turned off the wipers. "I don't have any problems saying that. I don't want to go."

She turned from me to the window so I could see only the back of her neck and her auburn hair pulled up in a swirl. She wore pearls. I looked from the windshield a moment to my wife in a blue satin dress, and to her bare, soft neck and those pearls and her hair.

I turned back to the windshield. The spray had built up enough. Cars in front of me were colored blurs. I turned the wipers back on. The spray, dirt, everything cleared. Paige turned from her window to me, and I could see her smiling. I didn't look at her, said nothing.

We got there as a light, cold rain started. We ran from the car to the door. We'd forgotten an umbrella.

The inside was like I thought it might be: red-flocked wallpaper trimmed in dark wood molding; red, white, and green carpeting with the restaurant's initials woven into the pattern. There were plenty of mirrors, chandeliers, paintings of Italian villas and street scenes. The wall behind the register was painted with a mural of the canals in Venice.

Just past the register was a black corrugated board on an easel, white plastic letters plugged into the board spelling out what was going on where.

Paige went to the board. "Bak–Mascotte. Here it is," she said. "The wedding's in the cocktail lounge–party bar."

I walked over to her, my hands in my pockets. I stood next to her, both of us looking at the board. I said, "A wedding in a bar. Great."

She took my arm and pulled me away from the board, away from the register. "Look," she said, "all I'm asking is that you come and at least smile and shake a few hands. So you might not like this place, and so you might not know anyone. I'm not even asking you to enjoy yourself. Just be here, all right?" She looked in my eyes.

I looked up, away. I said, "Fine."

A few people came in after us, looked at the board, then headed down a hall off the lobby. They were dressed as if they were going to a wedding, and so we followed them through the halls done in that wallpaper and the floors in that carpet and the ceilings with those chandeliers.

Then we were in the bar, dark and empty except for candles in fishnet-wrapped brandy snifters at the center of each table. We weaved in a single file around the tables, then came to a room off the bar where chairs had been set up. People were already sitting in there.

A short man with thick gray hair wearing a black tuxedo motioned with his hand toward the seating area. "I am Albert," he said, "your maître d' this evening. Would you please be seated?" He motioned with his hand again, smiled.

We walked about halfway up the middle aisle, found two seats in the row, then squeezed past three people to the chairs.

I leaned over to Paige, whispered, "First come, first served."

Paige turned her head from side to side, looking for people she might know. She tugged at my arm a minute or so later. "There's Wendy," she said. "Wendy Kasmarski, from the lab." Paige was smiling, looking across to the other side of the room.

"Great," I said.

Some music came through the speakers in the ceiling, and everyone got quiet. Then a door on our side of the room opened, and the groom and best man came out. They were wearing peach tuxedoes with cummerbunds and ruffles and bow ties and white shoes. Behind them was the priest. They went to the front, the priest taking his place behind a podium set up in the front of the room, the groom and best man off to the right. Then Albert came up the middle aisle, stood next to the best man. Albert gave a brief wave with his hand, and the wedding march came over the speakers.

Paige turned to me with this funny look on her face, trying to appear as though she knew the maître d' was the only logical person to be there, but at the same time showing me she thought it was a little crazy, his being up there. It was a funny look, one only I would know.

A photographer came out then, took flash pictures as first the flower girl came down the aisle, then the maid of honor, then Lora. Her dress was pretty, lace and pearls everywhere, daisies and white roses in her hands.

They made it to the front. The music stopped, her father leaned over, kissed her, and gave her away.

We all sat down, and I looked at Paige. She glanced up at me, her eyes all wet, and tried to smile. She took my hand, and we sat there through the ceremony, the photographer's camera flashing away, Albert up there all smiles, and Lora Mascotte and this Mr. Bak just staring at each other.

When the ceremony was over and the priest had introduced Mr. and Mrs. David Bak, and after we had all clapped and the two had gone down the aisle to more music over the speakers, Albert stepped down and held his hands above the crowd. He said, "Now, for your dining enjoyment, we will be serving hors d'oeuvres in the Appian Room, and then we will adjourn to the Napoli Room for dinner. Please, enjoy." He brought his hands together, bowed. Everyone stood, and we moved through the party bar down a hall and into another room.

Champagne fountains had been set up in there, long tables filled with warming trays of lasagna and stuffed cabbage and stuffed shells, plates of crackers and sliced cheese and Jordan almonds and petits fours. There was a cash bar in one corner of the place.

Paige and I got in line for hors d'oeuvres. All this time her eyes were going everywhere, looking for people. She took a couple crackers with cheese, put them on her plate, turned around and looked, then turned back to the table for two cocktail wienies.

I said, "If you want to go looking around, then you go looking, all right? There's a couple hundred people behind us and you're holding them up."

She stopped, her plate with only those few things on it, and said, "All right. I'll see you." Then she was gone, disappearing into the crowd of people already milling around the room.

I watched her go, and felt someone push me from behind. I turned around. A short fat woman in a pink and white caftan was leaning over the table and scooping stuffed shells one after another onto her plate. I turned back to the line, took my time as I went through.

Cocktail tables were set up along one wall. I went over, sat down. The floor in here was hardwood, a dance floor, and I wondered if we would be dancing later. I hoped not.

I ate my food. Occasionally I'd catch a glimpse of Paige: a flash of that blue dress, her hair, the gray, low-heeled shoes she wore. She never seemed to look toward me; all I saw of her face was her profile as she moved between people, talking and laughing. And there were those pearls, and her soft, white neck.

I'd eaten most of my food before I realized I didn't have a drink. I took the napkin off my lap, folded it up, then noticed some printing on it. I unfolded it, spread it out on the table. DAVE AND LORA, LOVE AND MARRIAGE had been printed in gold letters on all four corners of the thing, along with the date.

"Ain't it sweet," someone behind me said. I looked up, turned around. An old man stood behind me, a plastic glass of champagne in each hand. He was wearing an old short-sleeved yellow shirt, the collar frayed, and a blue and yellow striped bow tie.

He set one of the drinks next to my plate. "Saw you over here all by your lonesome with nothing to drink. Nothing sadder, they say, than a man who eats alone." He laughed. "These seats taken?"

"Well," I said, "my wife's out there somewhere making the rounds."

"There's two seats. I'll let her have one, I'll take the other." He laughed again, and sat down. "My name's Frank Lawson," he said. He reached a hand across the table to me.

I shook it, said, "Rick Wheeler." I put the napkin back on my lap, took a sip of the champagne. "Thanks for the drink."

"It's nothing," he said. He moved his chair out from the table, turned it sideways so he faced the crowd, then crossed his legs. He took a drink from his glass. "Saw you here and figured maybe you were in the same boat I was. You are." He smiled, sighed. "Mine's out there, too, sweeping the floor, making the rounds, doing whatever it is she does at these shindigs. We've been to weddings, funerals, bar mitzvahs, you name it and she'll be out there doing the do-si-do with people she's never seen before in her life. People she'll never see again, too." He turned to me. "So what's your story?"

I said, "I feel the same way you do. I don't know a single person here. I met Lora Mascotte once. She works with my wife at the university, but beyond that, nobody."

He smiled. "Take a good look at me, partner. This is you. This is you in a good thirty, forty years."

I laughed, and he took another sip of champagne. I looked at him. He was bald with a couple inches of white hair around the back of his head, age spots on his arms and hands and neck. A couple fingernails on one hand had gone bad, the nails brown to the tip where they disintegrated into white. He had wet, full eyes.

I said, "So why are you here? I mean, who do you know?"

He turned to me. I looked down at my plate. He said, "Oh, Davey used to be a bagger for me. I own a market over in Indian Orchard. What business are you in?"

I said, "I'm a salesman. RC and Schweppes."

"Hah," he said, "a salesman for RC. I remember back when you wouldn't have said RC first, but Nehi. I remember back when Nehi was the biggest thing your company ever had on its hands." He put the palm of one hand to an eye, rubbed it. "You know Jerry Landers?"

"Sure," I said. "He's got the route over on the east side. He your salesman?"

He turned back to the crowd, took a long sip off the champagne. "Yep," he said, and set the empty cup on the table. "Frank's Market is the name of the place. It's just a mom-and-pops, but I make enough money to have Jerry stop in twice a week. Frank's Market." He gave a silent belch. "Catchy name, huh?"

"I guess," I said. "It's a good enough name for a market." My plate was empty. Paige was still out there milling around. I looked out into the crowd, caught a glimpse of her with a drink in her hand. She was talking to a young couple.

"Frank's my *name*," he said, "or did you forget that? You were supposed to laugh. You're not all here, are you?"

"Yes I am," I said, and turned from Paige to him. "I'm here," I said, "but I sure as hell wish I wasn't." I looked back to the crowd. Paige and the couple were gone. "You know. You've been doing this for so long, like you said. You know what I mean. With all due respect, if I were you and I had to put up with this kind of stuff for as long as you have, I'd be mad as hell."

He stopped smiling. He uncrossed his legs, using both hands to pull one leg off the other. It seemed it took him an hour to move that one leg, but then he was leaning over the table, his face a foot or so from mine. His nose was pitted, red blood vessels running across it and breaking on his cheeks.

"Partner," he said, "you better learn to live with it. Put up with it. There ain't much you can do to change it. You look at me. I've tried, but what happens is you don't get the same person you married once you break her in. You look at me. I'm happy. I am." He leaned back then, and his old man's thick breath hung there in front of me. He gave this big grin, and I could see his stained teeth. "I'm about due for another." He picked up his cup, studied it. "How about you?"

I said, "Too sweet for me. Thanks." I shrugged.

"Suit yourself," he said. He stood up slowly, both hands on his knees. He picked up his glass, came around the table. As he walked past me he put his hand on my shoulder. It felt like a vise there, harder than what I thought that old man could have mustered. He let go. I turned around.

"Say hello to Jerry for me," I said, but he was already off into the crowd.

A few minutes later Paige came to the table with the couple she had been talking to.

She was smiling. "Who was that I saw you talking with for so long?" she said.

I said, "That was me in thirty or forty years." I smiled, too.

She laughed, and then the couple laughed, though I knew none of them knew why.

Paige said, "Rick, this is Wendy Kasmarski and her husband Larry. Wendy works at the lab with me."

Larry put out his hand, and I had to stand. "Great," I said. "This is just great."

Albert came into the room then, clapped his hands twice. The room went quiet. "For your dining enjoyment," he said, "everyone is invited to the Napoli Room next for a celebratory dinner."

We all filed out of the room again, Larry and Wendy in front of us. Paige was on my arm, and whispered, "I wish you'd cut it out. What's this forty years business?"

"Nothing," I said. "Nothing at all."

The Napoli Room was bigger than the last. We roamed around a while trying to find our table. We finally found the place cards at a table near the back of the room. Larry and Wendy's cards were at the same table. We all sat down.

The setting was nice enough: all the silverware you could need, a matchbox printed with DAVE AND LORA, LOVE AND MARRIAGE on the center of each plate. There were more of the printed napkins, and a large centerpiece of more daisies and white roses. At every place setting was a bottle of wine, a New York state burgundy, a peach ribbon around the neck of the bottle. I picked up my bottle, looked at it. There, printed across the ribbon, were

the words DAVE AND LORA, LOVE AND MARRIAGE. I looked over at
Larry, who was studying his bottle as well. Wendy sat next to
Paige, Larry next to Wendy. Paige and Wendy were talking, some-
thing about Lora's veil.

He set his bottle down. I said, "A bottle each. They went all
out."

Larry smiled and leaned forward. "Yeah, well maybe we'll
need a bottle each. I sure as hell know I need at least one to calm
me down after the drive down here."

I leaned over the table, too. "Where did you come from?" I
nearly shouted. I wanted to hear myself over the rising noise of
the crowds taking their seats, above Paige and Wendy.

"Colrain," he said, "up off the Mohawk. Took us over two
hours to get down here through all the muck and mud on back
roads. Then behind all the trucks coming down here on the 91."
He waved it all away with one hand, then picked up Wendy's
bottle. She turned from Paige and looked at him a moment, then
turned back to Paige. "I'll need this second bottle to prime me for
the trip back up," he said.

We laughed. I liked him. We talked for a while, then kept
talking while other guests came to the table and sat down. He
worked for Wang at their new offices in Holyoke. He was a pro-
grammer and worked the graveyard shift. They ran those programs twenty-four hours a day, he told me. He didn't mind so
much the awful hours he had to work, because he knew sooner
or later he'd work his way up to day shift, and the money was
good. In a year and a half they'd been able to save enough money
to put down on the house in Colrain. It was a fixer-upper, he said,
and so they had gotten a good price on it. His weekends were full,
though, working away on the house. It was a two-hundred-year-
old farmhouse, and needed all kinds of work done: the grounds
to be cleared of old farm equipment and boards and tree stumps;
insulation all through the place; new floors in one of the bedrooms
and in the kitchen and living room. "You come up for a weekend
sometime," he said, "when you feel like breaking your back for a
good cause."

Wendy turned from Paige then. "Larry," she said, "you're not recruiting him this soon, are you? You just met the man." She was looking at me, smiling, her hand on Larry's forearm.

"Hey," he said, and leaned back in his chair. "You have to take advantage of a good situation. That's all there is to it. He's healthy and interested. Heck, let's get the both of them up there for a weekend and put the two of them to work." He looked at Paige. His fingers were on the stem of his empty wineglass. "You look healthy, too. With the both of you up there we could get tons of stuff over and done with."

"Sounds good to me," Paige said and looked at me. She was smiling.

Wendy said, "We'll have a barbecue. If you guys come up there we'll have steaks and baked corn and chips. We'll make a party out of it. That is, after we do the outside stuff we've been putting off all winter because of the weather. Once it warms up, you guys come up and we'll get outside and work. It'll be fun." She turned to Larry. "You're pretty smart, actually," she said. "Recruiting this early." She moved her hand to his shoulder.

"Not really," he said. "Just an opportunist. I want to get the damned thing finished. Here before us sit two potential chain-gang members. Let's nab 'em."

We all laughed, and Wendy leaned into his shoulder. Larry put his arm around her.

"We're on," Paige said. She turned to me. "Aren't we?"

"You bet," I said.

Wendy held up her empty wineglass in a toast. She said, "Here's to chain gangs," and Larry, Paige and I held up our glasses, Paige laughing, me smiling and shaking my head, Larry with his arm still around Wendy.

We touched glasses, the sound lost in the noise of the room.

Finally Dave and Lora came into the room, and everyone clapped, stood up. Dave and Lora took their seats at the head table, then the waiters came around and opened as many bottles of wine as people wanted. Then a toast was made, a long, glorious one by the best man. It was a sincere, good toast, and he finished it by saying something in Polish. Most of the crowd laughed. I did, too, then drank off about half the glass. Paige elbowed me as we sat down, but I just smiled, took another drink.

Food started coming, first deep bowls of minestrone, then plates of antipasto, and then more toasts were made. More food came, this time plates of pasta, and then came prime rib and baked potatoes and peas.

"Prime rib?" I whispered to Paige. "What happened to our Italian dinner?"

Paige said, "Italian cows," without having looked up from her plate.

What she'd said wasn't all that funny, but I laughed. I laughed out loud so that some of the others at the table turned and looked at me, smiled, and went back to their food.

I turned back to Paige, and she was looking at me, a smile on her face right then that broke through the drive down, the people I didn't know here, this whole evening. I saw her new again, the one I'd quit college for, the woman I married. In her eyes, those green eyes, I saw the two of us, newly married, convinced we could make the world our own.

"What?" she said, this smile on her face. She tilted her head to one side, her hair falling off one shoulder. Light from somewhere in the room glanced off her eyes, shone through me.

I shrugged, looked down at my plate.

She gave a laugh, then placed a hand on my thigh. "Rick, what?" she said.

I looked up at her. "Nothing," I said. "I was just thinking. Remembering what it was like right after we got married." I shrugged again. "Being married. Thinking about why I loved you. Why I love you."

"There," she said, and brought her hand from my leg, placed it on my shoulder. She smiled, nodded toward the front of the hall. "Look at them up there."

I looked up at the head table. There sat Dave and Lora, talking, smiling. Everyone up there was smiling in between forkfuls of food and sips of wine. Then from somewhere in the room came the sound of a spoon tapping glass, and the sound was taken up across the hall, everyone tapping glasses and shouting, waiting for Dave and Lora to kiss.

Finally Dave stood, took Lora's hand in his, pulled her to standing. She looked as if she might be blushing, but then she threw up her hands in surrender, and they embraced. It was a long kiss, Lora leaning back, Dave holding her. Everyone cheered, continued tapping glass.

I turned back to Paige, and her face was right there, her eyes, her lips, her hair. The woman I'd married. She leaned toward me and we kissed, a long sweet kiss, her lips warm against mine, the sound of metal on glass ringing through the room.

Later, after the plates from dinner were cleared and six more toasts were made, the lights in the place went out and the waiters came through with flaming baked Alaskas. Paige and I were half-way through our second bottle of wine. The lights out, we turned toward each other again, kissed, and then I kissed her neck, smelled her perfume.

The lights came back on, and we grinned at each other, at our small secret.

A band set up in the far corner of the room: drums, electric guitars, electric piano, and bass. They played a few soft rock songs while we finished dessert and the waiters started in with coffee. Paige put her hand back on my leg. She and Wendy were talking again. So were Larry and I. I put my arm around Paige so that we were sitting closer and closer together, the four of us just talking.

The band played a fanfare, and Albert came out onto the dance floor. You could tell by looking at him, at how he held his arms in the air, at the fine crease in his pants, at the way he stood with his feet evenly spread, that he loved what he was doing. Who could blame him for being in the wedding?

"Now the first dance," he said above the crowd. He said it without effort, without seeming to raise his voice at all.

Dave and Lora got up from the table, kissed each other's parents. They came out onto the dance floor. Lora gathered up her veil in one hand, and then the band went into "We've Only Just Begun." I'd heard that song at at least a half-dozen weddings before, and I thought I would have been sick of it by that time, but it still worked. They started dancing, slowly moving around the floor.

"Mr. and Mrs. David Bak, ladies and gentlemen," Albert said. We all stood and clapped.

Lora's parents came down onto the floor and traded partners so that Mrs. Mascotte danced with David, Lora with her father. Then Dave's parents came down and did the same thing. Albert was introducing them all, and we ended up clapping the whole time.

"Now everyone," Albert said, "please join us in this marvelous dance, the first dance of their life together."

Before I could say anything, Paige had taken my hand and we were heading for the floor, and then we were there, moving slowly, Paige up next to me and holding me, and me holding her. She leaned her head against my chest, and her perfume rose up to me. I closed my eyes. The music just kept going, that old song playing over and over again. I opened my eyes every once in a while, looked down and saw her hair and those pearls, and the pale skin of her neck and shoulders. I looked up, saw Larry and Wendy not too far away, Dave and Lora across the room, and there, between people all moving with that song, was Frank of Frank's Market, huddled up against an old woman with silver hair wearing a paisley dress and thick, dark stockings. Frank had loosened his bow tie, held her hand in his, and the two of them swayed right to the music. Frank's eyes were closed. He was smiling.

Maybe that's me, I thought, maybe so. And I thought that that wouldn't be a terrible place to be. I closed my eyes, held Paige even closer to me, and kept dancing.

In April, then, I'd gotten the cold. It was a nasty cold. I thought it might have been caused by my tonsils, as I had never had them out. I thought that maybe I wasn't getting enough vitamin C. I also thought the cold might have been caused by recent drastic temperature changes, thirty degrees one day, sixty the next. But the cold, whatever the reason, was there in my throat and head and ears. I finally took a day off from work, and lay in bed.

I slept most of that day. Each time I looked at the clock, it was a few hours later: 10:13, 12:27, 1:52, 4:03.

Paige came home and stood next to the bed. I hadn't heard her come in.

"Any better?" she said. "Rick?" she said, as though I were asleep.

"I'm awake," I said. "No better." I was sweaty, and the sheets felt cold and filthy against my skin. I wanted a new set of sheets to sleep in, to warm me up, to make me feel better.

She sat on the edge of the bed. "Guess what?"

I wanted to tell her I didn't want to guess anything, that my throat ached too much to speak. Then I realized I didn't have to answer. Maybe my silence might signal her I didn't want to talk.

But she didn't pick up any such signal. Instead, she stood, put her arms out to either side, and slowly turned in a circle.

"Do I look any fatter?" she said, and smiled.

I watched her turning. It seemed it took her minutes to make
it all the way around. I shook my head.

"I'm pregnant," she said. "The results were positive."

I heard her words, but didn't comprehend them. I was con-
centrating on her face: the barely visible freckles across her nose,
gray flecks in her green eyes, her lips moving. For a moment I
thought I didn't recognize her. Do I know this face? I thought.

"Rick, honey," she said and leaned over me. "Are you all
right?"

I whispered, "I'm okay. My throat."

"Oh baby," she said, "we've got to get you to gargle with some
warm salt water." She sat on the bed and stroked my hair. I
thought I could feel her fingers on each strand, her hand moving
back and forth across my scalp. I closed my eyes, imagining that,
if I were sick long enough, I might be able to count the number
of hairs she touched.

Paige said, "You know, we'll have to find a bigger place.
Maybe even buy a house."

I was glad she was pregnant. We'd started trying the night of
Dave and Lora's wedding, the night we danced out there with
everyone else. We'd danced that number to the end, and then we
danced a couple polkas, and then to some old rock-and-roll songs,
and then we'd gone home. I'd even made it a point to stop and
shake Albert's hand as we left. He'd taken hold of my hand with
both of his, then shook and shook, smiling and thanking both of
us. Paige and I had held hands out to the car and all the way up
the interstate home, then up the stairs to our apartment. Inside,
we had held each other there in the dark, and slowly danced
around the place, ending up in bed where we made love, all
without words. Afterward we lay in each other's arms, and in the
darkness she said, "Do you know what it is you want?"

"What do you mean?" I said. I was looking at the ceiling,
trying to fish through the dark for familiar patterns in the stucco
up there.

"In life. Us. Our lives. What do you want?"

She said that, her words drifting up into the darkness separate and distinct. *What do you want?*

And I had lain there, just thinking. A few minutes later I said, "I don't know. Not just yet, anyway," my words insignificant, only air.

"I know," she said. "I know what I want." I looked at her, her head at my shoulder, and I wondered at her voice, her calm.

She said, "I want to have a child now. To make things different, change things. I want to make our lives count even more."

She hadn't yet looked at me, only lay there, still, and in her voice I found my center, my own calm. This was what I wanted, too.

She sat up in bed, and I could see her in the darkness, her silhouette. I reached up to her, put my hand on her shoulder and let it slip down her arm.

"What do you think?" she said.

"A baby?"

"Yes," she whispered, then said, "Yes." She took my hand, pulled me up to sitting, then reached over to the lamp on the nightstand and turned it on.

We were sitting across from one another there in bed, squinting back the light, smiling at each other.

I said, "Rugrats."

She laughed. "Yes," she said, "rugrats. And saggy breasts. I'll fail the pencil test, I know it. But I don't care."

"And dirty diapers."

"Smelly ones. And diaper rash, too. And spitting up. But I don't care. That's just a part of it all." She paused, still smiling. "You had dirty diapers once. You spit up. But look at you. No one gave up on you and you turned out pretty well." She took my hand, held it to her cheek. "What do you think?"

I was quiet, then smiled again. I knew the answer to this. I knew what it was I felt. I said, "I think I'm willing."

"That's what you have to be above all else," she said. "You

have to be willing to care for it. God, you have to be willing to love it. To change its diapers and wipe up after it and—"

"Don't push it," I cut in, and she laughed. Then she climbed off the bed and pulled me with her. "Come on," she said, leading me through the bedroom and into the bathroom. "There's something we have to do."

She took her diaphragm from the medicine chest. "Here's to a good and loyal friend," she said, pretending to hold back tears. She held the diaphragm in her hand as if it were some dead fish.

"You're crazy," I said.

"No," she said. "Just ready to start." She looked back at the diaphragm and said, "You've been a good mule, but you done threw a shoe," and I started laughing. I put an arm around her waist, took the diaphragm from her. I said, "Good-bye, Old Paint," and dropped it into the trash basket.

She laughed and turned to me, and looked in my eyes. "I love you," she said.

"I love you too," I said, and then we went back to the bedroom and made love again.

She brought me soup. I moved to sit up, and the room seemed to whirl. I stopped a moment, focused on the footboard, then sat up.

"Paige," I said. I had planned to celebrate her being pregnant by buying her flowers, then going out for an expensive dinner, then coming home and making love, but because of the cold we couldn't do any of that. I wanted to thank her, to kiss her and hold her. I wanted to talk about a bigger place, but the words all stayed in my head. "Paige," I began again.

"No, no words," she said. "You just eat this."

I brought a spoonful of soup to my mouth. I couldn't smell it or taste it, but could feel the heat in my mouth and throat.

I dozed the rest of the evening, waking up now and then. I gauged the evening's progression by what I heard: first phone calls to family, friends, relatives; later, the dishes and television.

Then I awoke, and the apartment was dark, Paige in bed next to me. The clock read 3:07.

My throat felt better; I could breathe through one nostril. I felt as if this was some kind of victory, and I moved to wake Paige. She mumbled a few words and rolled over away from me.

I sat up. A window shade was up, and moonlight shone through the window. I saw everything clearly there in the moon-bright darkness. There was my wallet on the dresser, Paige's lotions and perfumes, jewelry box and ring tray. The closet door was open a few inches, and I could see clothes hanging from the rod. Everything was clear, sharp, and this clarity, I thought, was just like that sensitivity to touch I'd had when Paige had stroked my hair and I had imagined I could count each strand. I thought I could see everything in the room, from my reflection in the dresser mirror to the faces in photographs hung on the far wall.

I was hungry. I stood up slowly, and felt my sinuses begin to drain. Though my throat was still raw and sore, my head felt better. I looked back at Paige, but decided not to wake her.

I went to the kitchen and opened the refrigerator. The sudden light from the bulb inside momentarily blinded me. I covered my eyes, then squinted and reached in for things for sandwiches. My arms full, I let the refrigerator door close gently, my foot under the door, guiding it along. I pushed my back against the door until it clicked shut. The click seemed extraordinarily loud.

I moved across the kitchen to the range and placed each item on the stove top, flipped on the stove hood light, and looked at all I had laid out.

I couldn't help but marvel at the colors. I picked up a wedge of orange cheese and studied it under the light, then unwrapped it and smelled it, taking in the deep, sour aroma. The sliced ham was a rich pink; I picked this up, too, and smelled it. There was yellow mustard and white mayonnaise, green leaf lettuce and soft, brown bread. I made two sandwiches, slowly put the food back in the refrigerator, then brought out a carton of milk and poured a tall glass. I put the milk away and turned off the light above the stove.

In the darkness I smelled the food, and thought that maybe the darkness enhanced the smell. The milk felt cool and smooth on the back of my throat; I took a bite of the sandwich, and thought I could taste each individual flavor: the tart mayonnaise, the sweet ham, the crisp, wet lettuce.

I looked out the kitchen window to the street and watched a car go by. The headlights were as bright as the sun, I thought, and the taillights like red flares. I stood at the window and wondered how many people were awake just then, and where that car was going and what the driver had been thinking the instant the car had passed. I enjoyed being up at this hour, so secretive, so quiet, yet with everything so clear to me.

I went to the front room with my sandwich and milk, and looked out the window to the courtyard of the apartment complex. No lights were on in any of the other apartments. I smiled and went back to the kitchen, refilled the glass, got the other sandwich. Back in the front room, I pulled a chair from the dinette set to the window, sat there to eat my food.

While I ate no other lights came on.

Later I went to the bathroom, got out of my pajamas, and took a hot shower, all in the dark. I took deep breaths, my lungs filling with the warm, moist air, and felt the hot water on my scalp, my neck, my back. I dried off in the dark, rubbing the towel hard against my body. I dropped my pajamas in the hamper, went to the bedroom and put on a T-shirt, underwear and a thick pair of socks.

Paige sat up in bed and looked around. Even in the dark I could see her confused expression, the moon so bright through the window. This time I thought her face was one I'd known all my life.

She said, "Rick? Honey? What's wrong?"

I climbed into bed. "Listen," I said. I took a deep breath to show her the cold was going away.

"What?" she said, and lay back down. "I don't hear anything."
A few seconds later I heard her deep, steady breathing.

I moved onto my side and propped myself up on an elbow.
Through the window I saw the silhouetted tops of buildings, telephone poles, trees and, beyond, those dark hills.

I remembered then that she was pregnant, and for a moment
felt ashamed and embarrassed I'd forgotten, felt I should have
awakened Paige to share and celebrate with her the food, the
darkness, the quiet. I looked at her face, her features so distinct
in the darkness, and smiled. I let her sleep.

I lay down and gently placed my hand on her abdomen. There
in the darkness I felt her pulse, and imagined it to be the child's
heartbeat. I felt that rhythm, and listened to the quiet music of
the dark apartment, and to my wife's breathing, and to the world
outside lit with the moon. It was this moment I would remember,
I knew, days, months, years from now, long after the cold was
gone. I took in a deep breath, the air cold in my raw throat.

TWO

The second Tuesday after Paige had gone I got up at five thirty, showered, shaved, and dressed. I was at the office by six twenty. I wanted to make sure all my display and merchandise requests were going to be taken care of. This was Thanksgiving week. I wanted my displays to be tight.

I came in the front door, stamped my feet on the mat. A few people sat around conference tables sorting through work for the day. The display men stood in one corner of the room, talking and smoking and drinking coffee. They were all young, nineteen or twenty years old, and dressed in jeans and work boots and RC shirts. Some wore company-issue Eisenhower jackets, that same logo on the front. Others had on down jackets or vests.

I'd started out as a display man. I did nothing my first year here except go around and build displays and merchandise existing ones. But I'd thought I was different. I'd done it hoping to get my own route, hoping to move up and make more money. These guys, though, looked as if they'd reached their peak. Cigarettes hanging from their lips, eyes creased closed and arms crossed as they complained or listened to each other complain, they looked as if they'd gone about as far as they could.

Off the main room was a hallway with three smaller offices for route supervisors, and before I could make it over to the display men to find out who was taking care of what on my route, I heard Mitchell cough and wheeze from down that hall.

"Ricky? That you?" he said. I heard his desk chair creak, and pictured him leaning back in his chair, hands behind his head, waiting for me to come down the hall to him.

I turned, went down the hall. I stood in the doorway. There he was, leaning back, hands where I'd thought they would be. His hair, black on top and gray at the sides, was like always: slicked back with Vitalis or Brylcreem or something, and there was the cigarette he always had, hanging from his lips. He had a thick, gray mustache stained yellow along the bottom edge from the cigarettes.

He sucked at that cigarette, and I thought how much he looked like those boys out there waiting to build my displays.

His cigarette burned down to the filter, the ash hanging there in midair an inch long before he stubbed it out in the ashtray.

"Yep?" I said. I put a hand in my pocket, leaned against the doorjamb.

"Ricky," he said. "I just wanted you to know what a fine job you're doing for the company." He leaned forward in his chair, shook out a cigarette from a pack of Marlboro Golds sitting on his desk. He lit it, leaned back. "Your sales are second in the division, first in this branch. You've placed more displays in your independents than anyone in this whole branch, my good man. You're averaging right in at thirty-two percent above projection. You're doing okay, in other words." He thought this was particularly funny, and took the cigarette from his mouth. He laughed, then coughed for it. When he got his breath back, his face was straight. I still hadn't said anything. "What's going on out there?" he said. "Why is everything going so great?"

He sat up at the desk, took a pen out of his shirt pocket, and started doodling. "I mean, it's great you're out there doing the job the right way." He was looking at the paper, drawing circles, then squares. "But I just want to know why."

"You want me to slow down?" I said and crossed my arms. "I can slow down."

"Oh, no no no," he said quickly, and looked up at me. I was smiling.

"No," I said, "it's just that we've finally got the right deal.

The right price. Somebody finally got off their collective fat butts and got the displays nailed down from above. All that left me to do was to ship the stuff in. I could think about the independents then, give them a little extra attention." I shifted my weight from one foot to the other, my arms still crossed.

"You don't sound like you're too excited about it," he said. He was looking at me, the second cigarette about finished. "You sound like you're sick or something. Are you still sick?"

"No, no," I said. I tried to smile again.

"Don't think I haven't been watching you," he said, "because I have. You don't look good. You look sick to me. Is Paige all right? She isn't sick again, is she?"

I wondered if someone had told him something. I hadn't told anyone, though, except Lonny.

"No," I said. "She's all right. I've just got my attention on work now. It's what I should do. I'm making the commission now for Christmas. Making hay while the sun shines, right?" I gave a small laugh, but it didn't come out as I'd wanted it to. It came out fake, dead, and I saw Mitchell's eyes pick up on that. His eyebrows went up, and then he went back to doodling.

"Family problems?" he said without looking up.

"No," I said, maybe too quickly. I uncrossed my arms, put my hands in my pockets. "Not at all. What makes you say that?" I was smiling again.

He dropped the pen on the blotter, leaned back in his chair again. "Some salesman." He was grinning, and I could see a row of brown teeth, as if he'd already died and had started decaying from the inside out. "Some, some salesman. I don't believe you. You've got problems back at the ranch, and you're taking it out on work." He closed his eyes, slowly shook his head. He was still grinning. "Most guys, they have problems, their route sales start to suck. What happens to you? Yours pick up." He opened his eyes, gave a short cough of a laugh. "Geez, what you should have done is to have had problems a long time ago, Ricky. That's what you should have done. Think where you'd be right now."

"Look," I said. I could feel my face getting hot. I took my

hands out of my pockets and let them hang at my sides. "Look, there aren't any problems, Mitchell. You understand. There aren't any problems. And I don't like what you're saying about my marriage." I was pointing at him now. "You know what we've been through. Every goddamn person in this branch knows what we've been through, so you knock off that shit about my marriage. All right?" I hadn't yelled, but my throat felt as if I had.

"All right, all right," he said, and stood. "I'm kidding, okay? I'm sorry." He looked down and shook his head. "I'm sorry about what I said. I shouldn't have. You've toughed out a lot of things. Different things than Sandy and me have." He looked up, put his hand out for me to shake. "It's just that you look so bad every day when you come in the door. Sales are great, fantastic, but you come in here every day like the walking dead." I still hadn't shaken his hand. "You better shake on this," he said, "or it's the first and last time you'll ever see me apologize."

I ran one hand back through my hair, and with the other shook with him. He said, "You'll make it through this one. Jeez, how can you not? You're a salesman. You're one of the best salesmen we've got."

I left Mitchell's office, and all the display men had already gone. I went from store to store that day, though, to find all my displays built and stocked, all the shelves merchandised. All I had to do was to come in, put up some bottle-hangers and carton-stuffers, then head to the back room and write up the order.

He was covering me, I knew. Mitchell was arranging a few extra perks, like all the physical work being done for me. Maybe it was because my sales were so good, I thought, or maybe he thought I needed time at home with Paige to work things through. But I knew it was for the first reason. He was covering me because of the sales I'd made. He didn't have time to screw around with my personal problems.

I ended up with another good day, way up over a thousand cases, and when I got back to the apartment it was still only four o'clock. I walked in the door, set the keys on the set, then went straight to the couch. I sat down, and called Paige's office.

"Neuroscience and Behavior," she said.

I was quiet a moment, astounded at that voice I hadn't heard in almost two weeks. She sounded like a different person, not for any change in her voice, but because I hadn't heard her in so long after hearing her every day for five years. It was a new voice again.

"Hey," I said.

She was quiet a moment, then said, "Hey."

"What's going on?" I was looking out the window, the sun already getting close to the tops of trees.

She said, "Nothing. I'm working."

I said, "It's good to hear your voice."

She said nothing, and then that bit of a high I'd been riding on all day, that bit that'd made me feel good because of the displays being built and stocked and that stuff about being a salesman, just fell through my hands. I'd planned this conversation out all day. I'd even rehearsed in the car a couple of the questions I'd wanted to ask, and a couple of answers she might want to hear. I had set up a sales presentation for her, and now I'd forgotten it all. All of it.

I said, "So where are you living? In case of an emergency or something."

"I really can't talk right now," she said. "All right? Jack's got a grant proposal he wants me working on and Tuesday is the deadline. I've got a lot of work and a lot of pressure."

"All right," I said, "but you can call me, right? You can call me when you get home to wherever it is you're calling home these days." I paused, then said, "This is home, you know. This is where you live."

She said, "Fine," and hung up.

I held the receiver in my hand, just looking at it, until the dial tone stopped and that high-pitched signal came across. I hung it up, looked out the window. The grass outside, down there on the front lawn of the complex, had finally turned gray. The sun

had already touched the trees up on the hill above the apartment
building, my apartment, my home, starting to grow dark like it
did every night.

At five thirty she called. I was startled at the ring of the phone
through the place. I was in the kitchen frying up some eggs when
it rang, and that loud noise banged off the empty walls into more
walls so that I ran to answer it, to stop all the sound.

"So what's up?" she said. Her voice didn't sound all that new
any more. It was still Paige, the same Paige I'd known all this
time.

"I wanted to talk to you," I said, out of breath.

"Go ahead," she said. "I'm listening."

"I wanted to know where you live. Like I said, in case of
emergency or something like that."

"Emergency. What kind of emergency?"

"If I got hurt at work, say. Or something like that."

She was quiet, then said, "I've got a phone at the office. Have
someone call there."

"What if you get hurt?" I said. "What if something happens
to you wherever you are and you can't get to a phone?"

"What is this?" she said. "Since when are you so worried
about accidents? What's all this stuff about accidents?"

I said, "I just want to know, you know? Where you are. Where
you're staying."

I heard her moving around. I heard the low pounding sound
of a grocery bag as she reached in and brought things out. I saw
her then more clearly than I'd been able to imagine her since
she'd gone. I saw her with the phone cradled between ear and
shoulder, saw her bring from the bag sour cream, milk, Cheerios,
eggs. I saw her moving from kitchen counter to refrigerator with
each item, then from kitchen counter to cupboard and back to
kitchen counter, the phone still on her shoulder. "It's like this,"
she said, and I listened. "What I want is to be by myself. You
know. I want to just be where I am for a while, quite a while,
maybe. And see what happens. Number one, see what happens
to me. Number two, see what happens to you."

I said, "What's happened so far? To you."

"What's happened to you?" she said.

"I asked first."

She kept on putting things away. I heard her fold up the bag, move to another. "I don't know. Something, but I'm not sure what. A week and a half isn't really all that long."

"A week and a half is a very long time," I said. "A week and a half is a hell of a long time. A plumber came and tried to fix a leak and he couldn't find it. Then he asked if I wanted to go hunting with him. That's what's happened to me so far. I'm still waiting to hear from him. And I've got displays everywhere. Schweppes. Somebody finally came through, and I've got displays in every chain, most of my independents."

"So I've seen," she said. She pulled something out of the grocery bag. "See this?" she said. "Can you see this? It's a bottle of ginger ale from one of your displays."

I said, "Oh, I see it. I remember putting that bottle up." We both laughed, then stopped at the same moment. "Tell me more," I said, "about what's happened."

"No," she said.

"It's somebody," I said, "isn't it? Someone else."

"Knock it off." She stopped, and I could hear her taking hold of the phone. She wasn't putting anything away. "I can't believe you," she said. "What is your problem? When are you going to stop this 'someone else' crap? You know me. You know why I've gone. Why I'm here and not there. You just don't want to face up to anything. We've got to talk about what happened." She paused, then said, "You know, we didn't die. I'm alive, you're alive. Or at least I hope you are. But I'm here alone and you're there alone and that's the way it's going to be for a while."

I said, "I don't know what you want. Seriously." For a moment I thought that maybe, really, I didn't.

"Don't lie," she said. "You're lying. You want me to spell it out for you? Let me spell it out for you. We were driving down to my parents' house, remember? And I was saying how bad I had to go to the bathroom, and you were treating me like a little girl, like a goddamned little baby, and you wouldn't stop. All the way from Springfield I'd felt like I had to go, but you wouldn't stop, remember? You kept going and going, just ignoring me until we were almost to New Haven when—"

"Paige," I said.

"—decided to pull—"

"Paige," I said again.

"—but it was almost too late and I had to run to the bathroom in order to make it. You sat in the car while I—"

I hung up. I threw the telephone across the room. It hit the far wall, and put a good half-dollar-size nick in the wall, right through the paint and into the drywall. White plaster dust and particles fell on the floor and on the phone.

We'd started looking for a bigger place after I got over the cold. It took me a few days, but then after I'd gotten better we went for dinner at the French restaurant on the main street in town. After that we'd gone to a club just over the Easthampton line, a club that played the music too loud and was too crowded, so that after pulling open the heavy oak door to the place and seeing what it was like inside, we'd turned and headed back to the car and home. We went to bed about eight, and got to sleep after midnight.

That Saturday we got up and made a big breakfast of French toast, eggs, sausage, juice, and coffee. Then we took off, headed for nowhere in particular, just looking for bigger places to live. That day we went south to a new development, Buttonwood. The homes there were all low ranches, unlandscaped with gray concrete foundations poking up beneath the homes. We drove up and down a few blocks, half the houses empty shells waiting to be bought. We turned around then and headed north.

We drove through a couple more developments, this time out on the west side, a place called Canyon Heights. All the homes there were split-level and were nice enough, but as we had turned into the place I'd seen a billboard advertising their prices. FROM $109,990, the billboard had read, and though we liked this place with its green, rolling lawns and trees about to bust out with new leaves, we knew we couldn't afford it. We went home after that place, didn't say anything to each other the whole way home.

Wednesday after that I got off early. I called Paige at the

university, told her I'd gotten home early and was wondering if
she could get off, too.

"Why?" she said.

"Why do you think?"

"To give looking at homes another try."

"Right," I said.

She said, "Come over now. Nothing's happening here."

It was in this way that we got into the habit of driving around
and looking at houses. Every afternoon I could get off I went
straight to the university, picked up Paige, and then drove to
different developments around, different hill towns, looking for a
bigger place. Weekends we were gone most of both days.

Late in April the weather started turning hot. We used this
looking for homes as an escape when the apartment, cooled only
by a box fan in the front room window, got too close. We'd stop
at a package store somewhere in town, buy a couple beers or RCs,
then head to places such as Agawam, drive up and down some
of the streets of professors' homes in Amherst and around Smith,
or by the cabinlike homes up in the hills behind Sunderland.

We talked about which homes we'd buy when we got the
money. We could never agree, and decided we would own different
homes, Paige the Tudor, me the Cape, then sleep over at each
other's houses. We would drive for hours, though we couldn't
afford the gas, then go back to the apartment after dark. Without
turning on a single light we'd undress and make love in the breeze
from the fan.

We looked and looked, never stopping anywhere, never going
into any of these homes. I didn't want to do that, didn't want to
squirm in front of some real-estate agent. But there was one home
in particular, one place we made it a point to drive past as often
as we could, maybe three or four times a week. We'd discovered
it one afternoon when we'd driven north on Route 10 to Whately.
The homes in this town were beautiful enough, and we wouldn't
have minded owning any of them, but I'd turned off 10 for some
reason and headed back into the hills.

We drove along an old road, bumpy with potholes; past farm-houses in cleared areas, cabins set in the midst of trees. We came over one hill and dropped down into a small valley where two farmhouses with barns sat on either side of the pasture at the bottom. The barns were three stories tall with stone basements that let out onto the pasture, the second level opening out to the hillside and the farmhouse. At the peaks of the barns were those intricate hex signs, all red and blue and gold. The pasture between the two barns could have been a lawn, it was trimmed so close.

We drove on, not knowing where this road would lead, not really caring. We passed a couple more old homes, then came to a deep woods, new green leaves shading the road until we came around a bend to the left. On the right the trees stopped, and we could see a mailbox on a brick stand, grass growing down to the edge of the road. A For Sale sign was stuck in the ground next to the mailbox.

I pulled onto the shoulder, slowed down until the car was even with the yard. We looked up the lawn to the house.

The house was a brown clapboard Garrison, the second story jutting out over the first all the way around. Next to the house was a three-car garage finished in the same color wood, and beyond that stood a small barn. Flowerboxes with geraniums and marigolds hung from the upstairs windows, more flowers planted in flowerbeds across the front of the house. It wasn't an old home; you could tell by the shingles and the shape the clapboard was in that it had been built just a few years ago.

Just then the front door opened, and two kids—two boys—ran out of the house, one chasing the other. They were laughing, and ran around the side of the house, back toward the barn. I put the car in gear, and we drove on.

When we got home that night we ate a simple dinner, then went to the bedroom. Without a word I undressed Paige, unzipped and then slipped off her skirt and slip, then unbuttoned her blouse. I unhooked her bra and took off her underpants. She then un-dressed me, and we stood there in the bedroom, holding each other. Then we slowly began dancing, neither one of us making a sound, both of us keeping the same slow time, the same slow rhythm, until finally we went to bed.

Afterward, we lay there facing each other. I said, "You know, we could never afford that place."

She breathed out, then rolled onto her back. She put her hands behind her neck, stared at the ceiling. "I know," she said.

A few minutes later I said, "Do you mind, really, our not owning a home like that? Or just any home at all?"

She was quiet a moment, then said, "No." She rolled over to me again. "Not at all, I guess." We were silent, until a few minutes later she said, "What matters most is the baby. That's what matters most right now. A house will come." She paused. "I hope so, anyway."

My vacation was the last week in May, and by then we'd been by that brown Garrison at least fifteen times. Each time we slowed down, each time we stopped, each time we saw some little sign of life: the kids—there was another one, a girl we sometimes saw—the lawn newly mowed, a garage door open.

We had joked about spending our vacation looking at homes we couldn't have, joked about visiting as many open houses as we could find, though we'd still not stopped for one. We joked, but both knew that down deep there was some truth about what we were saying, someting that wasn't a joke at all. But we'd decided earlier in the year to go down to New Jersey to her parents, and had already put a deposit down on a rental house on Long Beach Island.

The day came to leave. I had the suitcases in the trunk, a cooler and beach chairs on the backseat, a hibachi on the floorboard back there. I was in the car, waiting for Paige. It must have been seven already, the humidity and heat picking up, the bright green leaves on trees drooping with the weight of the air.

She'd had a bad case of morning sickness that day; she'd woken up about four thirty and thrown up, really thrown up. For the last couple of weeks she'd felt queasy, had once spit up a little in the sink, but this was the first time she'd actually vomited.

I'd gotten up after I heard the toilet flush. Like every morning the last two weeks I went straight to the kitchen, got out the saltines and brought a few to her.

She was on her knees, both arms around the toilet, her hair down in her face.

"You all right?" I said, and stooped down, the crackers in my hand.

She nodded, slowly took a cracker and chewed it up, swallowed it. "Just worse today," she said. "I guess this goes with the whole thing."

"Guess so," I said. I stood, patted her back, then went back to sleep.

When I woke up about five thirty, she was already showered and dressed, and was sitting on the sofa in the front room. She looked pale, held her hands between her knees.

"Are you really okay?" I said.

"Yes," she said. "Get ready for this," she said. "Get ready for my being sick. Some women are sick all nine months. Some women are sick from day one. We've just been lucky so far." She gave a little smile, shrugged.

I said, "Great," and went to the bathroom.

Now here it was seven already, and I wanted to go. I wanted to get down through Hartford before the morning rush hour, and I knew that, sitting there in the driveway at seven, we would hit rush hour head on.

I honked the horn, leaned out the window. "Come on, Paige," I shouted. She came down a minute or so later, still pale. She had a bottle of Diet Rite in one hand, a few saltines in the other.

I said, "Are you sick or not? Are you ready to go down there, or should we just stay right here the rest of vacation? Now we've got all that traffic to face, all that shit down there in Hartford to get through, and you don't even know if you're well enough to go."

And so we got into a fight right then and there, a fight over whether we should go then or later, a fight about her being sick; a fight over nothing, really. Just a fight.

We ended up not talking as we drove through town, not talking as we passed down through Holyoke and Springfield and across the Connecticut state line.

It wasn't until we'd gotten to Windsor Locks that Paige, her face turned away from me, said, "I have to go to the bathroom."

"Hold it," I said. I could see up ahead where traffic into Hartford was already backing up.

She said nothing. I kept driving. Traffic stopped, and we sat there, the air hot off the pavement.

A half hour later we were still in Hartford, just past the 84 interchange. Things were starting to pick up, a little breathing space between cars now.

Paige turned to me. "I'm still holding."

"We're just about to get out of this traffic, all right? Hold on. Just hold. We'll stop at Rocky Hill."

She turned in her seat, tried to pull her legs up under her. She couldn't.

The Rocky Hill exit came up some fifteen minutes outside Hartford. Paige was sitting with her ankles crossed, her hands on her abdomen. She was tapping one foot, but I drove on. I don't know why. I think because I was still mad. Because of the traffic we were almost two hours behind already, and I wanted to make up some time.

The exit passed by, and Paige turned to me. Her face was blank, as if she couldn't believe what I had just done.

"What in hell are you doing?" she said. She turned back toward the exit, then to me. "Just what do you think you're doing?"

"Making up for lost time," I said, my eyes on the road. I held the steering wheel with both hands.

"Goddamn you, you fool. I have to go to the bathroom. I'm about to burst. Stop at the next exit, you ass." She turned and faced front, crossed her arms.

We passed the next exit, and the next, each time Paige calling me an idiot, a fool, a loser. Each exit I wanted less and less to stop. It was a stupid thing to do. I thought she could hold it. She was telling me she couldn't.

Finally, after we'd turned onto the Merritt, I looked at her. Her arms were still crossed, but her head was bowed, and she was crying.

I looked back to the road. We passed a sign that read, SERVICES, 1 MILE.

I put the blinker on, took the exit. I pulled through the Mobil station to the parking lot beyond it, parked the car a few spaces down from the small, square brick building.

Paige looked up at me, tears on her face. "God damn you," she said. She opened her door, walked quickly to the building. She was bent over, holding her stomach. She'd left the car door open. I leaned over, pulled it closed.

I waited, watching cars on the parkway go by in my rearview mirror. I listened to the sounds insects made in the woods behind the gas station. Cars came into the station, filled up with gas. A woman in a gray business suit was making a call at an open-air phone booth next to the building. She hung up, climbed into a red BMW parked two spaces over from me, and drove off. Then a VW pulled in, and a man wearing cut-offs and a T-shirt got out. He had a golden retriever in the car. The man went to the bathroom, then came back to the car, let the dog out. They ran around the grassy area in front of the parking lot a few minutes, then the man opened the passenger-side door, went back to the grass where the dog was still running. He grabbed the dog by the collar, pulled him to the car, and lifted him in. The man came around, got in on his side, and drove off.

I looked at my watch. It was ten after ten.

Five minutes later there was no one around, no cars for gas, none in the parking lot. The attendant, I guessed, was in his office.

I got out of the car, wondering if Paige was all right. We hadn't had any breakfast yet, and Paige had only eaten those crackers and soda, as far as I knew. She needed more.

I thought of her eyes when she'd looked up at me after I'd pulled in. I thought of her wet eyes and of her asking God to damn me.

What she needed, I knew, was someone who could give her more than I could. I walked toward the brick building, and thought about how I'd gotten in a fight with her over nothing. It wasn't the fight that hurt, but the nothing that had caused it. It was my fault. And there was the fact we'd never be able to afford a house, at least not one like those we wished we could have, especially not the one at the top of the hill in Whately, the house we'd finally agreed we both could live in. I couldn't give her that.

About all I could give her, I thought as I came up to the door marked with a stick figure in a skirt, was what she had inside her, that child, that pulse I'd felt the night I'd had the cold. That pulse, that blood, that movement through her heart and into another that made her two people, part me, part her. A third. And this morning, when this woman had been so sick, I'd started a fight out of thin air, all for nothing. We'd gotten to this point, to this place in Connecticut, to this place in our lives no sooner. We'd just gotten here with more pain.

I knocked on the gray metal door. I said, "Paige, I'm sorry."

I listened. I heard nothing.

I said, "Paige?"

This is where I stopped it. This is where I always stopped it. There was nothing more I wanted to think about.

I stood up from the sofa, made my way across the now-dark room to the phone. I picked up the receiver, shook the dust off it, then put it to my ear. I heard nothing. I shook the receiver, banged the telephone on the floor twice. The dial tone clicked across the line.

The waitress, a girl in a beige apron and a red T-shirt and jeans, brought the first pitcher, set it on the table.

Cal leaned across the table, said, "Wheeler. You the big RC and Schweppes salesman. I knew that's what it was. I knew she up and left you." He leaned back, took the pitcher and filled both glasses. He spilled some of the beer on the vinyl tablecloth. "Whoa," he said, and laughed. "No use crying over spilled milk, but spilled beer is another thing, right?"

I smiled, took the glass. He raised his glass in a toast. "Here's to so much horseshit and holy matrimony," he said. He put the glass to his mouth, emptied it.

I took a drink, then put my glass down. I looked around the room. It was a small place, Joe's Cafe, and I'd never been here before. The walls were painted with pictures of saguaro cactus and burros and Mexican men with serapes, though Joe's was supposed to have good pizza. The place was separated into two small rooms, one with booths, the other with a bar and picnic tables. We were at a picnic table. A Celtics game played on the color set above the bar; pennants from everywhere hung around the mirror behind the bar, along the walls, from the ceiling.

It felt good to be in this warm room, with people shouting at the set and at each other. I'd called Cal and he'd said to meet him here in fifteen minutes. I had put on my jacket and walked down the hill from the apartment, crossed King Street and walked under the railroad overpass, then down Market. I ended up waiting for him outside for five minutes, but I was glad for the cold night air

in my lungs. Anything was better than the dead air in the
apartment.

The waitress brought the pizza, set it down in front of us.

"Ah," Cal said. "Linguica. Portuguese sausage." He picked
up a piece, took a bite, then made an O with his mouth to show
me how hot it was.

"I'll bet I'll die of heartburn," I said, and pulled a piece from
the pan onto my plate. The Celtics had just lost the ball, and
people at the bar shouted louder. Someone tossed a wadded-up
napkin at the set.

Cal swallowed. "What?"

"I'll die of heartburn."

"But what a way to go," he said, and took another bite.

We ate a couple pieces each, both of us watching the game.
A few minutes later a commercial came on. We turned back to
the table. Cal poured the last of the pitcher into his glass.

I said, "And it's not so much horseshit."

"It is too," he said. "Horseshit and holy matrimony. I know.
It's not like I'm blowing air out my ass." He downed half the glass.
"This was about a year and a half ago, when I took off on Molly.
But it wasn't like there were tears of despair all over the place.
Hah. No. I pulled the door closed behind me on the way out, and
the last thing I heard was the waffle iron banging on the inside
of the door. I'd seen it flying across the room at me and pulled
the door closed just in time." He took a bite of pizza, his eyes on
the set. He was telling me this story as if it were some kind of
joke, as though he'd probably told it a thousand times before, and
then I realized he probably had. "You could say there was no love
lost in this situation. Not by a long shot." He glanced down from
the set to me. He was holding the pizza with both hands, the end
in his mouth. He stopped, brought the pizza down and put it on
his plate. He picked up his napkin, slowly started wiping his
fingers. "But that don't help you too much, does it?"

I thought he'd forgotten what I'd told him when we first sat
down and he ordered the pizza, thought he'd forgotten I'd told
him how Paige cried the night before she took off, and about the

U-Haul boy coming up and moving things out, the two of them wrestling the refrigerator while I watched, and the sound of my wife's laughter coming up through the stairwell and into the empty apartment. And I thought he'd forgotten I'd told him he was the first one to know all this, the first one I'd told the whole thing to.

"No," he said, and dropped the napkin on the table. "This don't help you at all." He put his elbows on the table, folded his fingers together, and it was then I started wondering why it had been him I'd waited to tell. After I'd finished telling him what happened, he'd laughed and reached across the table and slapped my shoulder. Maybe that was why I told him. Maybe that was what I'd expected of him, and all I wanted.

Now here he was all serious and sober, and I looked down from him to my plate and the half-eaten third piece of pizza there.

He said, "I'm going to tell you this because I like you. We do good work together. You sell me a lot of product, then I sell it for more profit than you're making." He looked back down at his plate, picked up the pizza. He took another bite.

When we finished the pizza, I ordered another pitcher. He hadn't said anything more, and then we decided to move to the booth side of the place.

"I messed around on her," he said once we were sitting. He said it quietly, matter-of-fact. "I shouldn't have, plain and simple. As simple as that. This was a year and a half ago. Actually a year and eight months, but I'm not counting." He laughed a little, but not, I could tell, because it was funny. "This woman I messed with was a butcher back in the meat department. Jenny. She's not here any more. Shit, she left a couple days after we made it."

The next pitcher came. I poured.

He took a drink. He looked around the room. His eyes were already a little glazed over. He rubbed his nose.

"Shit," he said. "I've never been over in this half of Joe's. Same old crappy Mexican paintings."

I laughed, shook my head.

He took another sip, then held the glass in both hands.

"I was working closing back then, and I just kept seeing this

Jenny back in the meat department, back behind the glass wall that separates the case from the cutting room. I'd wave, and then she'd wave. She was no looker. No looker by a long shot. But there was just that flash, you know? That flash that hits you and makes your neck hot when somebody pays attention to you."

I nodded, took a drink.

"Things weren't easy at the home front, let me tell you. That was when I'd just started as assistant, and I was working twelve-hour days and closing to boot. And I wasn't seeing enough of my wife, and she wasn't seeing enough of me, and you and I both know I don't get paid doodley-squat. And here she's wondering why I should put up with shitty hours as an assistant with not much more money than I was making as a journeyman. We'd have these bouts every night when I came home, and then the next day I'd go to work and there'd be Jenny back there in her white apron with blood all over it, and wearing that white plastic construction hat, and waving at me or saying 'Hello, how are you?' She had pretty hair, I remember that much, but beyond that, nothing." He paused. "That's funny. I can't even remember what she looked like."

He unbuttoned the second button on his shirt, pulled the collar off his neck. He finished off the glass. I filled it again, then mine, then ordered another pitcher.

"One thing for sure," he said, "is that it wasn't any hayride when we finally did make it. Finally one afternoon she came out from behind that glass wall as I was walking past, and says, 'Why are you always coming on to me?' smiling and making like she was blushing. I said, 'Me? You're the one coming on to me.' And I was laughing, and there was that hot feeling coming across my face, and I thought that maybe she wasn't faking a blush, that maybe she was feeling like I was. That was the second I could see what was going to happen. I didn't know where, when, how, whatever. I just knew right then that we were going to make it.

"I said, 'And you a married woman.' And she says, 'You're not kidding me. You're a married man. But does that make any difference?' I said, 'I guess not,' and she turned and made her way back to the cutting room. She glanced at me as she pulled that sliding glass wall closed, and she was smiling. God, she was smiling. I just stood there with my mouth open."

He gulped down that glass. I finished mine, and felt the room getting hotter. We were drinking too much beer, but I filled both our glasses. I put both hands around my glass, felt the cool.

"That night I called up Molly and told her I would be late, that two of the registers had come up short and that I had no idea what time I'd be home. 'So tell me something new,' she said. That's it. She hung up, and I didn't even give a shit. I didn't give a shit what happened then. If there had been any sort of sorry in me for what I was about to do, it just took off.

"Jenny and me ended up driving around for thirty or forty minutes just trying to find a place to park. We were in separate cars, me in my B210, and Jenny in her old station wagon. The two of us were just driving around, me leading, trying to find a place where no one would bug us. We ended up at the baseball diamond over in Florence, on the other side of Route 9 back behind the high school."

All this time I was just watching him, listening to his story. I was trying to figure how his story might help me, and waiting so that I could tell him the rest of my own story.

"We parked, and we both climbed into the back of the station wagon, neither of us saying a goddamn word to each other. Shit, it was nothing. Nothing." He banged his fist on the table just hard enough to wash the beer around in our glasses. He laughed a little, wiped his hand across his forehead. "Shit, I even got a charley horse in my calf while we were at it. It was over in ten minutes, and still we hadn't said a word, and she's already buttoning up, zipping up, and I am, too. Then we're climbing out of the goddamn station wagon and then the headlights of our cars are on and it feels like the whole world, the whole fucking world has been watching us. That's what I'm thinking as I look out my windshield at the baseball diamond all lit up with the headlights of our two cars, all the way from home plate back to the chain-link fence and into the trees past that. She pulls out, then I pull out, and we're gone. We're over."

His eyes were still glazed, and it was starting to get hard for me to focus in on him, to listen to every word and put together what he was saying. I heard the words, knew what he was talking about, but I had been sitting and watching him for so long that I felt as if my body were just floating in the air, floating free, and that my hands and forearms on the table were the only things that kept me from floating away. I concentrated, moved a leg an inch or so, then the other, just to reassure myself I wouldn't disappear through the roof.

"I got home and Molly was sitting in the bathtub. She was crying. I came in and sat on the edge of the tub. That water in the tub was stone cold. She'd been sitting there for forty-five minutes, she said. She'd called the market to tell me to bring home some milk and ice cream and a stock clerk answered. He told her I'd taken off already. 'I know what you did,' she said. 'I just know. I just know.' She didn't say anything to me after that, just sat in the tub and cried in there until after four in the morning. Two days later she came out of her funk. The last thing she said to me was 'Get the hell out of the house.' That I made her sick just being around. That's when she started throwing things."

He stopped, leaned over the table. He put a finger to his forehead at the hairline.

"See that?" he said. "See this scar?"

I leaned forward. The place was dark, and I'd had too much to drink. I couldn't see anything. Still, I nodded. "Yep," I said.

"That's from a Tupperware juice pitcher she threw at me. Plastic. You'd never think Tupperware would do anything like that, would you? Just plastic."

He stopped talking, and we both just sat there. He was staring at the table, at the scarred wood. "Funny thing, though," he said, and took on a half smile. "Funny thing, but when I saw her there in the tub—" He paused, lost the smile. "When I saw her there in the tub, goose bumps all over her, and her crying, shivering, what I wanted to do was to help her up, give her a towel and dry her off."

He glanced up at me, and I looked away. He looked back at the table, then at the beer in his hands. "I wanted to warm her up, take care of her. That's what I wanted to do, but I couldn't. What I'd done kept me from touching her. And it's funny, but you'd think it would be the other way around. That you would try to do everything you could to make up for the loser you are. But it doesn't work that way. That's what's funny."

He was quiet then, and I knew it was my turn to talk. I wanted to tell him how we'd fought that day six months ago, and of the drive down to New Jersey and what had happened, but I didn't know where to start. I didn't know what to tell him, and then I wondered if he even knew Paige had been pregnant. Why should he? I wondered. Until a couple days before I hadn't even known his last name.

I said, "It's like this," and I stopped. I couldn't see how it was. "It's like this," I said again, and then I just shook my head, looked back at the table.

"This is what it's like," he said. He pointed at the table, tapped hard on it. "Right here and now. There isn't much else. That isn't a happy prospect, but that's it, and what you have to do now is learn to live with it."

He drank the last of the beer, set the glass down on the table. He gave out a big laugh, then reached across the table and slapped me hard on the shoulder again. "So what'll happen is that Thursday, Thanksgiving, you're coming over to my place for dinner, watch a couple ball games, right?"

I looked up at him. I wondered if he was right, if I'd just have to learn to live with what had happened. With *it*. I wondered if, after that whole story of his, he had helped me at all. I still wanted him to hear my story.

He was looking at me, then turned, shrugged. He got this grin on his face. "I've got a girlfriend now, maybe you know her. Carla. She's a checker at the store."

"Sure," I said. "I know Carla."

"She's going to be over. We're cooking up this turkey I got from the store. A twenty-five-pounder. I think there's going to be enough for the three of us. There's going to be more than enough. So you come over, right?"

I sat up in the booth, stretched my arms. I wondered what his place was like, and what mine would be like soon enough. I wondered how much this Carla had done for him. He'd just told me his whole story, and I could tell he was still stirred up over her, over Molly. Maybe, instead of him helping me out, I'd just helped him. It was no comforting thought.

"Sure," I said. "I'll be there. You can count on it."

Outside the sky was clear. I could see stars above us even though we stood a few feet from a lamppost. I shoved my hands deep into my pockets, curled my fingers into fists. I listened as Cal gave me directions to his place. I could hear people inside Joe's laughing and talking, could hear the television and the sounds of pitchers touching mugs. Except for the cold and the night we could have been inside.

Cal waved good-bye and headed off. I watched him fold up into the dark, then turned and headed for my apartment.

I walked down Market toward the railroad overpass. My legs were too long, I thought as I moved down the street. They were moving too fast for what I knew I could do after having drunk so much beer. A good gust of wind could come through here and I'd be blown over and I'd roll along the street like an old beer can.

I was already on Summer and making my way up the hill and along the row of old homes up there before I knew it. I stopped, looked around, amazed I'd walked as far as I had without tripping. There was the stoplight at the bottom of the hill, the Dunkin' Donuts, the Cumberland Farms, and the Mattress Barn. I couldn't even remember having walked across that intersection.

I turned back to the sidewalk and started walking. My legs weren't as long now, but felt short, made of stone. My feet felt as though they were blocks of granite, and it was my job to lift each one, move it to a certain spot on the next cement square of the sidewalk, then set it down. I concentrated hard on this task, but then I heard a door slam shut somewhere, and then I heard a car start. I looked up from the sidewalk, and saw nothing. The cold wind had just carried sounds to me from somewhere else.

I looked around. A house had white iron lawn furniture set up in the yard: a table, two chairs, a bench. A stiff wind picked up, rattled branches, threw dead leaves against the chairs and bench. I listened for more spent sounds, and heard nothing, just wind through the empty trees.

I pushed my hands even deeper into my pockets, leaned forward, and tried my best to run.

The apartment was, like always now that Paige had gone, empty and dark. She'd been gone a couple weeks is all, but it felt like a year and a half. Maybe a year and eight months. I closed the door and leaned my back against it, taking huge breaths.

There was no one there, but what had I expected? Paige? There was no one, and even deeper down into me, past that part that had hoped there might be someone there, I found one small truth: I *knew* no one would be there. That was the truth.

I sank down the door, my legs, the muscles in my thighs twitching from the running I'd just done, folding up beneath me. There in that empty room, that empty apartment, I started talking to myself, and I tried as hard as I'd ever tried anything before to listen to what I had to say.

Paige? Are you all right? I look around for the station attendant, wondering if he is watching me as I talk to the gray metal door on this small brick building. But he is nowhere around, and no cars are pulling in for gas. They just keep flying past on the Merritt, flying and flying.

I make a fist and pound on the door. *Paige?*

Now my hand is on the knob and I slowly push open the door. *Hello?* I move in.

There are beige tiles everywhere, on the floor, up the walls, with an occasional pink one thrown in. Sinks and a long mirror line one wall. Five or six stalls line the other wall, the metal sides and doors painted pink. There are signs of mold creeping up the grout between tiles on the wall, but the sinks are clean and white, the mirror free of water spots.

I look down the row of stalls. One door is closed. *Paige?* I listen.

I move through the room to the stall door, then put my hands on my knees and look under the door. Paige is sitting before the toilet. She is sick, I think. She's throwing up again.

Paige, hey. Open up. Are you sick? Open up.

I get down on the floor. I reach to touch her, just to touch her pant leg to see if she has passed out or not. I touch her, and she flinches, moves her whole leg as far up under her as she can.

Paige. I pull on the door handle.

Open up. Then I hear her. At first it sounds like nothing, like air around me, but then I listen closer, and hear the hiss of her silent crying, the quiet, quick breaths.

I stand up, shake the door handle. *Paige, open this up. I want to help. I'm sorry. Let me help.*

I hear the short, dull click of the stall latch. I pull on the door, and it opens out to me. Paige still sits on the floor. I stand behind her, look over her head into the toilet.

She has thrown up blood, is the first thing I think. My God, she has thrown up blood. The water inside the toilet is red. I put my hand on Paige's shoulder. She is still crying.

Paige. Paige, come on. We have to see a doctor.

No. Her voice is dark, still. I have not heard this tone before.

I stoop next to her, try and look in her face. Her hair is wet and stringy around her face, her face pale.

You're throwing up blood. We should go see a doctor.

I pull back a strand of hair. She stops crying, and gives an awful smile, only the corners of her pale lips moving up. Her eyes, still wet, stare at the bowl.

Look again.

I look. I bend over closer to the edge of the bowl, and look. There is something there in the water, a red mass sitting in the watery red. The thing looks like a round, red sponge, and then I realize what it is just as Paige says *Our child.*

Vomit moves quickly from my stomach and up my esophagus, and I just make it to one of the clean, white sinks before the acid jumps into my mouth and nose. And again.

A minute later I look up from the sink to the mirror. I run a hand back through my hair, and look at myself in this spotless mirror, and look and look and look. I don't see anything there. I see nothing.

Paige is sobbing now. I take a paper towel from the dispenser, wipe my mouth, then go back to her. She has both hands on the toilet seat, and she is crying into it.

Paige. Paige, come on.

I do not know what we are going to do. I do not know where we should go.

Paige.

No. She stops crying again. Her voice is cold, as cold as the steel pipes climbing from the bowl up the wall to the short, stubby handle. Cold.

Paige. I put a hand under her arm, try to pull her up. She is dead in my arms, her body limp. I put the other hand under the other arm, and pull her to standing. Still she watches the bowl.

Paige, we have to go. We have to get you somewhere. I am avoiding the bowl, avoiding looking down there and seeing that red thing in red water just resting there, dead.

She turns to me, her hands pressed to her face, her forearms and elbows flat against her chest. She leans into me, and cries.

I have my arms around her. I lean my head over, rest my cheek against her hair, my eyes closed. A moment later I open them, and I see right down into the toilet, right down to the fetus. The fetus.

Paige still cries, still leans into me. I know we have to go, to get out of this place. I take a hand from around her, then reach, reach across the stall to that cold steel handle against the beige tile wall. I look down at the fetus again. I think to say good-bye, good-bye to this red thing, but I do not. I pull down hard on the handle. I turn my head.

Paige stiffens in my arms, turns quickly to the bowl to see the last of the red water wash down into the pipes. She is quiet a moment, still frozen. She stares at the bowl, then slowly turns to me.

It is this look that kills me, this look she gives me then. There is no expression, no movement, only eyes open wide, lips parted, strings of hair.

In the moment it takes to blink and turn from this killing look, she changes, and her face is gnarled, her hair flying; she is hitting me, pounding me. Both fists pound on my chest, my shoulders, my face and ears, and still she pounds.

I do nothing, because there is nothing for me to do.

She hits me square in the nose, warm liquid pours out, and there is then my blood on her hands, her shirt, her face. My chest feels as if she has broken ribs, but I do not move. I only close my eyes, and let her hit me.

Finally she stops. I open my eyes. She is outside the stall, sitting on the beige tile floor, her legs bent at the knees and out to either side, just a little girl playing jacks, except that she is sobbing, her face in her hands, her hands stained with my own blood. And she is no little girl.

I slip down the stall wall, my legs buckling beneath me, pain in my chest, shoulders, face. I finally hit the floor, and I, too, cry. The only sound is our crying inside this bathroom and the cars outside, flying past this roadside stop.

The phone rang. The sound felt like an ax into the back of my head. My neck hurt, and I reached back to rub it. My hand hit something hard, and then I opened my eyes. I blinked a couple times, sat up. I'd fallen asleep on the floor last night, my back against the door. The hardwood floor was cold; I still had on the pants, shirt, jacket, socks, and boots I'd worn last night. I rubbed my eyes, turned my head to either side. The phone rang again, and I remembered why I had woken up.

I crawled across the floor. The phone rang again, then once more before I could answer it.

"Yeah," I said.

"Ricky?" It was Mitchell.

"Yeah?" I said. I looked around for a clock, remembered I hadn't taken off my watch last night. Seven o'clock.

"Ricky, where the hell are you? There's a route meeting, you know. We're all down here. Where the hell are you?"

"I'll be there," I said. "You don't worry. I'll be there. I'm running late. Sorry."

"Hustle your ass if you want to keep your job," he said, and hung up.

I sat there on the floor and heard the radiators start up. I heard the hissing, and just that sound, just that crack of air brought back last night. The hissing of pipes sounded like Paige's crying in the bathroom before I'd opened the stall door and looked down into that toilet, and here came the vomit again, now, six months later, so that I only had time to stumble to the kitchen sink before I threw up on dirty dishes there, thinking in those few seconds about my hand on that handle and pulling it down, and that red disappearing, and Paige hitting me and crying, and how this was where it had all come to: Paige gone, me here at the kitchen sink. I thought of Cal, and how I had to live with what had happened, and then it became a circle for me, one continuous movement from past to present and back again, what felt like no real hope for change, some kicking out into a future that might leave things done alone.

And yet Paige had still wondered, even to the last minutes before she had gone with the U-Haul boy that day, why I had done what I'd done, not the flushing of the death not yet born, but why I'd let it all fester inside me for as long as I did until I'd stopped talking, stopped touching her, stopped kissing her, stopped putting a hand to her waist, her shoulder, her face. She still wondered why.

THREE

shaved and showered, left my hair wet, though I knew it was probably only twenty degrees outside. I went downstairs, opened the front door of the building, and took a breath. I could feel the hairs in my nose freeze up, my ears and scalp go numb.

I made it to the office a little after seven thirty. I pushed open the front door.

Everyone was there, some thirty people, including the heads from Hartford. The salesmen were seated at the conference tables, the five or six heads against the far wall, just standing there as they always did whenever they came down. Mitchell and the other supervisors stood along the wall to the right, the wall with the posted sales. Cigarette smoke hit my eyes, sank into my lungs.

They all turned to me the moment the door opened. One of the heads, Lynn Andros, had been in the middle of something; he stood a few feet off from the other heads, his hand in the air in the middle of some gesture. He had stopped, and was looking at me like all the rest. He was a short guy with a flat face and small eyes below bushy eyebrows. I knew him. He'd ridden with me a few times. "Just checking out distribution," Mitchell always told me before Andros would show up the mornings he was going with me. That was the way the company worked: surprises all the time.

He was loud and stocky, but I liked him. No matter how shitty he was to you, you could look in those small eyes and see he was only interested in the number of cases you could sell. That was his job, and I sometimes envied him—like right then when

I'd come in late—because that was all he *needed* to worry about. That was his job. I knew he had kids: he'd shown me pictures of them when we'd stopped for lunch at a Wendy's one day. But I couldn't see him at home, couldn't see him having a fight with his wife over nothing, couldn't see him with a small child in his lap while he taught her how to tie her shoes. All he cared about was sales. He didn't have any family problems. He didn't have any problems at all, except you and why you didn't bring in the cases.

He slowly brought his hand down from mid-gesture, then put both hands on his hips. Smoke snaked up from a cigarette he held in one hand.

"Wheeler," he said.

I said, "Yes, sir," and brought my hands from inside my pockets, held them at my sides.

"Lovely afternoon."

"Sorry I'm late," I said, and put my hands together in front of me.

"You bet your sweet ass you're sorry," he said. He moved one hand up, the hand with the cigarette, and slowly pointed at the posted sales board. "You bet your sweet ass you're sorry. Do you think that just because you're forty-one percent over projection that you can waltz in here this late? Is that what you think?"

"No, sir," I said, and crossed my arms. My arms were useless. They could be cut off at the shoulder, and it wouldn't make any difference to those six company heads standing over there, or to those supervisors, or, for that matter, to the twenty or so salesmen glad it wasn't them standing here.

But he'd said forty-one percent. That was a new number. I thought about it, tried to remember what I'd done, but my head hurt too much to think. I needed coffee.

"Car trouble," I said.

He grinned. I knew he liked me; he'd told me as much when we were at a Food King once. He'd watched me get down on my knees and put point-of-purchase bottle hangers on every other RC and Diet Rite one-liter bottle we had on an end rack in that store. I put them on all the way to the back row. I'd had to reach my arm back until my shoulder hit the shelf strip. I was pumping it for him that day, giving him the lines about how conscientious a salesman I was, how I knew that no matter how much of a hassle it was to put up p.o.p., the Day-Glo bottle hangers really did increase sales. It was a load of bullshit, my telling him all this, but the thing was that he knew it was a load, and that he knew that *I* knew. That was what being a good salesman was about, after all. Who could tell the best lie. Who could pour on the shit most effectively, so that managers and consumers alike would really believe they needed to pour carbonated water and chemicals down their throats every day. We'd walked out of the store, my knees and hands filthy. All he'd said was, "I like your style, Wheeler."

Still, I couldn't figure him out. He was grinning, and brought his pointed hand back to his hip. He could go either way on me. He could just let me go, let me find a seat somewhere and disappear into it like everyone else, or he could turn me into some kind of lesson for the rest of the group. He was only interested in sales.

But forty-one percent. *Forty-one percent.* How did that number appear? I thought about it, and knew it was the work. Working my ass off. Selling and merchandising and selling more and working. Nothing else. Nobody else. Just me, working. *Forty-one percent.*

"January's coming, Mr. Wheeler," he said, and I knew then he'd already decided. I knew he'd already opted to murder me, but I wanted him to. It seemed only the next logical thing to happen. But forty-one percent. Here was the only thing I'd been paying attention to the last three weeks. I was here. I would see what I could do. I took a deep breath.

"January, and what happens then, Mr. Wheeler?" His eyes narrowed to slits. He was still grinning.

"All those Schweppes ends come down," I said.

"Exactly. Then what?"

"We're up shit creek, sir," I said, then paused. "Unless, of course, we shoot cases right back in where the holes are."

"Very good, Mr. Wheeler." Some of the men in the room moved papers, settled back in their chairs. Jerry Landers, two tables over, popped his finger, and I could hear the knuckle crack, the room was so quiet. I looked at him, saw his face turn from mine. He stopped shaking his finger. Springer sat with a new cigarette dangling from his lips, his eyes on the ceiling. Will Tremblay, with his black lacquered pompadour, cleared his throat, then pulled a pencil from behind one ear. They were all digging in. I had sat through enough of these meetings and had seen enough salesmen murdered. But this time it wasn't going to be me.

"How does one shoot cases back in where the holes are?" Andros said.

"One makes sure he has a damn good buy, and makes sure his bosses down in Hartford have that deal lined up and waiting for him. And one makes sure he has the real backup: the drivers, the display men, the merchandisers, everything to make sure he can make good on what he promises the manager."

Those six men at the other side of the room didn't move. Andros's smile seemed to grow wider.

"So," he said, "you've shot those cases right in. What is it you're shooting in, Mr. Wheeler? Do you have any idea?"

I stood there a moment, my arms still crossed, then looked down at the floor. "No," I said.

"Rule one, Mr. Wheeler: We're not late for meetings, are we? When we're late for meetings, we miss the whole goddamn purpose *for* the meeting. Purpose of meeting, Mr. Wheeler: what we're shooting in to fill the holes in January."

"I see," I said without looking up. Then I said, "But that's not the only thing to January." I looked up, saw Andros looking at me. His smile was tighter, tough. His small eyes shone, and I could see he was loving it. He wanted me to fight him.

"Mr. Wheeler, please be our guest. Tell us, Mr. Wheeler, what else January is for." He made a sweeping gesture with his hand. He ended by pointing his hand at the other heads from Hartford. "Please, Mr. Wheeler, let us in on your secret."

"It's saturation," I said, and put my hands back in my

pockets. I shrugged. "It's just saturation at that time. Common sense. I mean, you people down in Hartford pull through for us again, just like you did by getting us all these Schweppes ends everywhere, then we can shoot for saturation of the market." The words were hard and dry in my throat, and I had to force them out.

Andros sat on the edge of the table, stubbed out his cigarette, lit another, all without taking his eyes off me.

"I mean, we can quit worrying about the chains. Turn our attention to the independents. Turn back to them. We can go into all our mom-and-pops and give the shelves, the coldbox, the back rooms, everywhere a good workout. Rotate out the old product, clean up the shelves, put on shelf strips, clean up the coldbox, put in rolling can racks for them, stuff like that. Independents love that stuff, the attention. And they deserve it, you know, after the holidays when everyone was buying mixers at the chains. Then they see all this stuff we've been doing for them, and they give us a little end display in *their* place. It's just an end cap, maybe a side stack. Fifteen, twenty cases, but it's in there, and that's twenty extra cases out on the floor. And then, since we've cleaned up the coldbox, we ask them if they want a couple more brands to try out, maybe RC 100 next to the Diet Rite. And then, since we're putting in a couple more lines, then why not let us rearrange the whole damned box so that the RC and Diet Rite and Schweppes are right there at eye level and handle level. It's just cleanup for the month of January. Stuff you people downtown can't handle for us, stuff only we can do because we're down here at the bottom level. Saturation. Common sense."

The room was quiet, and I realized how long I'd talked. I thought about it for a second, and knew that was probably the most I'd said to anyone in three weeks, the most words that had come out of my mouth.

The quiet was broken by Andros, who started clapping. He held both hands in the air, clapping the fingers of one hand against the palm of the other, all the time looking around the room, grinning, nodding. He got off the edge of the table, then began making his way toward me, weaving around salesmen pulling in their seats so he could get by. Then he was in front of me, still clapping, still grinning.

"Very good, Mr. Wheeler, very good." He stopped clapping, brought his hands down, and turned to the group. "It's just as our private tutor has said here, gentlemen. Common sense. Use January, traditionally a slow month, for cleanup. Goodwill ambassadors. Brown-nosers, if you will. That's our business."

His back was to me. This was as good a time as any to move for an empty seat. I took a couple steps toward a table, and he turned.

"Mr. Wheeler?"

I stopped. "Yes?"

"Mr. Wheeler, a new rule. A rule which supersedes rule number one. This rule is: We don't 'quit worrying about the chains.' The chains, sir, are our meat, the independents our bread and butter. So we worry as much as we ever did about our chains. We can't eat bread and butter without meat, can we?"

"No, sir."

"Good, Mr. Wheeler. And once again, the old rule number one?"

"We're not late for meetings."

"Thank you. You may be seated."

He said a few more words to the group, words I wasn't listening to as I found a seat and sat down at a table. One of the men at the table pushed an extra fact sheet at me, the handout Andros had passed around before I got there.

Andros went back to the far wall with the other heads, and then a big, dark-haired guy who'd started out as a truck driver for the company some twenty-five years ago and who was now a vice president stepped up and started talking about some changes in truck routes. Andros lit up another cigarette, shook out the match, and looked at me. He grinned. I grinned, too, and shook my head.

～～～

When the meeting was over I started back to one of the small offices off the conference room where coffee and donuts had been laid out.

I got back to the office, took a styrofoam cup from a pillar of them next to the coffee machine, then poured in black, black coffee. I brought the cup to my lips, burned them with the first sip.

"Shit," I said, and turned from the machine.

Andros was standing there, just behind me. I almost spilled my coffee on him.

"Precisely what I say when a perfectly able salesman rolls in late to a meeting at which I'm giving a presentation," he said.

I moved away from the machine, let him pour himself a cup. I watched as he filled the cup, put in four spoonfuls of Cremora and then two packets of Sweet 'n Low. He sipped, winced. "But what you said, of course, is true. Common sense. January is slow, so start gearing up for spring and summer. Don't waste a minute. Never waste a minute of a day." He made a little toast with the cup, as if it were a glass of champagne, then swallowed two gulps of the coffee. He took a breath, then finished off the cup. He dropped it into a metal trash can next to the table.

He said, "Common sense. Common sense," and then he was straightening my tie, his hands at my throat. I just stood there, coffee in one hand, the other in my pocket. He pulled the tie snug beneath my adam's apple, and said, "Word has it you've got domestic difficulties, Mr. Wheeler. Problems on the home front." He looked at the knot, leaning his head one way and another, as if the knot were the center of things.

I said, "I don't like the fact it sounds like common knowledge."

He finished with the tie, smiled. "It's not. It's my responsibility, you know, to know what's going on. A salesman of mine has sales forty-one percent over projection, projection being, I'll remind you, ten percent over actual sales this time last year, for a grand total of fifty-one percent increased sales, then I want to know what's going on. And, of course, through my vast communications network—" he stopped, looked around, then nodded toward where Mitchell stood in the corner of the office talking to a couple of merchandisers—"I promptly and easily found out indeed what *was* going on."

"It's pretty straightforward," I said, trying to get back to business and something it seemed I might know something about. "You've got the deal on Schweppes. Mitchell's given me good backup. It's as simple as that."

"Common sense says work and family don't mix. Is that what your problem is? Are you trying to mix the two? You bringing it home?"

"No, sir," I said. "What's going on at home has nothing to do with work."

"Good answer," he said, "because they don't. Work and family don't mix. It's good to hear you're shooting in all those cases and that it's not because of home life. Or the lack thereof." He cleared his throat, grinned. "See you, then. Next week. Haven't nailed down the day yet." He turned to leave.

"What do you mean?" I said.

He turned. "I'm riding with you next week. We'll figure out when. One morning or another. Maybe your chains day, I want to make sure nobody's forgetting about the chains." He pointed toward Mitchell. "Talk to your supervisor. He knows all about it."

"One thing," I said. He turned full around to me. "One thing is, what do you care? What do you care about my home life?" As soon as the words left me, I knew this was something out of line, something I maybe shouldn't have asked. He was one of the heads up from Hartford, the chain accounts manager. Still, it was my life he was worried about, no one else's.

He came over to me, started straightening my tie, looking at it once again as if that piece of cloth around my neck were the center of the universe.

"It's my job," he said.

Neuroscience and Behavior."

"It's me again," I said, my eyes closed. It was a little after noon. I was at a pay phone outside one of my package stores. After the meeting a half-dozen or so of us went to breakfast at a Friendly's in town. We hadn't left until around nine. It had taken me those three hours since to work up the nerve to call again, even though everyone at breakfast had thought I was some sort of hero for standing up to Andros like I did.

"Oh," she said. I heard her lean back in her desk chair.

"I don't want to bother you."

"You're not," she said.

"Sounds like it."

She breathed out. "Have you thought any more about anything since I talked to you last? Do you have anything to say?"

I tried to imagine her at her desk. She put her hand on her neck as she waited for my answer.

I was quiet. Wind blew around me, under my coat. The pay phone was an open-air one. I said, "Yes." It was the truth, but I didn't know exactly what I was going to say next.

"Well?" she said.

"Well?"

"What is it?"

I turned toward the phone. I looked at the numbers below each button. "I have to see you."

"This is only the second time I've talked to you, do you realize that? And last time was a joke. Last time wasn't any kind of breakthrough for the two of us. I thought you might have called a few times more by now." She paused. "What I want is for us to talk on the phone a few more times before I see you."

"You could have called me."

"I didn't think it was my place. You and your pride. You and your goddamn pride."

"Isn't there anyone there? Someone's going to hear you."

"Don't you see what I mean?" she said. "This is it. This is exactly it. No one's listening. I'm here alone, but would that make a difference? No. You just care about whether someone's listening or not. I want to talk to you, and you're worried someone's listening." She paused. "And it's not like I've been sitting around and waiting for your calls, either."

"I wouldn't think you would," I said. "You've got so many other important things to sort out. Things you won't tell me about." I knew then where I was headed.

"I do. You're right. Poor Richard. Poor, poor Richard, who thinks the whole world is on his shoulders, that all the sins of the hopeless are on him. Other people have problems, too. Other people have lives, too. But you never even stop to think about that."

"What do you mean? What do you mean? What kind of problems could you have?"

"God damn you. God damn you, you son of a bitch. Don't you think I feel anything at all? Don't you think I feel something? Don't you think maybe I hurt, too? Or did you manage to forget that I was the one who miscarried. It'd been inside me. You think it was all your fault. You'd love to think the whole thing was designed just so you could feel pain, but that's not true. That's not true at all."

Her voice cracked, and then she was crying. "God damn you," she said, her voice high and shaking. "God damn you. I can't even think right now why I love you. Why I loved you in the first place. Not one reason."

We were both quiet, and I listened, said nothing, while she cried at the other end.

"I still love you," she whispered, then hung up.

I stood there at the open-air pay phone with the receiver in my hand. I was out in Florence, on the west side of town. I looked around. The package store was at the main intersection in Florence; across the street was a pizza parlor, a drug store, the post office. On the other corner was a clothing store for teenagers. All the stores were built, I supposed, in the 1880s and '90s, their storefronts extending up past the roofline so that all the buildings looked taller than they really were. I wondered why I had noticed this fact for the first time just then, but couldn't find a good reason. I just looked and looked at the buildings, thinking how fake that was, how misleading to make these fine, sturdy brick buildings look taller than they actually were.

I hung up the phone, then went into the package store where I sold the guy a twenty-five-case end stack of Schweppes for the holidays. Then I started in on rearranging his coldbox, emptying our space, cleaning it out.

Common sense, I kept saying to myself. I said it out loud there in the coldbox as I worked, pulling cold stock and putting it up on the shelf. "Common sense," I said. "Common sense, common sense," and watched my breath.

Common sense told me to go over to the university and wait for her to get off. I finished up my stops in Florence, where I sold two more displays. I found myself using those words in conversations with managers, owners. "Common sense," I heard myself say, "would tell you to put in a stack right here at the end of the chip aisle," or, "If I'd used common sense I would have sent in a little more club soda, what with tomorrow being Thanksgiving." The words were everywhere, so that when I finished my last stop, a market in Williamsburg, I climbed into the car, looked into the rearview mirror, and said, "Common sense."

I was at the university by three thirty. I pulled into the parking lot, drove past the empty security station. The lot was a permit-only one, but the guard, I knew, always left at three. I'd been here

enough times to know. I parked in a corner of the lot at the far
end of her building. I turned off the engine.

Her building was squat and ugly, built in the 1950s with
brick and steel and square angles. Every few feet was a window,
its frame painted primer gray. Her window was the third one down
from the front door. Plenty of days, especially when we'd been
going three and four times a week to look at that clapboard Garrison, I'd parked the car, walked over to the window and tapped
on it. Paige would turn from the typewriter or phone or whatever
she was doing and give me a small wave, just enough to let me
know she knew I was there. Then she would close things up—
put the plastic cover over the typewriter, unplug her coffeemaker,
straighten papers, graphs, anything left on her desktop.

I thought to go over to the window and look in, see what was
going on, what had changed. I wanted to know if our picture was
still on her desk, a picture of the two of us sitting on our sofa one
Christmas morning, me in a kelly green sweater Paige had given
me, Paige with her hair newly permed. Above her desk was a cork
bulletin board. She had thumbtacked birthday cards and things
I'd given her in the past, and I wondered if these things, too, were
still around. I knew there was a single glove of mine somewhere
in that room, probably on the floor of the closet. There was a
transistor radio in the shape of an RC can she had, too. I wondered
if all those things had been cleared, hidden away in her desk or
maybe burned in a small fire she had built in the trash can. I
could see her doing that.

But mostly I wondered if she were still wearing her wedding
rings or not, whether she'd finally done with them what I thought
she had when I owned Vermont, and tossed them in a garbage
disposal. Or maybe she'd thrown them out the window of the
U-Haul truck.

I sat in the car, and waited. Campus was empty, since
Thanksgiving was the next day. From where I sat I could see the
administration building, white concrete and recessed windows,
and beyond that a red metal sculpture of something I knew I'd
never be able to recognize. Below me, to my right, the ground

sloped down to the gray grass of the lacrosse fields. Farther down was the gym, huge and square and gray, parking lots next to it. Beyond that were the practice fields, and then the corn and tobacco fields began. In the distance were the violet foothills of the Berkshires.

Wind came up from the lacrosse fields, blowing dust and sand and salt from clear across the valley. I looked out across the fields, past the gym to those hills, everything peaceful and calm and motionless. You couldn't see the wind. You can never see the wind, I thought.

The sun finally hit the top of the gym, and long shadows that had been growing across the lacrosse field hit me, and then I was in shadow, and I was cold.

Paige came out of the building. She was wearing her trench coat, her hands deep in her coat pockets, her face and hair wrapped in a burgundy muffler. She walked slowly, looking at the ground, the wind whipping around her coat.

I waited for her to see the car, to see me, but she didn't look up from the ground, only moved her feet slowly, her shoulders up, and leaned into the wind.

She stopped for a moment, turned to look behind her. She still didn't see me, but then a woman came out of the building. I thought she looked familiar, her build, her hair. It took me a moment, the woman half-hidden in a thick down jacket and brown muffler around her throat, but I recognized her. Wendy Kasmarski, from the wedding, and then I knew where she had been staying all this time: with Wendy and Larry up in Colrain.

Paige waited for Wendy to catch up with her, and then the two made their way across the lot to a green Bronco. Wendy opened the passenger-side door and Paige climbed in. Wendy came around the front of the Bronco, and I saw Paige lean over, unlock Wendy's door. She climbed in, started the engine. A burst of black smoke shot out the exhaust pipe. They sat there a minute or so.

I started my car, too.

Wendy put the Bronco in gear, backed out of her slot, and

slowly moved down the row of cars toward the security station. I pulled out, too, and stopped at the end of my row. I watched them, now at the lot entrance waiting for traffic to clear. She pulled out, turning off to the right and, I knew, down past the tower dormitories and practice fields and gym to 116.

I pulled up to the entrance, watched until they were clear of the light at the intersection below the gym, then pulled out.

We drove north on 116, past the blocks of brick apartment buildings for grad students at the university, through the main intersection in Sunderland with its market, package store, and restaurant. I hung back from them what I thought must be just far enough so that Wendy might not spot me in her rearview mirror.

We crossed the old bridge over the Connecticut in Sunderland, the sun now down and making the water below us black. Bare trees lining the bank made the water look that much colder; I glanced down at the banks, half-expecting there to be a skim of ice a foot or so out into the river.

Then we were at the interstate entrance. I could either turn right and follow them, go all the way up there to Colrain, ducking behind cars, watching and following and feeling every car on the road knew I was following that green Bronco up there, or I could turn left and head down Route 10 through the trees and back to the apartment.

I sat at the stop sign, no blinker on. I turned right.

It was dark by the time we were off the 91 and at the traffic circle in Greenfield. I'd waited until then to turn my lights on, still afraid Wendy might see me, or that Paige, maybe turning to put her purse in the backseat, would look up, see me three cars back.

We made it through the circle, back under the interstate, and came out heading west on the Mohawk Trail. We passed a Stop & Shop, the parking lot filled with cars, shoppers picking up last-minute items before Thanksgiving. I wondered how much

Schweppes was being sold in there, then turned back to the row of cars in front of me, the taillights once more like red flares, Paige in a green Bronco five or six cars up. We started the climb up the mountain, the small-town spread of lights in Greenfield below us, the cold, black night of the forest ahead.

Another day Paige and I had been driving this road to Wendy and Larry's in daylight, the trees green and alive. We'd had the windows down, sunglasses on. It had been a month since she'd had the miscarriage.

We'd gone from the gas station on the Merritt into New Haven and the first hospital we could find, Paige crying all the way.

They took a look at her, said there was nothing they could do, that the bleeding should stop in a few days. I remember a nurse practitioner looking at Paige, a metal clipboard held against her chest, and saying, "Things like this just happen. You wouldn't believe how often this happens."

We went on down to New Jersey to her parents' house in Old Bridge instead of going to the beach apartment we'd already rented. We ended up spending the whole week inside her parents' house. I remember how cold that week was; the air conditioner went nonstop, and our clothes, even those clothes in suitcases, were always damp. Paige's parents at work each day, we wandered around inside or watched TV, neither of us saying anything, not even asking what the other was watching on the set. That empty house felt like a cave, and my mind had already started frosting over with black thoughts about what had happened, about Paige, about me.

We drove home that Sunday, took the 95 past all the industrial garbage along the coast to the 91 just to avoid the Merritt, and that gas station.

Paige's bleeding hadn't stopped a couple of days after we got home, and she came back from the doctor's with the news she was having a D & C done the next day. I didn't know what she was talking about. Then she explained it, and asked if I would go down there with her, wait for her.

I told her I couldn't get off work, which was a lie. I just didn't want to. I even went to the phone, Paige in the bedroom, and made like I was calling Mitchell, trying to talk him into it. I never connected lines with him, my finger on the disconnect button as I punched in the numbers.

I sat on the couch after I hung up the phone, and cried. Paige came in, put her arms around me for the first time since we'd been in that bathroom.

"It's okay," she said. "We can have another someday. We can."

I let her think what she was thinking, let her believe I was crying about whatever it was she wanted.

Wendy ended up going with her to the University Health Center, and then invited us up to their place in Colrain for the weekend.

"She says there's plenty of work to do up there," Paige said at dinner. "And that it gets awfully lonesome up there. They'd like the company."

I said, "Of course Larry knows, right?" I hadn't started eating yet, just looked at the pork chops and corn and mashed potatoes in front of me, my hands in my lap.

"I imagine."

"Who else have you told?"

Paige stopped, put her glass of iced tea down. "A couple of people."

"I haven't told anyone yet." I picked up my fork, put it down.

"You don't have to tell anyone, if you don't want to." She had stopped eating.

"I know that," I said. "You don't have to tell me that."

That Saturday we were climbing the mountain at the edge of the
Berkshires, blue-green squares of corn across the valley. We followed the directions Wendy had given us, turned right at an apple
orchard 3.2 miles from the base of the hill, onto an old asphalt
road.

Apple trees lined the road now, low, bent branches spreading
out over the grass, those trees perfectly still as we banged over
potholes in the road. A mile or so back we came to a fruit store,
a building that had been a barn at one time, but which now had
signs hanging in new windows advertising prices on peaches,
oranges, apples, cheese.

Paige said, "Let's stop here. We have to bring Wendy and
Larry something for putting us up this weekend."

I pulled off the road onto a gravel lot, parked the car.

Inside, old coldboxes lined one wall, big white enamel things
with thick glass windows and wooden handles. I turned to Paige.
"I wonder whose route this is," I said, and went over to the coldboxes.

I looked things over. We had lousy distribution in there: only
one facing each of RC and Diet Rite cans. I knew I could get
more in here if the place was mine.

Paige was picking through some fruit set up in bushels along
one wall. On the shelves above the fruit were tins of maple syrup
in eight or ten different sizes. There were preserves and jams and
jellies along another wall, spices and dried flowers and boxes of
Mason jars along the other. A refrigerator case filled with blocks
of cheese sat in the middle of the room.

Paige put a few apples, oranges, and peaches into plastic
produce bags from a roll hanging above the bushels. Then she
went to the refrigerator case, started going through the cheese.

"What do you think?" she said without looking up.

"Of what?" I went over to the case, stood across it from her.
I started picking up pieces, too.

She held a cellophane-wrapped wedge in front of her, read the label.

"This place."

"Lousy distribution," I said.

She took the cheese and put it in the blue plastic basket she'd picked up at the door. "I like it," she said. "This is fresh stuff. A little expensive, but good stuff." She looked at me. "What else should we get them?"

I picked up a wedge, tried to smell it. I couldn't for the cellophane, and then I was thinking about that night when I'd had the cold, when we'd first found Paige was pregnant.

I dropped the cheese back into the case. I said, "You think of something. You know them." I turned and headed for the door. "I'll be out here," I said. "I'll be at the car."

I left her there, a wedge of white cheese in her hand, a blue basket on her arm. I pushed the screen door open, stepped outside into the humid morning. The door had been lighter than I had thought it would be, and banged against the side of the barn.

I went to the car, leaned against the hood. The orchard in front of me sloped down the hill, stopping somewhere down there where thick stands of trees began. I wondered what it would be like just to go and walk through those orchards, ducking below low-hanging branches, kicking through the high grass, all the way down to those trees.

We followed Wendy's directions up into the hills, each road narrower than the one before, through Colrain, past farms and pastures, a graveyard, modern homes built in odd angles, until we were heading up a ravine on a road wide enough for one car. I slowed down and honked the horn at each curve in the road.

Paige was leaning forward in her seat, her back straight, her fingers reaching forward and just touching the dashboard. She said, "We're looking for a dirt road off to the left. There's a small bridge across that stream, and the dirt road crosses it."

A little farther up the ravine we found a dirt turnoff, and the bridge. A half-dozen mailboxes were nailed to a post just before the bridge. I turned in.

The road here was even steeper, and wound up the hill through thick stands of trees a few miles, finally letting out on a meadow. The road ran alongside the meadow.

At the top of the field sat a farmhouse, white with a stone basement exposed on the near side. The roof line bowed a little at the center.

The road ended next to the house; past that were trees and a trail wandering back into them. I pulled into the rock and gravel driveway in front of the house, parked behind a green Bronco and an old maroon Jeep.

Paige leaned over to me, pushed her sunglasses up into her hair. She put both hands around my neck, kissed me full on the lips. She pulled away, said, "That's for getting us up here safely." Then she leaned forward and kissed me again, this time longer, this time even sweeter. She pulled back. "That's for you, just because. And because I love you." I took her hand, squeezed it hard.

Two dogs came running through the trees above us, barking, wagging their tails. I opened my door, and the two of them were there at my feet, my knees, my chest, a black Lab and a golden retriever.

"Hey," I said, and laughed. I pushed them off me, shook their heads in my hands. They started barking louder then; one of them, the black Lab, ran a few feet back up into the trees and brought back an old branch. He dropped it at my feet, and both dogs sat. They barked, waiting, tensed up, watching me. I picked up the stick, threw it as far as I could in the opposite direction, down into the meadow. They both took off through the high grass.

"Good riddance," Larry said. I turned. He had come around the far end of the house, and was wearing a gray and maroon UMass T-shirt. He had on Levis and work boots scuffed and muddy, and a pair of canvas gloves. He worked off one of the gloves, put out his hand. We shook.

"Glad to see you," I said. "Long time no see."

"Not since the wedding," he said. "Let me tell you, it took both those bottles of wine plus another somebody left on the table just to get us home."

"You're crazy," I said.

"Not really. I just had Wendy drive us all the way home. The drive was no problem for me. I kind of enjoyed it, me sleeping there on the backseat."

We laughed, and I turned to Paige. She was next to me, her sunglasses back on.

Wendy came from inside. "You're here," she said. "The cavalry has arrived." We all laughed at this, too. Wendy, barefoot and wearing khaki shorts and a madras shirt, slowly stepped across the gravel, her hands in the air as if she were on a tightrope. She made it to Larry, and he put his arm around her.

I put my arm around Paige, then, too. We all turned to the meadow as if it were the next thing to do.

The house was at the crest of the hill, the meadow stretching out below us. The road we'd come up bordered it on one side, the west, trees lining the other two sides, the house at the top. There were no roads except for the one we'd come up, no homes, no cars. Nothing. Just a ridge of hills due north, the top of the ridge maybe three or four miles off. Trees, all shades of green, covered the hills.

We all looked at the view without a word, the four of us there. I don't know what the others were thinking, but I was wondering what was over the ridge, whether we'd gone far enough north to make that quiet land over there Vermont, or if it were still Massachusetts, where I lived with my wife and my sales route and the ghost somewhere of the baby we'd lost. That's what I was thinking.

Larry said, "Hope you're ready for work."

"Larry," Wendy said. "Let them relax a minute."

"I'm ready," I said.

Paige said, "Me too."

But we just stood there. The dogs, down in the meadow, were fighting over the stick, each with an end in its mouth, each shaking the stick as hard as it could to wrestle it free from the other.

We worked. Larry had rented a rider mower, and we took turns, one of us on the mower, the other in front, walking slowly through the grass, picking up boards, sheetmetal, bottles, anything else that had accumulated over the past two hundred years. We cut grass the rest of the morning. There was no definite lawn to cut, just high grass all the way around the house, and then down into the meadow.

Above the driveway was a fallen-down stone fence Larry discovered while using the weed-eater he'd also rented; once we'd finished the grass and took out the weeds surrounding the house, we started in on the fence.

We worked on putting that fence together the rest of the afternoon, and there was a simple pleasure I found in putting rock on rock, and in sweating, and in being outside, that I'd forgotten had been there, a pleasure that maybe I'd never even known existed. My hands ached from gripping rocks through canvas gloves. My back and shoulders hurt, too; I could feel my shirt sticking to the small of my back. I felt the cool breeze blow across it, and imagined the dark stain there.

I stopped a moment, my hands on my hips, and looked out across the valley.

"You think that's Vermont over there?" I said.

Larry stopped, ran his arm across his forehead. "Nope. It's only a couple miles farther over, though," he said. "Wendy likes to think it's Vermont. I've never told her different." He laughed. "She tells everybody we know that we can see right across to

Vermont from where we live, as if she could throw one of these stones a few feet and have it land in another state." He took a couple of steps back, sat on the fence. "But no, it's not."

"But it might as well be. I mean, for Wendy. So I guess it really is Vermont over there, if she thinks it is." I sat down, too.

"Whoa," he said, "don't get philosophic on me now." He put his elbows on his knees, leaned forward. We both sat there, the only sound birds and insects. Every once in a while we heard the girls laughing from around the back of the house where they were planting some vegetables and flowers along the basement wall.

I shook my head, looked down at the grass at my feet. "I guess I am," I said. "But you can't help it up here."

"I know," he said. "This is the first weekend we've worked outside since we bought the place in December. We did all the inside work, or as much as we could afford, all winter and spring. Now we get outside and we look out across this land, this land *we own* now." He smiled, slapped his knee. "Hell, you want that to be Vermont, it's Vermont."

We were quiet a while, and then I told him about how I'd owned Vermont once. I told him the whole story, about her rings, about the beer and the ashtray, even about the girl in the car and how I'd thought I could have her if I wanted. It felt good to get words out, out into that clear, blue air, even though I knew they would drift off with the breeze and disappear.

He waited a few minutes after I'd finished, and then said, "I know what you mean. We have fights. We have fights just like that. But now we live up here, where are we supposed to take off to?" He stood, tapped the toe of his boot on a rock. He reached down, picked it up and started in on the fence again. "The best we can do is just go to opposite ends of the house. We've done that. Just gone and sulked at opposite ends for a couple of hours or so. Or just taken off with the dogs up into the woods. Grab a flashlight and go." He wedged the stone into place, pushed with one hand to make it move a fraction tighter in place. "There's nothing up here, so we have to deal with each other whether we like it or not." He leaned over, picked up another stone. I was up and working, too, on the other side of the fence. "Robert Frost has this poem, and it says that good fences make good neighbors. Hell, we don't have any neighbors to have good fences for. But I think I like the fact nobody's up here. It makes us closer."

He picked up a stone, held it above the fence for a moment. He looked at that rock like it would say something, and then he put it into place, picked up another. I had a good idea what he was thinking about, knew that there was more he wanted to know. Or maybe he was wondering how he could help, what he could say. I could have told him that his listening to my story had been enough, that those words out into the valley hadn't been wasted, because he had listened.

We kept on, stone on stone, until the sun went behind the trees.

For dinner we barbecued steaks and baked corn in the husk. We sat on lawn chairs outside, eating that food and looking at the trees, the house, the rebuilt fence. We had big jugs of Gallo wine and Tupperware tumblers, and we ate and drank until all the food was gone. Then we sat there, the dogs chewing on bones we'd tossed them. Mosquitoes started in on us then, and we moved inside to the kitchen.

We sat down at the kitchen table, an old Formica-topped thing with steel legs. The backs and seats of the chairs matched the table, yellow with gold flecks. Larry set a jug of wine on the table.

A huge, wood-burning stove sat against one wall in the kitchen; another wall was all cupboards and counter space. The third wall had a refrigerator and sink with more cupboards. The last wall had a picture window, one that looked out on the meadow and the valley. It seemed that everywhere we were—building the fence, mowing, barbecuing, and now, just sitting—that view was with us.

The sun was already down, but it was still light enough in the kitchen for us to see one another. I turned to Wendy, said,

"So that's Vermont over there, huh?" I glanced at Larry. He smiled, brought his tumbler to his lips.

"Actually," she said, "I've looked at maps, and it isn't. Larry thinks it is, but it's not. So I just humor him."

I looked at Larry. He sat there a second, the glass in midair. He blinked, turned to her with this look on his face. I couldn't help but laugh. I laughed and laughed.

Wendy reached over, put a hand on Larry's shoulder. "It's true, you know. Sorry to have to burst your bubble."

"What's so funny?" Paige said.

"Nothing," Larry said.

After a while, Wendy said, "So, you never said how your drive up was." She was leaning forward, her hands on the table. She was, just like the rest of us, looking out the window.

"Beautiful," Paige said.

"Scary," I said. "Bumpy."

"No kidding," Larry said. His chair was turned from the table so that he faced the window. He was leaning back in the chair, his feet out in front of him and crossed at the ankles. "We take that little jaunt every day."

"How can you guys do that?" Paige said. "I mean, every day down and back up, down and back up. Think of the gas. Think of the time."

"We think about that too much already," Wendy said, "and then when I get to the top of this hill I get out of the Bronco and I slap my hand as hard as I can on the side of this house, and it doesn't fall over." She took a drink from her glass. "That sounds crazy, but I do it every time I get home. Then I come inside and look out this window. And that's that."

Larry said, "Scares the hell out of the dogs, her banging on the house."

We all smiled, and then Paige said, "Oh." She got up from her chair, headed for the front door. "I forgot something." We turned to watch her head outside. I heard the car door slam, the dogs barking at her. Then she was back inside with the bag of stuff we'd bought at the produce stand.

"We brought you something," she said, and pulled out a white box tied with a string. She made a big production of it, first taking the jug and filling everybody's glasses, then setting the box on the table and carefully untying the string. She pulled the lid off the box, and said, "Fudge."

"Fudge," Wendy said. "Did you get it from Ferguson's?"

She shrugged. "I don't know. Did we?" She looked at me.

I said, "The only thing I noticed was the crappy-ass distribution we had in there."

Larry said, "The produce stand on the way in."

"Yep," Paige said. She lifted up the box, held it out to Wendy. She took a piece, cupped her hand beneath it, took a bite.

The room was near dark now. I stared out the window, focusing on nothing, just looking. Folds in the hills, bumps and rises and depressions all started turning darker and darker, changing first to a sort of blue, then to blue and black, the trees melting into one another. Only those nearest the house and those on the far crest—those trees in Vermont, I thought—were clear and distinct. The window and the little light left out there made me feel as if somehow the air were drawing the light from inside out. I felt like light was leaving the kitchen as the place slowly grew dark, the stove disappearing into a black square, the cupboards, sink, refrigerator all disappearing as the land outside drew everything through the window and out to it. The sky to the left, to the west, was yellow, a dark yellow that faded to orange to blue to violet across the window, across the valley. I tried hard, but I couldn't tell where one color started and one ended. I wanted to do that, wanted to put my hand up in front of me and outline one color, then the next. I felt that would make things clearer for me, that things would straighten out if only I could straighten out the colors.

The second jug was empty. The colors in the sky were disappearing, replaced by a new one, a black that slowly crept across the window from east to west, taking over the sky, the land, the kitchen. I needed to say something, to utter some words that might hold things up, that might remind me I was still alive.

I said, "Are there any ghosts up here?"

There was no sound for a few moments, and then Wendy said, "We don't know."

From somewhere Larry had gotten a cigarette. He struck a match, lit the cigarette, shook out the match. The tip of the cigarette moved around in the dark as he dragged from it, held it, flicked the end. "People have lived in this house continuously since it was built. Two hundred years. Somebody's bound to have been attached to it one way or another."

Paige said, "I wonder how many people have lived here. I mean, altogether, how many."

The room was black now, and our voices came from nowhere, just the air around us. Fireflies, white sparks, started appearing down in the meadow and in the trees.

Wendy said, "Look at the fireflies," but we already were.

Larry said, "The people who lived here before us were renters. They were hippies. Real live hippies. There were about eight or ten of them." The cigarette jumped from one point to another, then the tip brightened, and I could see the barest profile, dark amber. "They had a few sheep, a few goats. The living room, you know? This room off the kitchen . . ."

Though I couldn't see, I knew he was pointing to his right to an empty room off the kitchen that had a door leading outside. They had kept the room empty, Wendy had told us earlier when she'd shown us around the house, simply because they didn't have enough furniture yet.

"During the winter," Larry went on, "they used to keep the sheep and goats in there. Can you imagine that?" He was quiet. The cigarette flew up to the table, stubbed itself out in the now-empty fudge box. "I can't imagine that. You wouldn't have believed the mess, the shit in this place when we bought it."

"Who was the owner?" Paige said.

"God, that's a sad story." It was Wendy. I heard her chair creak, imagined her leaning back, her eyes on the view. "He's a lawyer down in Amherst."

"Why is it such a sad story?" It was me then. That was my voice in the room.

"Because," Wendy started, then stopped.

Larry said, "Because his wife died. Right here in this house. She had a brain hemorrhage." He paused, breathed out. "They'd bought the place just for summers. They had two kids. Two boys about four and six. They had this place fixed up pretty nice, too, from what he told me when he showed me the place the first time. But they were up here for the summer, I guess about four years ago, and she just had this hemorrhage, and there was nothing anyone could do. She was thirty-three years old."

Wendy said, "The sad thing is that after she died the guy just couldn't come back up here. He couldn't bring his boys up here after that, and then he rented it through an agent to these hippies. He didn't even know who they were. Then one day last fall—it took him three and a half years before he could make it up here again—one day last fall he decides to just drive up and take a look at the place. He comes up here and finds the place a wreck."

"Goddammit," Larry cut in, "he didn't find it a wreck. He found it a shithouse." His chair creaked then, too, and I felt the weight of his arms on the table. I could feel in this black air his anger. "Imagine you come in here and you find goat and sheep shit all over the floors. There's stars and rainbows and half-moons painted all over the walls, and down in the flowerbeds, down where your wife used to plant bulbs every fall, there's these huge marijuana plants, and there's a hammock strung up in the living room."

"Larry," Wendy said.

"Well," he said, "can you imagine that?"

I didn't know if he was expecting an answer from me or not. Paige was quiet, too. Outside, the black had taken over the sky, and stars were appearing, at first glancing light, as though magnificent fireflies had flown clear of the trees and stopped there, above the black valley.

"Imagine there are all those things and more: a couple junked cars down there in the meadow, ten people walking around up here, people you've never met. A couple busted windows, and those animals everywhere. Imagine this is your house, the house where you and your wife and kids lived summers, and before the kids, just you and your wife. Imagine how you had the place before all this shit." He paused. "Imagine that this is where you used to make love with your wife, and that this is the place where she died, right up here in these hills."

He stopped. I listened closely, and heard the pounding of blood through my head, the high-pitched sound of blood through veins and arteries. I imagined it then, saw myself with Paige and two boys. They played catch in the yard, both of them wearing shorts and striped T-shirts. Paige sat on a lawn chair and looked at the view, a glass of something cold in her hand. I watched. I imagined Paige and me making love up in the master bedroom, the windows up, all around us the sounds of these hills at night.

"Imagine," Larry said, and the high-pitched drone in my head disappeared, broken with a simple word. "Imagine," he said again, "that this is the house where you conceived your children. Those two boys. And that those two boys who'd been found up here at the top of this hill in the bedroom upstairs on a couple of nights like this one, with the stars everywhere, imagine that those two boys, and this house, were all you had left of her."

"Larry," Wendy said, this time her voice lower, firmer.

"What?" he said.

Wendy said nothing, and a moment later Larry said, "Oh, Jesus. Oh." He pushed his chair out, leaned back again. "Oh, Jesus, I'm sorry. I'm sorry, you guys."

He moved around in his seat a little more, movement I couldn't picture.

"I just wanted you to know how he felt, you know? Coming up to this pigsty."

Wendy said, "He kicked them all out that week. They tried

to give him a hard time about it, but he was a lawyer, and he knew what to do. He could handle things like that."

Paige said, "Lawyers."

A while later Larry said, "Anyway, we got the place for a steal because the guy just wanted to get out of it altogether. He just wanted to forget the whole thing, all the grief those jerks had brought him, and he wanted somebody to guarantee him they were going to fix it up. He comes up here about once every other month now, by himself, just to see what's going on. He's pretty pleased. He just walks around inside here and touches the walls, the stove, the fireplace. He's generally here not more than half an hour. He has a cup of coffee, and then he's gone."

"That's the sad story," Wendy said.

"That is," Paige said.

I said, "He sounds like your ghost. Like he'd be the ghost you end up with."

Larry chuckled a little. Paige leaned her head over to me, and I put an arm around her out of reflex.

We sat there another half hour or so, no words among us. Only the house around us, and the hills, and the black.

Paige and I made love that night, upstairs in a bedroom darker than the night outside so that I couldn't see her face, couldn't see her below me as we moved together. Insects and the air around were the only sounds, and our movement. The windows were open, and the warmth of Paige and the cool night gave me a chill from my legs to my neck, through my whole body. I wondered if, too, the semen I gave to Paige that evening weren't cold as well, cold and dead inside her womb, that womb already waiting to try for another child.

Afterward we pulled apart. Paige reached up to me, brought my head to her breast, and held me there while she cried.

"What?" I said.

She said, "Nothing," and I knew she was right in this.

I put a hand to her face, felt where tears had slipped down.

She turned from me, pulled the sheet up around her and held it tight against her body. I rolled over onto my back, put my hands behind my head.

When she had fallen asleep, I sat up in bed. I turned and put my bare feet on the floor, then stood and went toward the window, the only piece of light in the room. The floor moaned beneath my weight, but Paige did not awaken.

I put both hands on the sill. The window was old, divided into twelve panes. I looked through the glass, saw that each pane was the original, trees and stars and black hills all bending and rolling as I moved my head back and forth behind the glass.

Here was the view again. The meadow down there, fireflies gone, more stars above now. I stared through the old glass at the older trees and even older hills and at the ageless stars, and then I thought of Paige behind me. I thought of my own fresh seed inside her, thought of it slipping from between her legs while she slept so that it would be of no use to her, which was, I realized, as I wanted it.

I looked down into the meadow then, and saw a child there in the high grass just beyond where Larry and I had stopped mowing.

I blinked, rubbed my eyes, swallowed. I looked through another pane of glass, then another and another, hoping it was only bubbles in the glass, waves thicker in one place than another. But nothing changed.

A child played down there in the yard. I could not tell if it was a boy or a girl, but it was there, moving around, jumping, dancing, its hands now above its head, now moving in a circle, its hands on its hips. A small child. There.

I thought I was drunk, or that I was going mad. Then I thought, Why not? Why couldn't I have this ghost? Why not let me have this child here in the woods? Maybe that was the child I'd killed already, I thought, the child I'd caused us to lose. Or maybe it was the child that might have been if my seed had taken inside Paige this night. Or maybe that was me down there, the ghost of love for Paige and for a life I would not know, that had disappeared, finally, here in the hills this night, disappeared with the colors I couldn't define.

I watched that child ghost down there, and knew it was me, the me I'd no longer seen in the mirror at the women's restroom where I'd not let Paige say good-bye to that child, where I'd ceased to be with the quick, determined pull of that handle.

FOUR

The orchards were white with snow, black, leafless trees in rows I hadn't been able to define in the summer for the grass and leaves and dead blossoms. The asphalt road seemed bumpier now as I drove, Wendy and Paige a hundred yards or so ahead of me.

We passed the fruit market, closed now, and drove on through stands of more leafless trees, more and more snow around us. Though it had all melted in town, snow was still thick here, and light from stars and the moon banged off the white. The light from my headlights seemed an ugly yellow, insignificant.

I wondered what Paige was thinking right then, if she thought at all about our drive up here last summer, or if this drive had become a given, just a thought buried under what projects she'd left undone at work that day, or what she might help prepare for dinner.

The road dipped back into black trees, started down into Colrain. I could see lights back in the trees and down in the valley, lights in homes that had been hidden in the foliage last summer. The town seemed bigger.

The road leveled off, and I was heading toward a four-way stop, the main intersection in this small town. Wendy's Bronco was already there, the blinker on, waiting. I slowed down, hoping she'd turn off and head out to her place, but a few old locals, bundled up in parkas and heavy boots, were slowly making their way across the intersection. Wendy sat waiting for them, and I ended up a few yards behind her, my blinker on, stopped.

My headlights shone on the Bronco, and I could see the back of Paige's head. She had taken off her scarf and hat, her hair down around her shoulders. She turned to Wendy, and she was smiling. There she was, her hair, her face, her nose and mouth and eyes. She was smiling, then said something to Wendy. Then Paige laughed, her mouth opening, her head tilting back, her hair falling off her shoulders. Wendy said something, turned to Paige, and they both laughed.

Wendy gave it the gas, slowly moved the Bronco through the intersection. I watched until I couldn't see their taillights any longer, then cut my blinker.

I turned right, circled back through the intersection in something of a U-turn. I parked on the street, turned out my lights.

Across the street was the Colrain Inn, an old two-story building with a wooden porch out front. A blinking yellow plastic sign hung above the porch and front door of the place. I got out of the car, walked across the street and went inside.

At least I knew where she was. That was something I could take with me back to the apartment.

I stayed in that bar until after eleven, then went out to the car. It took me a few tries to find the right key for the ignition. They all seemed the same to me. Then I found it, turned over the engine, let it run until my breath stopped fogging up the windows.

I didn't wake up until after one the next day, Thanksgiving. I lay there on the sofa bed, the sheets around me, tangled up around my feet. The room was filled with light; I opened my eyes, saw from where I lay the brilliant blue sky.

I sat up. Cal had told me to come over to his place a little after two. I went to the window, stood at it and looked down at the dead grass.

I thought about Lonny, wondered if he would ever call me, ever show his face here again. I hadn't seen his truck around the building since then, but I'd worked every day, killed myself every day. It was no wonder I hadn't seen him. He could have come in and replaced my old toilet, and I would have never known.

I turned, went back to the bathroom and looked at the toilet. As far as I could tell, it was the same one.

I took a shower, shaved. While I was looking in the mirror, pulling the razor across my face, I thought of calling Larry and Wendy and asking to speak to Paige. I wondered what would happen, wondered if they would play stupid and say she wasn't there. Then I wondered if she would even want to talk to me. That was something I hadn't even thought about.

Cal's apartment was on the other side of Route 9, down Market Street past Jack's Seafood. I drove over there, the streets all deserted, shops and stores all closed. His building looked as if it had been a dormitory or boarding house at one time: it was big and square, four stories with those gray asphalt shingles from top to bottom. I pulled in to a muddy dirt lot behind the place, got out and stepped around ice-crusted puddles, then up a few steps to the front door.

I went up two flights of old wooden stairs, the finish worn off, wood splintered up. The banister on the second flight was wobbly; a few of the ribs had been broken out. I made it to the third floor, Cal's floor, and started down the hall.

On one door was a poster of Che Guevara, on another was painted a double-edged ax, beneath it the words WE SHALL NOT FORGET—LESBIAN WOMEN UNITE. Another door had a flyer advertising a contradance to be held the night after Thanksgiving.

I got to Cal's door, 3E, and knocked. I looked both ways down the hall.

Carla answered.

"Rick," she said. "Come in, come in." She stepped back from the door, waved me in.

Carla was a beautiful woman. I'd seen her most days I went into Cal's market, there in her lime-green smock and black pants.

She was thin, I could tell even with that ugly smock on, but not too thin. Her skin was almost white, and her black hair was blunt cut, her bangs always perfectly straight across her forehead. Single strands of gray hair fell here and there.

Now she stood in the doorway wearing a striped knit dress, nice makeup that made her lips fuller, her eyes even more blue.

I stepped in. The door let into the kitchen, and I smelled the turkey. I felt as if I hadn't taken in that aroma in years.

"Your coat, your coat," Carla said. She closed the door behind me, then had her hands on my shoulders from behind. She helped me off with the coat.

"Carla," I said. "You look great. That dress."

She hung the coat on a hook on the back of the door. "Like it?" she said, then turned around, her hands out to her sides like some model. When she'd made it around to me, she put her hands on my shoulders again, then gave me a small kiss.

"Happy Thanksgiving," she said.

I said, "Happy Thanksgiving," and took a step back from her. I bumped into the door. Carla laughed.

"What's with you?" she said.

"It's you," I said. "It's that dress. I never see you in anything but that smock and those pants at the market."

"Oh God," she said and laughed. She went to the kitchen counter, picked up a knife and started chopping a carrot. "Don't even mention that thing. Don't even mention that godawful thing. This is a holiday. Lime is not my color."

"What's going on out there?" Cal shouted from another room. He came into the kitchen through a doorway at the end of the counter. He had a bottle of beer in his hand, and wore a pair of brown corduroys and a navy blue sweater that took away most of his beer belly. "You goofing around with my woman in here?" He smiled, brought the bottle to his lips.

"Admiring her from afar," I said. "I was telling her I'd never seen her in civilian dress before. Just in that smock."

"Cut it out," Carla said. She put the knife down, turned and leaned against the counter. She crossed her arms. "For one thing,

I'm not your 'woman.' Have more respect." She pointed her finger at Cal, said again, "Have more respect." She turned to me. "And another thing. I said not to mention that smock. It makes me think of work. And about those awful black polyester slacks I have to wear. And old women with outdated coupons. Those are not things I want to think about today."

Cal threw his arms around her shoulder, pulled her to him. "Spunky wench," he said. He laughed, but Carla made a fist and pounded his chest.

"Now cut out that shit," she said. "I'm serious." She pulled away from him. "Quit showing off in front of Rick." She turned to me. "He's not like this at all when nobody else is around." She looked over her shoulder at him. Cal shrugged, held his hands palms up.

"Oh, you guys get out of here," Carla said.

Cal grinned, and went into the other room.

I started through the kitchen to the doorway, but Carla put up a hand to stop me as I passed her.

She said, "We're glad you're here. We're glad you came over today. He acts like a tough, but he really wanted you over today."

I looked at the carrots, then at her. "Thanks," I said.

She turned back to the carrots. I went to the doorway, stopped. "Can I say that things smell good in here?"

She smiled. "Only if it's not some sort of sexist remark."

"Things smell good in here," I said. She laughed.

Cal was already sitting on the couch in the other room, his back to me. A color portable set sat atop two blue plastic milk crates against the far wall. A ball game played on the set. I looked around for another doorway leading out of the room, but there wasn't one. There were just these two rooms; a living room, a kitchen.

"Incredible," he said. "At this rate it'll take four hours for one football game. I don't believe it." He tipped up the bottle, finished it off.

I came around the end of the sofa. It was an old thing, a blue bedspread thrown across it. I sat down, and sank into it. Two white parson's tables served as coffee tables. Cal had his feet up on one of them.

A couple of pictures hung on the wall above the set, cheap seascapes you could buy anywhere. The wall closest to me, on my left, was bare except for a Dr. Pepper clock in the middle of it, the numbers 10, 2, and 4 in red. Below that, on the floor, sat three rows of concrete-brick and plywood shelves. The shelves were filled with records, some books, a couple of boxes. On the top shelf sat an expensive-looking stereo system: cassette player, radio, turntable, all silver and black. Two walnut speakers sat on either side of the bookshelves.

The opposite wall, the one closest to Cal, was mostly windows, big, square panes. Beige, water-stained curtains had been pulled back, and I could see trees out there, the top story of the house next door, this one with powder-blue shingles instead of gray.

Below the window was a beautiful light oak dropleaf table. An arrangement of small green and orange gourds and dried flowers sat in the middle of the table.

Cal said, "That's about all she left me."

He hadn't turned from the set, hadn't taken his eyes off the game. He knew, though, that I was looking around, taking things in, wondering.

I turned to the set. "What's that?"

"That table. That's about all she left me. That and my records. And my clothes."

"I guess I made out. I got a sofa bed, a black-and-white portable, my clothes, and a couple sets of towels. There were sheets on the sofa bed when she left. Lucky, I guess."

He laughed, though still not looking at me. I didn't want to, but I laughed, too.

Carla came in. "What's so funny?" She had three beers and a plate of crackers and cheese. She pushed Cal's feet off the parson's table with her leg, set down the plate. "Sit up, you," she said.

Cal sat up, turned toward me and pointed at the wall behind us. "At least you got something of a bed. Mine folds up into that wall over there." I turned around, saw two large doors in the wall.

Carla sat down between us. "So," she said. "Two happy fellas. How nice."

I said, "Just comparing scars."

"Like most men. Just comparing scars." She took a drink from her bottle.

"What's with you?" Cal said. "What's your problem?" He pushed himself back into the corner of the sofa, away from Carla.

"I'm tired of hearing about your ex-wife. We all have battle scars."

"Well, sorry."

"You should be."

I cleared my throat and said, "This is a nice place. I like the windows. The light in here."

"It's too small," Cal said. "Way too small. Sometimes I feel like jumping out the goddamn window it feels so small."

"So it's small," I said. "You've got light in here."

"True," he said.

We watched the game. Every now and then one of us sat up, took a cracker and a slice of cheese, eased back into the sofa.

After a few minutes, Carla said, "So, how are you doing?"

I said, "Me?"

She looked at me, smiled. "Who else in this room has been newly single-ized?"

"I'm doing okay," I said. "Sales are up."

"Thanks to me," Cal said.

"Sales. Is that all you guys think of?"

"Pretty much," Cal said.

"Guess so," I said. We laughed, looked at each other. She straightened her dress out over her knees. "Has anything official been done?"

"No," I said. "Not that I know of." I looked at the set. I wondered what he'd told her. Everything, I imagined. Everything I'd told him, anyway, which was all old news. There were plenty of things he didn't know about.

I took a drink, held the bottle in my lap. "At least now I know where she's been hiding out."

"Where?" Cal said.

"Oh, last night I went over to her office. At the university." I put my arm on top of the sofa. "I guess I followed her after she got off."

"You followed her? You men. Men are crazy. You make it sound like you're some sort of private detective."

"That's what I felt like." I paused. "I thought I could work up enough guts to talk to her as she was coming out of the office. But I chickened out."

"Aww," Cal said. Carla hit his knee.

She turned to me. "Keep going."

I said, "But I don't even know why I started."

"Because we're all in the same boat."

I turned to her. She was looking at me. I said, "You're divorced?" After I said it I realized I wasn't surprised at all. Maybe there was something in how she acted that told me she was divorced: her independence, her always touching Cal. Her hand was on his thigh right now.

I started feeling cramped there on the couch. I felt like there were too many of us on that thing, three of us sunken down into the frame. I brought my arm down from the top of the sofa, put my hand in my lap.

"Of course I'm divorced," she said. "Would you think a brainy, beautiful woman like me wouldn't have been swept off her feet by some clown at least once in her life?"

"She's been married twice. Of course, she's been divorced twice, too," Cal said.

Still looking at me, she pointed a finger at Cal. "Mathematical genius."

Cal said, "I just want to hear more of your goddamn story. More cloak and dagger. Where the hell is she hiding out?"

I struggled up off the couch. I picked up a cracker, a slice of cheese. I went over to the bookshelves, squatted, started flipping through the records. My back was to them.

I said, "She's staying with one of her co-workers. This woman and her husband live up in Colrain."

"Colrain?" they both said at the same time.

I stood, my back still toward them. I looked up at the Dr. Pepper clock. "I see Ed Travis has come through for you."

"Freebies," Cal said. "Comes with the territory."

Carla said, "You followed her all the way up to Colrain? I hope for your sake you got to talk to her."

"At least for your car's sake," Cal said.

"It's not that far," I said. "And no, I didn't get to see her. I stopped at a bar in town. The only bar. I had some drinks, then went home." I turned around. They were sitting closer to each other now, Cal's arm around Carla, Carla leaning into him. They were both watching me. I said, "There's nothing to say anyway. Nothing I want to say to her."

"That's all right," Carla said. "It's okay to feel that way."

Cal looked at Carla. He said, "You don't think he's aware of that? I told you all about our talk at Joe's. He'll be fine. Just look at him. He's got a beer in his hand. There's a ball game on. Food in the oven. He's all right."

I looked at the set. I said, "How do we get out of this?"

"Out of what?" Carla said.

"Out of talking about this. Out of going over this again and again." I turned back to them. I tried to give a convincing smile.

"Bad news, brother," Cal said. "This'll be the topic for the rest of all time and eternity, whether you're talking about it or not."

"Some help you are, Cal," Carla said. She pushed herself off his chest. "One way is to come back to the sofa here, and sit down." She patted the sofa where I'd been sitting. "Just to sit is a good way."

I went back to the couch, sat down. I put my feet up on the parson's table in front of me. We watched the game. It seemed the best thing to do, the best advice I'd gotten in a while.

Cal cleared his throat, said, "Why there's no chairs for the table is another story."

Carla was in the kitchen. The first ball game over, she'd given us the job of setting the table.

"Go ahead," I said. We were standing at the table, pulling the leaves out to full size. The leaves fell into place, then Cal squatted next to the table. "See the legs under here?"

I put my hands on my knees, leaned over. "Yeah."

"Those are called barley-twist," he said. "Barley-twist legs. Molly and I bought this table just after we got married. We'd gone to some big antique warehouse down in Hartford we'd heard advertised on the radio or somewhere. But we couldn't find any chairs for it. The guy at the warehouse said he hoped he'd have some coming in sometime, but the place was all the way down in Hartford, and we couldn't see driving down there again and again. We just took the table and went home."

We stood. I followed him into the kitchen. He went to a drawer under the counter. Carla had the turkey out of the oven. She was stirring juices from the turkey in a pan on the stove.

Cal pulled the drawer open, fished through a couple dozen pieces of loose silverware and utensils. "Aw, to hell with it," he said, then picked up two handfuls of silverware. He turned, nodded toward a door in the corner of the kitchen. "That's the bathroom. There's chairs in there. Bring them all out."

I went to the door, opened it. Inside was a toilet, a small sink, a shower stall. Four beige metal folding chairs leaned against one wall. I picked up two in each hand, then banged along through the kitchen past Carla and into the other room.

"I'm impressed," Carla said.

"So anyways," Cal said once I was in the room, "we finally rounded up four chairs that matched the stupid table. It took about eight months of going to every antique store and tag sale we could find before we found this set of barley-twist chairs. We found them at this place up in New Salem, believe it or not. Saw them advertised in the paper. The chairs ended up costing more than the table, but Molly had to have them."

I started unfolding the chairs, wondering why he'd had me bring out all four. He stood at the table, the silverware spread out across it. He started picking through it. He pulled out four forks, then four spoons, then four knives.

"So when we split, we had this beautiful, beautiful table-and-chairs set. But she was so whacked out, she'd gone so far overboard that all she wanted was the chairs. I told her to go ahead, take the table, too, but she wouldn't. She says, 'I want you to think about us and how you screwed everything up every time you look at this table without the chairs. This is a symbol,' she says."

Carla came in, said, "I can understand that. It's easy to see."

"It's crazy," Cal said. "I found out later she'd sold off the chairs after she moved back to Worcester to live with her parents."

"That's not crazy, that's practical," Carla said. "You're so burned up about it, why didn't you sell the table? Could have meant a few extra dollars."

"It's a nice table," Cal said. He stood back from it, his hands at his sides. He let out a deep breath. "It's a goddamn beautiful table," he whispered, and took another breath. He moved a hand to the table, gently placed his fingers on the wood. "That's what it is," he whispered, and just looked at the table, touched the grain.

I looked at Carla. She shrugged, turned to Cal.

"If it's such a nice table, why'd you forget a tablecloth to protect it?" Carla said.

I said, "And why four place settings?"

Carla looked at Cal, then me, then Cal again.

"Cal?" she said.

He turned and went to the kitchen. "Don't have a shit," he said. "I'll get the tablecloth. The silverware's not going to kill the table." He was in the kitchen, opening drawers, cupboards.

Carla looked at me, smiled. "He didn't tell you?"

"I guess not."

"Well," she said, "we're having a friend of mine over, too. Rose is her name. Rose Plavny."

"Oh." I went to one of the parson's tables, picked up a half-empty bottle I'd left there when we'd started on the table. I looked down into the bottle, gently shook it so that the beer swirled.

"We're not trying to fix you up. We just thought it would be nice to—"

"It's okay. Don't worry."

She held her hands in front of her, looked down. She was still smiling, though I could see by her eyes and the corners of her mouth that she was forcing it. She looked up at me. She said, "Excuse me while I kick Cal's ass."

"Don't. Don't worry about it."

She was still a moment, then went to the table, started collecting the silverware. "He was supposed to call you and ask if you wouldn't mind. We just thought it would be nice." She had the silverware from the settings in one hand, then picked up the odd pieces with the other. She went into the kitchen. I didn't hear anything except the silverware drawer opening then slamming shut. I couldn't hear any more cupboards or cabinets being opened up, and I imagined Cal had found the tablecloth. Then I heard some tough whispering, Carla at Cal.

Cal came out a second later. I sat down on the couch. The pregame show for the next game was on, the announcer checking in with headquarters for final scores and updates.

Cal popped out the tablecloth, a forest green thing with bright red poinsettias all over it. He let it fall to the table. His back was to me the whole time. Then he went back into the kitchen, came out with the silverware. He began putting each piece where it had been before.

A minute or so later there was a knock at the door.

Cal hurried out of the room. I stood, put the bottle down. I tucked in my shirt wherever it felt loose. I put my hand through my hair. The door opened in the kitchen.

"Rose," Carla said.

"Rose, Rose, Rose," Cal said. The same old Cal. "Let me take your coat," he said. "How much can I get for it?"

I heard this Rose laugh. Carla didn't. They started through the kitchen, and then Carla was moving into the room, Rose behind her.

She was a little taller than Paige, long brown hair falling in curls on her shoulders. She had a dark complexion, her irises black from where I stood. She wore a pair of khaki slacks and a black turtleneck. She was pretty.

Carla said, "Rose Plavny, this is Rick Wheeler. Rick, this is Rose."

She held her hand out first. I took it. Her hand was cold in mine, fragile.

Rose smiled, said, "So this is it. No matter how hard Carla and Cal have tried to make this seem not like a date, it still is."

I laughed, and held her hand a moment longer than I should have. I let go, put mine in my pocket. "Real lovebirds, these two," I said.

Carla laughed, then headed back to the kitchen. Cal had hung back in the doorway between the two rooms. Carla brushed past him without looking at him.

"I'm sorry I'm late," she called to Carla. "But Jason's father was an hour late picking him up."

Cal and Carla left us in the room while they got things together in the kitchen. Mostly Rose and I stood smiling, said a few things about the weather. Carla brought out the twenty-five-pound turkey, then she and Cal alternated bringing out bowls and plates of more food: mashed potatoes, gravy, applesauce with cinnamon, peas and carrots, acorn squash with brown sugar, rolls, stuffing.

Finally everything was out, and we sat down.

Cal said, "Wait a minute," then stood, went back to the kitchen, and came back with a bottle of spumante. He sat down, popped it open. We passed our glasses to him, and he filled them.

"A toast," he said. He held up his glass. Rose and I did the same. Carla was the last to lift hers. She still hadn't looked at him.

He cleared his throat, glanced at Carla. His face was serious, straight. He said, "To friends on Thanksgiving."

We all touched glasses, took sips of the spumante. Carla smiled a little, then Cal leaned over, kissed her cheek. She blushed.

We talked. Rose had been divorced for three years now; she worked part-time at an insurance agent's on King Street; she had known Carla since high school down in Holyoke; each had been maid of honor at the other's wedding.

"I mean at Carla's *first* wedding," Rose said, and laughed. "She asked me to be it for her second one, too, but I told her there really wasn't a need for a matron of honor at a courthouse wedding."

"That's not true," Carla said, laughing. "Not true, not true."

There was a great difference between the two of them. Rose sat back in her folding chair, relaxed. She ate her food slowly, smiling and talking quietly. She held her champagne glass with two fingers at the stem, gently tipped the glass and took small sips. But here was Carla, sitting straight up, her back never touching the back of her chair. She ate little, and ate it quickly. She did most of the talking, her blunt-cut hair waving around while she told us the story of that second wedding: "A disaster. A run in my stockings. A head cold. Bill had the flu. We both had to be back at work the next day. A complete disaster from day one. From hour one. A worst-case scenario." She leaned over the table toward me. "That one, Rick, lasted four months. He'd been fooling around on me since before the wedding. Some Smithy, no less."

Cal, who'd been carving and serving and eating all this time, said, "Men."

We all laughed. Carla put a hand on her chest, threw her head back. Rose shook her head, looked at me. I looked down at my plate, then at Carla. I watched her laughing, and wondered how long she'd been divorced, how long ago those four months had been. And I wondered if Rose was so quiet and, it seemed, so much more sure of herself than Carla because she'd been single for three years, and hadn't remarried. But I just shook that idea out of my head. They were just two people. Two different women.

Cal said, "So how's Jason?"

"Jason," Rose said, "Jason, Jason. He's a sweetheart. We're sitting over at the apartment waiting for his father to show up, and he said, 'Mom, there's nothing I want to do less than do Thanksgiving with Dick.' Jason's only five years old. I nearly cried."

I said, "Your son calls your ex-husband by his first name?"

She was cutting up a piece of turkey. She speared a piece. "His father thinks it's really quite hip and groovy to have his son call him that. Jason comes home from his once-a-month weekends with his father, and calls me Rosie for about the first thirty seconds. I won't let him get away with it."

"Her ex is a jerk," Carla said.

Rose laughed, said, "Yours are real clowns too, you know."

They both laughed.

Cal said, "Be nice."

Rose settled down, turned to me. She tilted her head a little, let her curls fall, then pushed them back over her shoulder. "Do you have any kids?"

I said, "No." I looked at my plate, pushed some things around with my fork. I was full, and hadn't known it. I said, "I'm not sure if I'm lucky or not."

"Lucky," Rose and Carla said at the same time. They started laughing again.

I pushed my plate a few inches away from me, leaned back in the chair.

～～～

When we'd finished, Rose volunteered herself and me to do the dishes. Carla started to say something, but Cal put his hand on her forearm, said, "Don't blow it."

She shrugged, and then Rose and I were standing at the sink scraping dishes. Carla hung around in the kitchen a while, wrapping and putting away leftovers. Then she was gone.

"You didn't say much in there," Rose said.

I opened the cabinet beneath the sink, found the garbage can there. I gathered up the turkey bones, dropped them in the trash, then closed the cabinet. "I just didn't know what you knew about me and what you didn't," I said. "I didn't want to risk repeating old information."

She started running dishwater in the sink, took a yellow plastic bottle from the counter and squeezed in soap. "Real sketchy," she said. "The RC salesman for Cal's store, right?"

"Somebody's idea of the most important information about me."

"There's other things." Suds started up in the water. She took a wooden dish brush from behind the faucet, shook it in the water to build up more. "Newly split up. You're a great friend of Cal's."

"Great?" I started looking around for the dishrack, remembered it was next to the garbage can. I got it out, set it up on the counter. "Until a week or so ago I didn't even know his last name."

Rose smiled. She started putting glasses in the water. "He's like that, from what I can gather. It took Carla six months just to get him to go out with her, just to go to a movie. Shy and retiring, I guess."

"You ought to see him in action. At the market."

She turned the water off, then went to the refrigerator, pulled a dishtowel from the handle. "You wash," she said. "I'll dry." She stood next to the counter, one hand on her hip.

"That's not fair," I said. "Let's compromise."

"Shoot," she said.

"I'll do half, you do half. There's a lot of dishes."

"Deal," she said. We started on the dishes.

A few minutes later we hadn't yet said a word to each other. Then she said, "So how long?"

"Two weeks," I said. "About."

She said nothing. She just stood next to me, rinsing silverware, then putting it into the rack. A moment later, though, she put a hand on my back, patted my shoulder, then went back to rinsing. It was a small thing, and meant only what it appeared to be: consolation, a touch.

We finished the dishes. The kitchen looked good; we'd found places for all the pots, pans, dishes, and glasses. Whether they were the right places or not we didn't know. We only put things where they fit.

Rose hung the dishtowel back on the refrigerator handle. I'd ended up washing all the dishes. I didn't mind. It was something to do. We headed into the other room.

The room was dark except for the light from the set, a football game still playing. We came around the front of the sofa, and stopped. Cal and Carla lay across the cushions, asleep. Cal's head was back, his mouth open, quietly snoring. Carla, her head on his chest, lay with one arm around his neck, the other hanging off the edge of the sofa.

Rose turned to me, put a finger to her lips. We went back to the kitchen.

She went to the refrigerator, opened it up and poked around until she found a can of coffee. "I'm making some coffee," she said. "You want some?"

"Sure," I said. "I'm beat myself." I stretched, my hands in fists. I saw a pie on top of the refrigerator.

I went over, took it down. It was pumpkin, a store-bought thing. "Look at this. I'll bet he lifted this from his own bake shop."

Rose was pouring water into the Mr. Coffee on the counter. She turned, laughed. "Cut it up. Shoot, if they're going to sleep we might as well dig in."

I cut up the pie.

~~~~

We were just talking about things. The fresh coffee had brought
me awake, and it seemed I could talk, laugh, listen, better than
I had in a long time. We were leaning against the counter, plates
in our hands, mugs on the counter. The kitchen window was
black now, steamed over from the radiator beneath it. Rose told
me about some classes she was taking through continuing ed at
the university. She was trying to finish up the prerequisites at
night so that she could, someday, quit working and go back to
school full-time.

"If it wasn't for Jason, I might be able to do it, go ahead and
quit work now, but he's just too small. I can't see leaving him all
day long by himself. As it is this part-time stuff breaks my heart.
I want him to be a little older and in school all day before *I* take
off for school all day." She took a sip of coffee.

"Who takes care of him now?"

"Oh, my mother. Three nights a week I'm at school, four
mornings a week at the office."

I took a bite of pie. It was old, the skin on the top of the pie
almost too thick. I looked at Rose, leaning against the Formica
counter, her feet crossed at the ankles, relaxed.

I tried to imagine how I would approach Rose if she were a
customer, a store manager or something. She would be difficult
to sell to, I knew; most managers got off on belittling you by
making you feel your product couldn't sell and that they lost all
kinds of money on you. You had to follow them around the store
like a lost dog behind some kid while they went first to a register
to okay a check, then to the floor where they'd chew some clerk
out for something, then to the back room to take a look at your
stock. You saw a lot of a manager's back as a salesman. Cal was
something like that, but there had been something different in
him, something that showed me he wanted to be friends. We were
about the same age; he was assistant manager, which made him
a peon in the manager's eyes, much as I was. I'd seen through
him at the start, seen that his yelling at everyone was for him a

joke. He didn't take himself as seriously as managers did. I knew then that that was it, that Cal didn't take himself seriously, yet at the same time he went through the motions of a good, pissed-off manager. A good manager would never have let me into his office, then pulled off his shirt so that his fat, white belly was exposed. A good manager would never have laughed with a salesman after he'd bitched at three bag boys for screwing around.

I was a lot like Cal. I did my job, and I was a good salesman, but it'd seemed so often, even more since Paige had gone, that I was just doing it. Going through motions. I wasn't taking myself seriously. How could I? Paige was gone. There wasn't much left to take seriously. Yet my sales had gone up, and the more they went up the less a part of things—my route, my markets, my being a *salesman*—I was feeling. I was outside, watching myself sell case after case.

Now Rose. I watched myself watching her. As a salesman, how would I approach? What tactic? She knew herself; she wasn't any manager who took himself so seriously that he'd become a robot. She wasn't like Cal, either, not taking herself seriously enough. She would, I knew, demand the truth from me. I would have to face her while she waited for me to deliver facts, and then I'd have to wait while she gave a just answer. There was no way I could bullshit her. No way I could fake her into buying things.

I looked down at my plate, took another bite. I tried hard to swallow, my throat tight, as if a square rock had lodged there. I looked away to the steamed-over window.

Rose said, "Carla and I said at dinner that you were lucky you didn't have any kids. We said that for different reasons."

I said, "Oh?"

"And I saw what you did, your reaction. I saw you push your plate away. You can ignore me if you want. But if you, you know, split up because of some problem about kids, I'm sorry if I said anything wrong."

"You didn't say anything wrong. I was full. I was done with dinner."

"Of course," she said, and I knew then that I'd made a false

move. I'd started feeding her a lie instead of the truth. She put
the mug down, took a bite of pie without looking at me.

I said, "There were plenty of things. A problem about kids
among them." I wondered if she would believe me this time.

"You don't have to say anything, really. This is a tough time.
The toughest, maybe."

We finished off our pieces of pie. I glanced up at her a couple
of times, saw that her irises were a dark brown, darker than her
hair.

We washed the plates off, put them in the rack. It was my
turn to talk now.

I said, "It's been pretty rough, sure. But I've been working
hard."

She nodded, smiled. She held her mug with both hands.

"Sales are way up. I've got displays most everywhere. Cal's
market's the best one on my route. And I've had plenty of things
to do. Sales meetings. Building displays. Things. I've taken time
out to call her a couple of times, too."

She tilted her head. "How did that go?"

"Miserably." We both gave a short, small laugh. "There's not
much chance, actually," I said, and then heard how quiet things
were in there, the only sound the patter of the announcer in the
other room.

"But a plumber came by," I went on. I went over and poured
myself some more coffee. "Crazy old guy. Told me a lot about
toilets, though. Mine's about shot, he told me." Rose was smiling.
"We made a date to go out hunting, too. So that'll be something.
I'm just waiting to hear from him."

Cal came into the kitchen, then, scratching his head.

"Hear from who?" he said. His shirt was pulled out, the tails
hanging down below the sweater. Carla was behind him. They
were holding hands, both blinking back the light. Carla's dress
was wrinkled, her hair messy.

"Here they are," Rose said. "Mr. and Mrs. America."

"America's favorite couple," I said.

Cal walked over to the Mr. Coffee, Carla to the cupboard for two mugs. She brought them down, Cal filled them.

"Hear from who?" Cal said again.

"A plumber. A guy who came to fix a leak that was supposed to be somewhere in the bathroom. Crazy. He asked me to go hunting with him sometime."

Cal yawned, put his hands around his mug. "What's his name?"

"Lonny. Thompson."

"You know that old fart?"

"Sort of," I said. "Know him?"

"Sure," Cal said. We stood across from each other, Rose and I on the sink side, Cal and Carla on the Mr. Coffee side. Carla still hadn't said anything. She stared off at the cabinets as she sipped her coffee. "He's the guy who comes out whenever something breaks down at the market. Saved my life more than once. My life and a couple hundred boxes of popsicles. He's good people."

Carla looked up from the cabinets, said, "Pie? Do you want some pie?"

"Carla," Rose laughed. "You ought to go back to sleep. Look next to you."

Carla slowly turned, looked at the half-eaten pie on the counter next to her. "Oh."

"So you're going hunting with that old fart."

"I guess I kind of forced him into it. I asked him if he hunted. He said he did, then said I could go with him."

"Hunting's about all he talks about. He lives for it. For that and fixing pipes. He must do okay."

Carla, still staring, said, "You men. All you talk about. Hunting and fixing things."

We played four-handed poker the rest of the evening, Ohio Blue Tip matches for chips, until Rose looked at her watch, said, "It's almost ten. Jason's coming home from his father's soon." She finished off her coffee.

We all stood. "I'm going to head out, too," I said. "The stores'll be shot tomorrow, everybody, even you"—I pointed at Cal—"bitching and moaning about Schweppes displays."

Carla said, "You can walk Rose to her car then."

Cal said, "Uh-oh."

Rose rolled her eyes.

We were at the door, our coats on, when Carla said, "Wait a sec." She went to the refrigerator and pulled out some things wrapped in foil. She gave them to me. "Turkey," she said. "And rolls and stuffing. You eat this stuff. Turkey goes bad fast."

"Thanks," I said. I gave her a hug, then shook Cal's hand.

He said, "Glad you came. You and Rose both."

"I'm glad I came, too," Rose said. She kissed Carla, then Cal.

The two of them followed us out into the hall, and at the top of the stairs Rose and I turned, waved back at them standing just outside Cal's door. They stood a foot or so apart, Cal with his shirttails still pulled out, his hair messed up, Carla holding her coffee cup with both hands, her lips at the brim, her feet bare on this splintered floor. Their eyes were expressionless, as though they had felt certain we would not turn and look at them again, each lost in some way, alone in thought. When they saw us they both smiled; Cal raised his coffee cup in salute, Carla waved. Then they turned to each other, leaned over and kissed, a measured kiss, as if they were doing it for us. They turned and waved at us again.

Outside the mud puddles had frozen over, tire tracks through the wet ground frozen into gnarled, hard lines across the lot.

"Be careful," I said. Rose was a step or two behind me. "Where are you parked?"

"Right there." She pointed to a VW bug, gray in the light from the lamppost.

We got to her car. She found her keys, opened the door and sat down. She left the car door open.

My hands were in my coat pockets. The palms were sweaty

and cold. "So. Do I ask you for your phone number? Is that what I do?"

"You could," she said. She had her hands in her pockets, too. "You can call me up. We can talk some more. Talking's a good thing."

She gave me her number. My stomach hurt, and the cold started seeping into my eyes. I repeated the number a couple of times.

"It's in the phone book, if you forget." She pulled her door closed, rolled the window down a few inches. She started the engine. "Got to go. Jason'll be home any minute. You can call me."

"Great," I said, leaning over to speak into the window.

She pulled out, flipped her brights on and off a few times, then left. I heard her tires breaking ice all the way across the lot.

Paige isn't here, Rick," Larry Kasmarski said.

I was sitting on the sofa bed, the phone in my hand. I was about to head out the door for the route. Wind rattled the storm windows; I could see through the window breaks of blue in the stone-gray clouds outside. A few small flakes blew past the window like broken feathers.

I didn't know what I'd wanted to say to her over the phone. Other times I'd called I'd felt some need to talk to her, to try and do something. But my calling her now was a reflex. I'd thought of it as I'd put my hand on the doorknob on my way out.

"Where is she?" I said.

"Rick," Larry said.

"Where is she?"

I hadn't slept the night before. I had thought of Rose: thought of our going out together somewhere for dinner, our dancing, our going back to her place, wherever that was, our making love. I thought of her body: large, dark nipples, firm breasts, taut, smooth stomach.

I had lain there in the dark and begun to masturbate when I saw that those places I'd imagined Rose and me going to were places I'd been with Paige, saw that the things we'd done were things Paige and I had done. Then I saw that that woman, that body I'd imagined, wasn't Rose, but Paige. Paige's soft, lean neck, her hair, her warm thighs and legs around me, her soft hands on my back as I moved into her.

But nothing happened. I had not been able to come.

There were things I wanted to apologize for, I knew, right that moment, right there over the phone, even though I was afraid to name them. There were too many now, and the thought of naming each thing I'd done and then apologizing for it overwhelmed me. I wanted to cry at all this, and wanted it all forgotten.

"Rick," Larry said. "Wendy and I are already in this deep enough as it is. You know, well. You know we care about you two, and we don't like seeing what's happened—"

"Larry," I cut in, "where is she?"

"She's not here," he said, his voice going quiet. "She told us not to tell you. She's gone to New Jersey."

"Jersey?" I said. I put my hand back through my hair, remembered trying to count the hairs when Paige had touched me that way.

"She's staying down there, well, until whenever. I don't know. Until she knows."

"New Jersey."

"Yes," he said. "Listen. Come up here when she comes back. You guys can stay up here. You two have to talk."

"Who are you?" I shouted into the phone. "Just who the hell are you, Larry? What do you think? I'm supposed to listen to you and to everyone else, right? Everyone in the whole world I'm supposed to listen to."

"Rick," he said.

"Forget it, Larry. Thanks a whole lot, Larry. You really care. You really care about us, I can tell," I shouted. I hung up.

My displays were blown. The shelves were empty, stock was low. I worked at each stop. I filled the shelves, threw p.o.p. on cans, bottles, two-liters. I rebuilt six displays that day, throwing over three hundred cases altogether. I wrote giant orders for the chains. If they needed twenty-five cases of ale, I sent them forty; if they needed fifty cases of club soda, I sent them eighty. I went into stores, killed myself there, then left. I didn't talk to any managers, clerks. I didn't even look for Cal when I was in his store. I just put up product.

On the way out of the parking lot at my last stop, I saw Lonny. I was sitting at the entrance, waiting for traffic to clear, and here came the beat-up red truck, Lonny sitting alone in the cab, still in his hat and coat and those glasses. He was in the far lane, moving along pretty fast, and I honked the horn, waved. I wanted him to see me, remember who I was. Rick, the one with the leak somewhere. I honked the horn again, kept waving, but he passed right in front of me without even looking. I watched that old truck head south toward downtown, watched until I lost it in traffic. Someone honked at me then, and I looked in the rearview mirror, saw a woman in the car behind me. She had on big, white-framed sunglasses, and was yelling at me.

I looked at the road, saw traffic had cleared, and slowly pulled out.

I came into the office with the biggest day yet. Bigger than I'd ever had.

Mitchell came out of his office down the hall while I was in the middle of posting my sales on the board. With each new number I put up, I could hear him behind me, moving, giving a low whistle, shaking his head. When I was through I turned around. He stood there with his arms crossed, then put out his hand.

I shook it. He put his other hand on mine as we shook. He was still looking at the board.

"Holy shit," he said. His eyes were red. I thought he might start crying any second.

I didn't say anything, let go his hand. I went back to the stock room, gathered up some more p.o.p., then headed for the door.

"Ricky," Mitchell shouted from his office after I'd gotten the front door open. A few snowflakes fell inside the door, melted there on the linoleum.

"What?" I yelled.

He leaned out into the hall. "Good day."

"That's all?" I said.

"And Andros is riding with you on Monday. Be here early."

"Bring him on," I said. "Bring that bastard on. I want him."

Once home I phoned Rose.

"Rose," I said. "What are you doing tonight? Let's go out to eat and then dancing or something."

She said, "I'm baby-sitting."

"Who?"

"Jason. Who do you think?" I heard her say something then, a few small words. "That's right," Rose said to him. "Take that to the kitchen."

"Then I'll come over."

"No," she said. "Slow down."

"I can't," I said. "I'm a salesman. Salesmen can't slow down." I tried to laugh.

"Tell you what," she said. "Jason and I are going to the Quabbin tomorrow morning. You can come with us, if you want. It'll help you relax to get out there."

I took a breath. I sat on the sofa bed, still unmade. I put my elbows on my knees. I looked at my black steel-toed shoes, my blue polyester pants and light blue company-issue shirt. I said, "All right. Where? When?"

It was the best I could hope for. Don't press.

FIVE

I walked down the hill to the Dunkin' Donuts the next morning, just as we'd planned. Her VW—yellow, I could see now, not gray—was parked there. I went inside.

She and Jason were sitting on stools at the counter. "Good morning," I said. Rose turned to me, smiled.

"Have a seat," she said.

I sat down. Jason was on the other side of her. He held a carton of milk with both hands, sucked at the straw. He didn't look up at me, only sat there, a half-eaten chocolate frosted donut on the counter in front of him. His feet dangled below him, moving to some rhythm.

Rose had a cup of coffee and a plain donut in front of her. "Jason," she said, "this is Mr. Wheeler. I told you about him. He's going on our picnic today."

He pulled the straw out of his mouth, his legs still going. He said "Hi" without looking up. He put the straw back in his mouth.

"Nice to meet you. We'll have fun today."

He put the milk down, picked up the donut with both hands, took a bite.

Rose turned to me. "It's still early. He's got to get warmed up. Once he's warmed up, watch out. He'll be all over the place."

"No problem," I said.

One of the girls working the place came up behind the counter. "Just coffee," I said. I turned to Rose. "I can still drive."

"No problem. I'll drive."

We finished, then got into her car, Jason in a booster seat in the back. We drove down King to a sandwich place, went in and ordered sandwiches and chips and sodas for later. I bought, though Rose got out her purse and made like she wanted to pay for hers and Jason's. "No," I said. She shrugged, put her wallet away.

Jason stood behind her, one hand holding the edge of her coat.

We drove downtown, then turned onto Route 9, the sun full in our eyes. The highway passed over the Connecticut, then through fields silver with frost in Hadley and up toward the old homes and across the commons in Amherst, the ground there, too, covered in frost like fine white ash. Then we were outside Amherst, driving through thick stands of bare, stiff oak and maple, dull green pines.

Rose turned the radio on. She said, "The heater's not worth much in this thing. Maybe the radio will take our minds off the cold." I still had my hands in my pockets, my shoulders hunched. My feet were cold, too. I breathed out, saw wisps of air.

"Jason," she said. "You warm enough?"

"Okay."

I pulled my hands out of my pockets, put them up under my arms. I settled back in the seat, looked out my window.

Paige and I had been along here often enough. Most every fall, in fact, we'd come out here, pull off on one of these side roads back into the woods, and take pictures of the foliage. During the summer we were out here with the windows down, just driving, going to the Quabbin to sit on rocks by the water and let the cool breeze off the lake, wind from all the way up in Vermont and New Hampshire and even farther north, wrap around us. We'd gone there one winter, too, and sat on those same rocks, felt the bitter wind tear into our faces like razors. We'd stood there only a minute or so before we went back to the car. We sat in there and drank coffee from a thermos, steam from the coffee clouding up the windows. The next day we'd read in the newspaper about a doe park rangers had found out on the ice; apparently she'd wandered out there, then had fallen, unable to get up again. The rangers had found her frozen and dead the day before, the day we'd been out there. Paige had cried, I remembered, cried with the newspaper spread out on the coffee table. I couldn't remember what I'd done. I just remembered the cold wind slicing right through our coats, and the black coffee and the steam.

We were at the intersection in Belchertown. Jason said, "He doesn't say a lot, Mommy."

"He's not asleep," Rose said.

I said, "I heard that."

The light changed, and we went on. Rose said, "You know, you haven't told me much about you."

"And you didn't even wash half the dishes. I did them all."

"That's true."

We were at the entrance to the park.

"Are we there?" Jason said.

"Yep," I said. I turned in my seat, looked at him from between the front seats. "What are you planning to do today?"

He said nothing, looked out his window.

"Jason," Rose said.

"I brought a frisbee, some cars. Stuff."

"Sounds like fun."

"Maybe."

I turned around. We were coming up to the main building, a huge red brick building with white trim sitting behind Windsor Dam. We drove along the road on the dam, the water to our left.

The Quabbin was always bigger than I remembered it being. Each time I came out here I realized I had forgotten how long and blue the reservoir was, stretching miles to the north, the shores up there just smudges of green and brown. Hills rose up all around the reservoir, trees growing down to the stone shore, a bone-gray strip of dead ground circling the lake. The lake itself was something of a W in shape, the left arm reaching north and a little west some twelve or thirteen miles, the right arm around twenty miles long and reaching up toward New Hampshire.

The wind hadn't picked up yet; the water was still. We followed the road to the east along the edge of the lake.

She turned off the road onto another that rose up from the lake and led to the top of a hill on the peninsula. At the crest of the hill stood a viewing tower, what had once been, I'd always imagined, a fire lookout. A hundred yards or so below the tower was a gravel parking lot, and Rose pulled in, cut the engine. Ours was the only car there.

"All out," Rose said.

Jason was standing in the backseat. "Let's go, Mr. Wheeler, let's go." He pushed on the back of my seat.

I opened my door, started to climb out. Jason squeezed between the car seat and me before I had both feet on the ground. "Hey, wait," I said. I reached behind the seat, pulled out a red frisbee.

Jason was gone, running to the tower.

Rose and I followed him up the path. She had her hands behind her back. I held the frisbee in one hand, tapped it on my thigh with each step toward the top of the hill.

"What are you thinking about?" I said.

"What I can tell you."

Jason was at the top of the hill. "Don't go in the tower until we get up there," she called to him. He started running in circles.

The grounds around the tower had been neatly trimmed, and sloped a few yards down the hill facing the western arm of the reservoir. We got to the top and saw Jason running along the edge where the grass, now brown, had stopped being trimmed and gave into tall brush. He ran back and forth, back and forth in some game he'd already invented.

"We're going up into the tower now," Rose said.

He froze, turned to us. We three were the only people there on the hill: a boy near the brush, this woman in an olive corduroy coat, me with a frisbee.

We climbed the flights inside the square building. The top level, windows on all four sides, was already warm from the sun. Jason went from window to window. "What's that?" he'd say, wait a moment for an answer, then move to another window, ask the same question.

We tried to answer him as best we could. "The mill in Holyoke," Rose said. "Windsor Dam," I said. "The road." "Our car." "The eastern arm of the lake."

Finally he gave up the questions, seemed to slow down. He stopped at one window, looked at everything.

"See what I mean?" Rose said. "He's wound up now. It'll be a long day."

I leaned against the railing around the stairwell. We were at the east window, the sun still low. She turned to the window, put both palms against the glass.

"We used to come up here all the time, Jason's father and I, before Jason was born. Once we came up here in the middle of fall. This place was incredible, the whole lake. The trees. We were right here, right here in the tower." She turned her head, looked at me, waved me over to the glass. I pushed myself off the railing, went over and stood next to her. "See that part of the lake over there?" She put a finger to the glass, tapped it.

Due east was the lower arm of the lake. In the morning sun the water there was white, a strip of silver.

"That part of the lake doesn't look all that far away, does it?"

"No," I said. "Maybe a mile."

"Hah," she said. "Guess again. This one fall afternoon Jason's father and I were up here in this tower, and he decides we'll walk down to the water down there. 'Fine,' I say, and we're off. We skip across the lot down there, then take off on a trail that goes back into those woods on the other side of the lot. And we go, and go, and go. At first it's not so bad. We're just having fun kicking through the leaves. He had a camera, and was taking pictures.

"And then, when we got to the bottom of this hill, and had lost all sight of water, and after he had started cussing out every branch, root, and stump we passed because he thought we'd never get to the water, we nearly fell into this hole in the ground. It was about six or seven feet deep, thirty or forty feet across both ways. This hole just came out of nowhere. Then we stood back from it, looked at it. It was a cellar. From one of those old homes that had been built up here ages ago. I thought it was beautiful, scary."

She still held her palms against the panes, as if she were attached that way, her palms taking in sun and warmth, storing it up somewhere inside her. Her eyes shone in the sun. Her hair had turned to gold.

"I looked closer at it, walked around it a few times. Vines grew down into the hole, and somebody had thrown an old stump in there. There were beer bottles down in there, too. Junk. But at one end of the thing I found a stone staircase that led down into it.

" 'Don't go down into that,' he says. 'Let's go. Let's get back to the car. This is crazy.'

"I just ignored him, though, and stepped down into the hole. 'Let's go,' he says. 'You're crazy.' But I walked around down there. I went to one side of it, pushed back some growth, and found the wall. It was brick, all beautiful red brick, and it was cold. I put my hand on the bricks, and this is going to sound so corny, so silly, but it was like I *knew* that house. I *knew* from that damp, cold brick what the place had been like. I saw men bringing in wagonloads and wagonloads of bricks. The men were dressed in old clothing—white shirts with big sleeves, vests, pants with suspenders, slouch hats, and they all built the place. And here was this house, up here in the middle of the woods, the top of the hill just behind the house a mile or so, and below the valley and trees and deer and birds for years, centuries, until the government bought out the land so they could put in a reservoir so that Bostonians could drink clean water. Then that home was torn down, all the bricks thrown in the back of some dump truck and driven out of here, just like the place had never existed.

"Jason's father looks down at me. 'Fuck this,' he says, and takes off.

"I just stood there, one hand on the wall. I looked up out of that hole at the trees, the red and yellow and orange leaves just waiting to fall from that blue, blue sky, and I didn't give a damn.

It was the first time, the first time I really, *really* didn't give a damn about Jason's father. I didn't.

"I found an old branch at my feet, and I picked it up. I started digging out that brick I'd had my hand on. It took a while, but I managed to get it loose enough so that I could work it out of the wall. I broke two or three fingernails in the process, but then I had it. It was cold and heavy and damp. Dirt all over it. I climbed up out of the hole, went back up the hill with this brick in tow. When I got back to the parking lot, he was sitting in the car, the engine running. My door was locked, and he made me knock on the glass before he pulled up the little knob. He said he'd been thinking, and that he hadn't seen me there.

"He looks at this filthy old brick in my lap, and he says, 'What the hell is that for?'

"I said, 'Nothing. I wanted it. Let's go.' "

She turned from the window then, leaned against it. She crossed her arms. She was smiling, then leaned her head back, looked at the roofbeams. "God, that brick used to drive him nuts. I took it home and treated it like it was a new puppy. I washed it, dried it, found a nice little place for it in the kitchen, as a sort of bookend for some cookbooks I had on the counter. He'd take it and throw it in the trash every once in a while, but I always found it, dug it out. He'd tell me it was silly, that it was ugly there in the kitchen."

She looked down at her feet then, her hair falling down around her face. She shook her head. "My first little act of defiance." She looked up, out the window to the west. "It's still there in my kitchen. Still there, holding those books up, doing nothing, really, except collecting dust. People have things like that. People have little things like that that meant something to them a long time ago but that, in the long run, don't turn out to mean much. I don't know. It's a brick. It sits on my counter at home. It's not ever going to move, either. I don't want it to." She looked at me, her face half in the sun, her right eye filled with light, almost crystal.

I thought of my ghost up there in Colrain, that child dancing somewhere, perhaps, right now, through grass. I wanted to tell Rose about it. I wanted to, but didn't know how.

I said, "I've got something like that. At home somewhere."

Jason ran around the railing to me, took the frisbee from my hand.

"Let's play frisbee," he said. He was off down the stairs, skipping the last step at each landing so he could jump, his tennis shoes slapping the concrete.

We followed him down. Rose said, "What is it?"

"It's a quarter," I said. We were walking down next to each other, our steps in unison. "A quarter my father gave me. He gave it to me a couple days before he died. I was twelve."

"I'm sorry."

"That's okay," I said. "Me too."

We made it to the bottom of the stairs and back out into the light. Jason was already out there on the grass, throwing the frisbee up into the air, trying to catch it. It would wobble a few feet up into the blue, then fall through his fingers. Once or twice he might catch it.

I watched him there. I thought about my being twelve and losing my dad. I hadn't thought about him at all since Paige had gone.

"It was a car wreck," I said. She didn't look at me. "He gave me this quarter, and then we went up to his and my mother's bedroom. My father got some nail polish from the dresser. He opened up the stuff, then painted a couple stripes of red nail polish across both sides of the quarter. He told me that, after I spent the thing, I might some day get that quarter back in change somewhere, and I would be able to tell it was mine because of the nail polish. I wondered exactly how I was supposed to tell it was mine. What if someone painted up theirs, too? But I never asked him that. The next day I went out and bought a can of soda with that quarter. And then the next day my father was driving home from the bulk mail center in Springfield where he worked. He was coming down North Main in Wilbraham, where we used to live, and some drunk college kid broadsided him."

I was quiet. Jason threw the frisbee a few feet out in front of him, went to where it landed, then threw it a few feet farther, working closer to the brush where the lawn ended. We both watched him.

I said, "But the quarter. About five or six months later I was at the market, and I got this quarter back in change. I looked at it, and I couldn't believe it. It was the same year, and it had these chips and spots of red nail polish in places. There was no way I could tell if it was the same one or not, but still. I kept it. It's at home."

"Good," she said.

What I didn't tell her, though, was that I didn't know where it was. Or if I still had it. I tried to remember where it might have been, where it might have gone. In a drawer. In the top of a closet. I couldn't remember. It was probably with Paige right now, or with our things, wherever she had stored them. But that seemed right. She was the only one I had ever told about the quarter. I hadn't even told my mother, who had died a year after Paige and I got married. Only Paige knew. And now this woman, this Rose Plavny.

At least I hadn't told her what had occurred to me as we watched her son moving closer and closer to the brush: that what she'd decided to keep, that brick, represented something she'd gained, but that quarter had always meant something lost.

Jason was at the edge of the high grass now. "Mommy," he said. "Watch."

He brought the frisbee back, his arm nearly reaching around himself, then brought it forward with a quick snap of his wrist. The frisbee flew up over the brush, and a small gust of morning wind lifted it. We watched as the red frisbee was carried higher into the blue, off to the west, then down the hill, where it ducked behind green pine, and disappeared.

"I found it," I called up the hill. Jason waved both arms above his head. Rose shouted, "Thanks."

I took a few steps up through the brush, then threw the frisbee up to them. Rose caught it, then played catch with Jason while I made my way up from the trees and high grass to the lawn. We played with the frisbee for a few minutes, then went back to the car.

Rose drove down off the hill and back onto the road skirting the lake. A little farther on we came to a pullout on the left, a scenic lookout over the water. Rose turned into the pullout, parked. We got out; Jason was once again out of the car before we were. He climbed up on a stone wall at the head of the parking spaces, started walking back and forth on it, hopping from stone to stone.

Next to the wall a round green sign hung from a post. The sign read:

ENFIELD LOOKOUT

OVERLOOKING FORMER SITE

OF TOWN OF ENFIELD

FORMERLY KNOWN AS

QUABBIN PARISH 1736–1786

SOUTH PARISH OF GREENWICH 1786–1816

TOWN OF ENFIELD 1816–1938

Jason stopped at the post, looked up at the sign. "Mommy, what does that say?" he said.

Rose read the sign to him. The first breezes had begun to pick up, white cumulus clouds starting to form to the north, roiling up one on another.

Jason said, "What does that mean?"

"It means," I said, "that there used to be a town down there. Years ago. They took it away, though, when they put in the reservoir."

He looked at me. "There's a town down there under the water?"

"Not now, actually. It *was* there."

He looked at the water. He put his hands in his pockets. He said, "I'd like to swim down there. I'd like to see if there's anybody down there. Look for skeletons."

Rose whispered to me, "I felt like I lived down there the last year of my marriage. Like I lived underwater."

We both laughed then, though what she'd said, I knew, was something of the truth. Maybe that was what made it funny.

Jason turned to us. "What's so funny?"

"Nothing, nothing," Rose said. She leaned against the car. "You just keep looking for skeletons down there." She looked up at me, crossed her arms, and smiled.

"I wasn't sure about going for Thanksgiving dinner with someone I didn't know," Rose said. "It took Carla a while to talk me into it." She put her elbow into my side, and I made like I was ticklish, bent over and away from her. "You're not bad company," she said.

"You're not too bad yourself," I said, leaning on the fender again. "And Cal never even told me you were coming. I didn't know you were going to be there at dinner until about a minute before you knocked on the door. I almost jumped out the window." I gently elbowed her, and she laughed.

"Disappointed?" she said.

"No." We were standing closer to each other than we had been before. Then we happened to look at each other at the same time.

I quickly looked back at the lake. I wondered if this was what it was about, if this same, strange childishness that I'd thought was finished in me so long ago was just how everything started each time.

Rose looked at the lake, too. "Jason," she said. "Be careful." She pushed herself away from the car, went over to him, put an arm around him. Their backs were to me.

Later we continued the drive around the lake, and she told me about her father, who, at age sixty-two, had been in his first fistfight the week before. He had fought with a man half his age at the bank downtown over who was next in line for the next available teller. Her father had been proud, Rose said, that he'd thrown the first punch on the younger man. I told her about how the first time I ever met Paige I'd had my fly down, and how I tried so nonchalantly to zip it back up while we walked past the pond and Memorial Hall to our next classes. She told me about some insurance agent who worked in her office who was always putting the moves on her.

"I mean," she said, "he parts his hair in the middle, and has it feathered back on the sides and over his ears. Incredible. He always carries a little brush in his suit coat pocket, too."

.   I told her about how, before Paige and I had been married, when I was working as a cook in a restaurant in Springfield, I'd stacked wicker onion-ring baskets on top of the exhaust from a deep fat fryer. The cook station was visible from the booths in the restaurant, and then a minute or so later the baskets went up in flames.

"The manager came back into the cook station and showered the place with a fire extinguisher," I said. "Then people who'd seen the whole thing from their tables in the restaurant started putting their coats on and taking off. The manager came out and tried to stop them. 'No problem,' he said. 'No biggee.' But they all just filed out, one after another. Even Paige, who'd been waiting for me in the lobby, took off."

We laughed. They were small stories, irrelevant as far as I could see, but it was the telling of them that did something. I rolled down my window once it was warmer outside, took in deep breaths of fresh air, as if it had been me, too, who'd been living at the bottom of the reservoir all this time. I hung my head out the window, whooped a couple times for Jason. He bounced up and down in his seat, laughing. "I want to," he said. "I want to, Mommy." But Rose wouldn't let him into the front seat while the car was moving.

"Rose," I said. "Come on. Let him up here. He can't roll his window down."

She glanced at me then, both her hands on the wheel. "No," she said, her lips barely moving. She looked up into the rearview mirror. "Jason, you settle down. That's how people get killed."

I knew then that I'd overstepped something I didn't know much about, and I sat back in my seat, put my hand out the window. I tried to make it slice through the air without letting it catch too much air above or beneath it. I tried to keep my hand right there in the middle, cutting straight through the air.

We had lunch later on; Jason had seen a picnic table far back up in the woods. Rose drove a little farther ahead, then made a U-turn, drove back to the spot.

"There, Mommy," Jason said. "There."

We could see a picnic table back there, one off by itself and not far from a backwater finger of the lake. Rose parked the car. We got out, ate lunch surrounded by bare trees, Rose making sure Jason sat next to her, and that his jacket was on tight, and that he ate.

The sun was behind the trees across from my apartment by the time we got back. Jason, his seatbelt across his waist, lay across the backseat, asleep; after lunch we'd played more frisbee, collected different leaves, tried to skip stones across the water below the picnic area. Later we'd driven to the dike, and the three of us had climbed all over the granite boulders and slabs that lined the shore. The breeze had made its way into a steady wind off the lake, and by the time we'd finally finished scuffing across the rocks, the wind had begun to cut. Rose had been the first to mention going home. Jason had begun to cry. I didn't say anything, just waited for Rose's next move.

I looked back at him in the seat, the light failing. I said, "He's a good boy."

"He's the greatest there ever was." She was looking at him, too.

I said, "What's it like? Being a mother. A parent."

"Nothing like it," she said, still watching him. "You have to live it." She turned to the front. "It's pure hell sometimes. Especially for me. Working, everything." She put her hands on the wheel. "It's just like I said the other night. Carla and I said you were lucky you didn't have any kids. Carla said it because I don't think she could ever have one. At least as long as she's who she is right now. She's got her own self and her own problems to worry about. I think I could have five more kids, though. I think I'm okay. I think I've figured myself out pretty well to where, if I had the time and the money, I would have a half-dozen more.

"The reason I said you're lucky is because you're divorcing. That's too much on a kid. It was on Jason. He just doesn't look the same any more. He doesn't look as innocent, I don't know, as *soft*. I've said this to his father, and he in all his infinite wisdom said Jason's growing up. But I know it's something else that's happened." She stopped, blinked. She looked at me and smiled, embarrassed. "God, I talk too much."

I thought of telling her right then, *now*, about the miscarriage, about that death. I wanted her to look at me, to feel something she could give to me about the word *parent*, about the word *father*, and have me understand. I wanted her to tell me.

She said, "So. Thanks for the good day. It was good to talk. I found out a lot."

I turned, put my hands on my thighs. "I learned a lot, too. But there's more I want to know." I rubbed my palms back and forth on my legs.

"Is this you asking me out again?"

"I guess so. If you want."

"I think I want to," she said.

I stopped moving my hands, leaned over toward her. Her face came closer to mine. I closed my eyes, felt her lips on mine: warm, gentle. Then it was over, and she was looking out the windshield, her eyes on the road.

"Call me," she said.

"I will." My hands were moving on my legs again.

She smiled, dropped her head. "Go on, get out of here."

I climbed out, watched the car pull away.

Is this it? I wondered. This? All over again. A game. A game I dreaded going into, playing with someone who knew so much more than I. I knew so little.

Her car slowed down at the intersection down the street, her brake lights blinking on and off in the brittle darkness, beneath this inescapable sky as she eased the car down the hill.

Monday morning Lynn Andros was waiting for me. I was not late, was, in fact, early. Still, he had beaten me to the office.

It was only six fifteen. None of the other supervisors had even gotten there yet. But there was Andros, sitting at one of the conference tables, legs crossed, ashtray in front of him. He was wearing gray flannel slacks and vest, a blue dress shirt and black tie. He dragged off the cigarette, held the smoke in his lungs for several seconds. He was turned to the side, his profile to me. He didn't move as I scraped my feet on the doormat, let the door close behind me.

I went to his table, dropped my route book on it.

He still hadn't turned to me, and said, "Wish I could have been here Friday."

I said, "Why?" I pulled off my jacket, dropped it on the back of a chair.

"They're calling it Good Friday down in Hartford. Yours was the best day from Hartford to Brattleboro."

"Great," I said. "You want some coffee?"

"Already had two cups." He held up an empty styrofoam cup he had had in his lap.

I went down the hall to the coffee room. Two full pots of coffee sat in the machine. I poured myself a cup, went back to the main room. "How long have you been here?"

"Half an hour." He still hadn't moved. "Thought a salesman

like you, Mr. Shining Star, would get up early, be here early and get out." He put out his cigarette.

I went over to the conference table, leafed through the merchandising paperwork to see which displays had to be rebuilt, which stores had to be stocked. I found my request forms in there, put them on top of the pile so they'd get done first.

I said, "It all has to do with working your ass off. Just forgetting everything else and working your butt off."

He turned then, put both hands on the table, looked at me. "Mr. Mitchell, your supervisor, also informed me Friday that you wanted him to 'bring the bastard on.' Presumably, the bastard is me."

I stopped. I put the papers down. I picked up my coffee cup. "What I meant was—"

"What you meant," he said, "is that you were ready for me to ride with you." He smiled, that same grin he'd had when he'd pinned me to the wall last week. "Well sir, the bastard is here. And the bastard doesn't care whether a salesman calls him a bastard or not. The bastard only cares about your sales. A salesman may call me whatever he likes, so long as he brings in the cases." He stood, still smiling.

"I was pretty high that day. Friday. I was wired from all the sales. Wired from everything that happened that day." I thought about the phone conversation I'd had with Larry Friday morning, about how that had set the day in motion.

"Regardless," Andros said, "the bastard is here to ride with you. Shall we ride?"

"Fine," I said.

I got my coat from off the chair, picked up my route book. Andros went to the coatrack behind the front door, put on his suit coat. He picked up a black briefcase he'd leaned against the wall. A briefcase, I thought. He'd never brought a briefcase along any other time he'd ridden with me.

Once in the car, he opened up the briefcase. It was empty except for a yellow legal tablet, two pens and a dozen or so fact sheets, the same sheets he'd passed around at the meeting.

He took the fact sheets out, closed the briefcase. He turned, put it on the backseat.

"These," he said, "are for you. Today's your chain day. We will hit most all your chains today. This is the new fact sheet, new since the meeting last week. Since we haven't made the new fact sheet public yet, these are the only copies out in circulation." He put his hands in his lap, looked out the windshield. His profile again. "We want to see what you can do with it. Take me out and show me how you sell. Use this new fact sheet, and sell."

I looked at the sheet, glanced over the numbers. It was for two-liters, RC, Diet Rite, RC 100. There were some good numbers there, especially the retail price per unit: ninety-six cents.

"Ninety-six cents a bottle. That's a good price. I can sell that." I looked it over a little longer. "What ads are nailed down so far? If I knew some ad dates I could use that for a little leverage."

"No ad dates. Not yet."

"What about chain approval? Have any chains decided to go with this yet?"

"Mr. Wheeler," Andros said, "this is not an official fact sheet in any regard. Nothing has, as yet, been nailed down. What this is, however, is a chance for me to see you in action. Cold turkey, as it were. You're on now, Mr. Wheeler. We're going to go to your chains, you're going to go in and sell this deal, and I'm going to watch you. Every case you sell we'll back up and offer at the price you show them on the fact sheet."

"What's this about?" I put the fact sheets in my route book, closed it on my lap.

"It's possible," he said, "that your sales are due only to the fact all your chains were directed to buy and display Schweppes this year. It's possible you didn't *sell* at all, just filled orders."

I said, "That's bullshit."

"I'm not one of those accusing you, not that anyone is accusing you of anything. We just want to see some real selling. We want to see how you do."

"You only have to look at my locations, where my displays are. All ends, most of them from the ground. Nobody told anyone in the stores where to locate displays. That was my job."

He was quiet, then took a breath. "Again, Mr. Wheeler, no one is accusing you of anything here. We want to see you in action." He turned to me. "Now let's go."

I put my route book on the backseat, started the car. The sky was still black. I turned on the headlights, backed out. I would show him. For whatever reason he was riding with me, I would show him.

Again, as on Friday, displays were shot, shelves empty. I started out the day by going to those markets I knew would have had the worst damage, those up and down King Street. At the first market, a Stop & Shop, I spent forty-five minutes rebuilding the front end display. I ended up using every case of Schweppes I had in the back room. Still, the display wasn't finished. There were holes here and there where I could have put up another five cases ale, another seven club soda.

I cleaned up the empty cases I'd wheeled out, came back to the display and put up some bottle-hangers. All this time Andros was just hanging back, watching me. He'd say something every once in a while, tell me a tray or one of the stacks wasn't exactly in line, point out a bottle I might have missed facing.

When I finished with the display I went to the shelf, faced all the product there. I wrote up a merchandising request form, wrote up the next order—fifty cases ale, eighty club, forty tonic, along with everything else—and then went to track down the manager.

The manager, a tall guy with short, wavy hair, wearing the company-issue blue polyester sport coat, gave me the typical stuff: first he was too busy because the store had just opened and he needed to give a final check on the condition of the floor. I followed him as we walked from one end of the store to the other. Then he had to okay a check on register two. Then he decided to bag two or three orders.

Finally we got to the back room. We'd lost Andros.

The manager stood there, hands on his hips, looking over my area.

"There's no product here," he said. "What's going on?" He kept looking at the area, walking back and forth in it.

"Terrific sales," I said. "Your end display up there is taking off. I've got a few extra cases coming in—"

"How many?" He stopped, looked at me.

I read off how many cases of what I was sending in. "Then I'm having a merchandiser follow the truck. As soon as the product's delivered, he's going to be in here, rebuild the display and fill the shelves."

He looked down, started pacing again.

"One more thing," I said. I opened up my route book, pulled out the fact sheet. "I want you to take a good look at this." I handed it to him. He grabbed it, held it with both hands.

I glanced around the room, looking for Andros. I didn't see him. I wondered if he were watching from somewhere, maybe back in the shadows behind the baler, or if he were just out on the floor, waiting to see how I'd done. My guts were twisting into knots just knowing, though, that he was out there somewhere, judging me.

I said, "This is a little way down the road. This is for January second. But you can see it's a price that's going to move product."

He said, "Ninety-six. That's good."

"Here's the thing," I went on, glancing around for Andros, seeing no one. "Here's the thing. I'm the only salesman with this buy-in. Nobody else has it. I'm the only RC salesman with this deal."

"What about my headquarters? What do they know?" He looked up from the paper.

"Nothing," I said. "Not yet, anyways. But I've been given the go-ahead from my headquarters to sell this to you. What we want is to plug this stuff right back into where the Schweppes is now. That comes down after New Year's."

"I know that."

I stopped. I moved my weight from one foot to the other. "Your profit's fourteen, right?"

"That's what this says."

"And you'll sell two-liter at ninety-six. That's for sure."

"Maybe." He was still reading the sheet, though everything was in big, bold letters and numbers there. Not much to read. There were even little pictures of two-liter RC and Diet Rite bottles on the sheet.

"You're the only Stop & Shop on my route. You'll be the only one with this deal nailed down early, so that when your head-quarters gets hold of this big deal coming down, you'll be there already with a display lined up." I was pouring it on now, stroking this guy. "You'll be Mr. Shining Star."

"Cut that shit out," he said. "Just put me down for two hundred. Half RC, half Diet Rite." He snapped the paper down, folded it in half. He looked at me, his mouth closed.

"Fine," I said. "Two hundred."

He turned, walked away through the double doors and out onto the floor.

I took a deep breath. Not a difficult sale, but typical. If it was a sale. I still wasn't sure what was going on.

I started making a note of the sale, then realized I didn't know where to record it. Did I write it on my order sheet? Just put it on a slip of paper? Write it on the back of a carton stuffer?

I looked up from my book. Andros stood in front of me.

"You forgot to press him for RC 100. A third line. Could have meant another one hundred cases, Mr. Wheeler."

I closed my book. "Come on, Lynn. What's going on? Show a manager a slip of paper that has some pictures on it and I'm supposed to sell it to him. Come on."

"And don't, Mr. Wheeler," he said, "worry about where you're going to write these sales down. You saw the yellow tablet in my briefcase. It will all go down there."

"Two hundred cases," I said. "You make sure it's two hundred cases."

Things went like that all day long: merchandising and stocking the shelves, finding the manager, following him around, getting him into the back room, bringing out the fact sheet. Andros always disappeared just before my presentation, then reappeared after the manager left. Things went well; the only chains to turn down my offer were a Waldbaum's and a D'Amour's. Both managers flatly refused when they found their own headquarters hadn't backed the deal.

The last stop was Cal's Price Chopper. It was a little after two already, and I wondered if Cal were still at work. We went to the front door, Andros behind me, and then, as he'd done at every stop so far, he hung back, looked around, started wandering through the store as if he were any man in a three-piece suit come to the market to look at dog food, the *TV Guide*.

I went to the Schweppes end on the bread aisle. I'd hoped a merchandiser might have been there by that time, but no one had come yet. The end was shot.

I took out a carton stuffer, wrote down how many cases of what I'd need to fill it. I glanced up, saw Andros at the end of the aisle. He picked up a loaf of bread, examined it, then put it back down.

I went to the back room, put my book on the product. The truck had already delivered: stock was piled six and seven cases high in my rows. A good deal of it would go up.

I had to go to the bathroom then, and so went back out onto the floor and down to the back corner where the milk and meat cases met. I pushed open the bathroom door, glanced behind me for Andros. I didn't see him.

I went to a urinal. I heard the door open, but didn't turn to see who it was. Then Cal stood next to me in his wrinkled white shirt and lime-green vest. He unzipped his pants, went at it.

"Who's your shadow?" he said.

"You won't believe it," I said. "Chain accounts manager. Up from Hartford just to ride with me today."

"What for? He's acting like Mr. Comparison Shopper, but he's about the most conspicuous clown in the store. Worse than you in your RC outfit."

I zipped up, flushed. I went to the sink and rinsed my hands. "He's watching me tread water with some new deal we've got going on. I've got to talk to the manager and sell him after I fill up the display and shelf."

"Shit," he said, bending his knees and zipping up. He didn't flush. "Sounds to me like some sort of test. You getting canned?" He laughed. "Wouldn't that be a kick in the ass for the old Schweppes man. You lose your wife, then get canned."

"No," I said. "I don't think that's what this is about." After I'd said those words, though, I wasn't sure. Maybe it *was* about losing my job. Maybe there'd been complaints of my overstocking my back rooms, my writing orders from the house that Wednesday Paige left. Maybe I'd finally shot in too many cases. But no, that was impossible; that's what sales was about from my end of things: shoot as much crap into the store as possible. Stack product so high you'll lift the roof, Andros had once told me.

He tucked in his shirt. "So what's the deal?"

I took a paper towel from the dispenser, told him about the fact sheet and how little I'd had to go on all day. Just the numbers on the sheet and as much talking and ducking and evasion as I could get in.

"Listen," he said. "Listen, you just follow my lead. You just sell it to me."

"I can't," I said. "You know I've got to go through the manager. You know that."

He looked at me, tilted his head. He put his hands on his

hips. "When are you going to find out? How many times have I told you? When are you going to finally realize I don't give a flying fuck? I'd thought you'd figured that out by now."

I looked at him, put my hands in my pockets, then looked at the tile floor. Gray tiles; no pink ones anywhere.

He said, "Anything you sell to me, I can get the manager to okay. If I don't, I don't. You blame it on me, the whole thing. Just do me this one favor, okay? Come on. Just let me screw around with this for once."

I was still looking at the tile. I said, "I never know if he's watching or not. It's like he hides."

"Let him hide."

I took a breath, looked up. He stood with his hands on his hips, then put them in his pockets, elbows locked, his arms stiff at his sides, and suddenly his face seemed more serious than I had ever seen it. Eyebrows knotted, lips closed tight, he was waiting for some sort of agreement between us, a pact in this. He was waiting, looking at me.

I said, "Let him hide."

He grinned, rubbed his hands together. He leaned his head back, let out a laugh, and looked at me again. "I'll lead," he said.

"Wheeler dealer," Cal shouted. He banged open the back room doors on his way in from the floor. I had the last stack of product on a hand truck, the last five cases I needed to finish filling the display.

"Cal," I said, maybe too quiet. "Cal," I said again, louder. I let the cases down.

He reached over, slapped my shoulder. "What shit are you going to pile up in my back room this time?"

I felt Andros's eyes somewhere in the room. I didn't want to do this, didn't want to lie to him by letting myself sell to Cal. This assistant manager. Then I saw Cal there, saw in his eyes as he waited for an answer the joke in it all: our sales, our jobs, our lives.

I said, "Two-liters. Ninety-six cents. Want in?"

"Show me some paper," he said.

To hell with Andros, I thought. "No paper. No nothing. Just word-of-mouth down from those bastards in Hartford. So far all I know is that there's RC, Diet Rite, and RC 100 two-liters at ninety-six cents the first of the year."

"Done," Cal said. "One twenty-five each RC, Diet Rite, and RC 100."

"Great," I nearly shouted. "Great. We'll put it up where the Schweppes is now." I pulled the hand truck back, started wheeling the cases down my row toward the back-room door.

"Done and done, you son of a bitch," Cal laughed. He followed me out onto the floor, left me when a check okay came over the speakers.

Andros said nothing when we got out to the car. He opened his briefcase again, wrote something on the tablet.

I said, "In case you didn't hear in there, that's one twenty-five each RC, Diet Rite, and RC 100. I didn't forget the RC 100." I smiled. I was almost laughing.

He gave a tight smile, closed the briefcase, then nodded for me to go.

We made it back to the office at four. Andros was first out of the car; the office door had already closed behind him by the time I'd collected my route book and sales orders from the backseat.

I went into the office. Eight or ten men sat around at the tables, all of them looking at me. I looked down the hall toward Mitchell's office, saw Andros duck in there. I looked back at the others, shrugged with my hands out to either side, then went down the hall.

"No problem at all," I heard Mitchell say from inside his office, and then he was out in the hall. "Andros wants to talk to you in there," he said as he passed me. He whispered, "Alone." He gave me the okay sign with his fingers, a cigarette jammed between his index and middle fingers. "You're doing great," he whispered.

I went into the office. Andros was already in Mitchell's chair, the tablet out on the desktop. He said, "Close the door."

I put my route book on the corner of the desk, turned and pushed the door closed.

"Eight hundred fifty cases," he said. He hadn't looked up. "Eight fifty. Not bad at all." Still not looking at me, he took a mechanical pencil out of his suit pocket, then drew dark lines through the last three numbers on the list. I looked at the numbers: 125 RC, 125 Diet Rite, 125 RC 100. Cal's stop.

He looked up at me. He was not smiling. "Of course your charade at the Price Chopper won't count. I'm not sure what you think I know of the ways of the world as far as Price Choppers go. I'll fill you in. I know the responsibilities of every position in that chain. I know what the chairman of the board's job is right down to the bag boy's. You ought to test me sometime, see if I really do. One thing is for certain, however: one does not sell end displays to assistant managers. Assistant managers don't buy our product. The manager does."

He leaned back in Mitchell's chair, springs creaking. "So what will happen tomorrow is that you and I will return to your beloved Price Chopper and sell to the manager. Not the assistant. Not a cashier. Not a produce man. The manager. And you won't pull any more jokes on the bastard from Hartford."

"Yes sir," I said. He sat there, his eyes still on me. I looked up at the fluorescent lights of the ceiling. I said, "So is this about me getting canned, or what?"

I heard springs creak again. I looked down, saw he was leaning even farther back in the chair. He had his hands clasped behind his head. He was grinning, that same grin. A tough grin.

"Hardly," he said. "Hardly, Mr. Wheeler. I'll be riding with you again tomorrow. We'll be visiting your independents after our little jaunt over to Price Chopper. The rest of the day I'll be watching your 'saturation' techniques in the mom-and-pops."

"Why?"

He sat up, both hands flat on the desk. His mouth was straight.

"I'm breaking every code of ethics I know of, Mr. Wheeler, but I like you. We like you. I feel I can be assured of your confidence. Am I correct?"

I shrugged. I didn't know what he was leading to. He could tell me anything he wanted. "Sure."

"Come the first of the year, Mr. Mitchell, your supervisor, will be relieved. We hope his leaving our company will be a mutual agreement."

I swallowed, sorry I'd told him he could tell me. I didn't want to hear this. I picked up my route book from the corner of the desk, put one hand in my pocket.

"Sit down," Andros said. He motioned to a chair against the wall behind me. I turned, sat down.

"Well?" he said.

"What?"

"What do you want to know?" He took his hands off the desk, put them under the table.

I said, "I'm not sure. I'm not sure I want to know anything. Except why."

"Sales," Andros boomed. "Sales. *Sales*. They're down. They're sad here. Yours are the only good sales this district has had this year. You've shown the cases are out there. We've studied printouts from your route, and your cases aren't all from big chains. There are cases to be had. Plenty. Mitchell isn't doing his job out there."

He relaxed then, picked up the pencil, leaned back. "He's an old-style salesman. He plays loose. He gambles. He lines up displays to be built, stops to be merchandised, then only hopes the work gets done. And he should be out there making some sales himself. A salesman has a tough time with a manager, the supervisor should be out there, show the salesman how it's done." He was quiet a moment, then said, "And salesmen shouldn't be building so many of their own displays."

"He's been good to me," I said. "He's covered me, for the most part. Plenty of times I've gone out there and found things already done for me."

"Of course," he said. "Wouldn't you want to cover your best man? Look at you now. You're defending him."

"I'm not defending him," I said, and was amazed at the truth I'd given him. I didn't care about Glenn Mitchell. I put the route book on my knees, my palms flat on the cover. "I'm just telling you what's happened. I'm just trying to figure why."

"And I'm telling you. The point is, if he covers *you*—sends out merchandisers to build your displays especially—then when we in Hartford notice you, Rick Wheeler, making all these big sales, Mr. Mitchell says 'Look at me. I covered him. I helped him. I had all his displays built and maintained. Therefore, I'm a good supervisor. I'm doing my job.' Fact is, Mr. Wheeler, that your sales started picking up long before Mr. Mitchell took it upon himself to cover you. According to our printouts, they've been picking up since mid to late July."

Of course, I thought. Though I'd not known that fact, it was only logical. Since last summer.

"Another fact," he said. "We want new blood." He looked at me, his face still straight. "We're looking at you."

I sat back in the chair, my palms hot against the plastic cover of the route book.

"Except for your little joke there at the Price Chopper, you've shown me how close, how safe you are. You gambled there at the end, and you lost. You play tight. That's the way you should. Work your ass off, don't wait for someone else to handle things. When was the last time you remember Mr. Mitchell going out to one of your chains, one you were having particular problems getting some promotion in for whatever reason, and selling the manager for you? When?"

I was quiet a while, then said, "I can't remember."

"You see what I mean."

He was quiet then. He was waiting for me to say something, I knew.

"You're looking at me," I said.

"Right at you."

There was a knock at the door. "Lynn?" It was Mitchell.

"Come on in," Andros said. He looked at me. He didn't blink.

Mitchell came in. Andros still looked at me. He was wondering what I'd do, how I'd act with Mitchell in here, the man whose head was about to roll. He wondered, I knew, if I would choke up. He wanted to see how good a salesman—an actor, a liar—I really was, how I could piece my way through this moment.

Mitchell passed in front of me, coughed, then turned to me, smiling.

"Mr. Andros giving you hell?" he said, laughing. He coughed again, this time onto the back of his hand; the other was in his pocket, fishing around for his disposable lighter, I figured. He didn't have a cigarette. "If he is, you probably deserve it," he laughed.

I hadn't taken my eyes off Andros yet, and we held a stare. I said, "Hell, all right. Nothing I can't handle, though."

"Good for you," Mitchell said. He was lighting another cigarette, his face all screwed up with the first new smoke. "Makes you tough."

Andros said, "Tomorrow, then. I'll ride with you again, visit your independents. You can show me some of your common sense."

"Early," I said.

Maybe Paige would have danced. Maybe she would have made us go out to dinner. Maybe she would have only hugged me, held me, quiet at the news I would be a supervisor. But I would not know.

I called Rose, gave her the good news.

"You're welcome for dinner," she said. "Nothing special, but if you want you can bring over a bottle of wine. We're having baked chicken and rice."

"I'll be there."

She gave me directions. "Congratulations," she said.

She lived in an apartment in a big Victorian four stories high with a gabled roof, a turret, a screened porch. Everyone I knew lived in apartments, I thought.

Except for Larry and Wendy Kasmarski.

I walked up the granite steps to the beveled glass door, went inside. The foyer made me feel as if I were inside someone's home: a worn, Persian rug, landscape paintings on the walls, a polished brass lampstand. Stairs led up from the far end of the foyer. Rose lived on the second floor.

I went up, knocked on the door. I heard a deadbolt slide back, the scratch of a chain.

Paige, I decided, would have danced.

"Rick," Rose said. She pulled open the door.

I came in, handed her the bottle of wine. "So this is where you hide out," I said.

I looked around. We were in the living room, a big room with plenty of furniture and plants. Jason sat on a Big Wheel in the middle of the room, the television on. He was watching an old episode of "Andy Griffith." He didn't move.

"Jason," Rose said, "here's . . ."

But he had already turned to me and was up, running across the room to the couch. He reached under it, pulled out the red frisbee. Before Rose or I could say anything, he had flung it across the room at me. I missed it, and it hit a lampshade, nearly toppling the lamp.

"Jason," Rose said. "Not in the house. Not in the house! How many times do I have to say that?"

He stood next to the couch, leaned against it. His face was turned from us, but his eyes were on me. "I just tossed it," he said. "Not hard."

"But not in the house. At all," Rose said.

I said, "Later we'll play. If not after dinner, then another day."

He shrugged, rubbed the toe of his tennis shoe on the floor. "Okay," he said, and went back to the Big Wheel, sat down and watched the program.

Rose turned to me. She smiled. "Some salesman. You must be some salesman. Good job."

"Thanks."

We looked at each other for a long moment, then Rose said, "You're welcome," and led me into the kitchen.

She opened the refrigerator, brought out a head of lettuce, a tomato, celery. She said, "You can make a salad, can't you?"

I said, "Supersalesman can do anything."

She laughed. I cut up things for the salad.

We bumped around in the kitchen for a while, smiling, but saying little. Something was going to happen that night. We both knew it.

The dining-room table was in the front room, off to one side and under the windows. When we sat down to eat, there was again that moment when Rose and I looked at each other longer than we should have. Rose looked away first, picked up her glass of wine. She said, "Here's to sales. May they always increase."

I lifted my glass. Jason, seeing us, picked up his glass of milk, made us touch our glasses to his before we could take a drink.

It was after eight when we finished dinner. Jason cried a little when Rose told him it was too late to go out and play frisbee. He looked at me, said, "But you said—"

"Wait a minute," Rose said. "We never promised anything, but if you stop crying and start being my big boy you can take a green zombie bath tonight."

"Oh," Jason said, and wiped both eyes with his hands. "A zombie bath."

Rose looked at me and smiled. "A couple of drops of green food coloring under the faucet makes a zombie bath. A treat."

"I'll remember that," I said.

Jason was already down from his seat and heading into the back of the apartment.

Rose and I stood at the same time. She put her silverware on her plate, then picked up her glass.

"Mommy," Jason called from the bathroom. "Bring the zombie stuff."

"Go," I said, and took the plate from her. "You go zombitize him. I'll clear."

"Great," she said, and leaned over, kissed my cheek. She smiled, then turned and started down the hall. "Thanks," she said.

I stood holding our plates, watched her walking away. I smiled, and went into the kitchen.

I rinsed the dishes, put them into a portable dishwater pushed back into a corner. Then I squeezed some dish soap into the pans and the casserole dish, ran some hot water in, and let them soak.

I went into the big room. The TV was still on, "Wheel of Fortune" now.

Photos of people hung on the wall: Rose with Carla, Carla in a wedding gown. Neither woman looked any different than now, except that Rose's face was thinner. There were pictures of Rose years ago, a baby in her arms, two silver-haired women on either side of her in front of a church somewhere; four pictures of Jason at different ages, those Sears portraits where the child sits on the shag-carpet-covered table; a picture of a newborn, probably not over a week old, its hands in fists, its eyes swollen shut. Jason.

I looked at all the pictures of Jason, from oldest to youngest, and you could see, really *see* that that baby, the one with spiky black hair on its head, eyes shut, was Jason. A person. A boy I knew.

I found my way to the bathroom. Jason, already washed and in pajamas, stood on the toilet seat brushing his teeth, Rose behind him, her hand under his jaw. They were looking in the mirror. Slowly Jason worked the toothbrush around in his mouth. Rose was giving him directions. Neither had seen me.

"Now rinse," Rose said. She leaned over to the counter, picked up a glass of water, gave it to him.

Jason turned, saw me. His mouth was full of foam. "Watch," he said to me. He took a mouthful of water, leaned his head back and started gargling.

"Cut it out," Rose said. "Spit it out."

He kept gargling, his head back, one eye watching me.

I said, "You better cut it out."

He closed his eyes, kept on.

"Jason," Rose said. "Stop it. Now. Spit it out before I spank you."

But Jason only kept on gargling, until finally Rose, one hand on his chest, the other on the top of his back, forced him to lean over the sink. Jason spit out the foaming water, most of it missing the sink and splashing on Rose's combs and barrettes, makeup case.

"That was smart. That was really smart," she said to him.

Jason looked at what had happened, then to Rose and back to the counter. His mouth, the bottom lip, started quivering.

Rose took one arm, then spanked him while he stood there on the toilet. He began crying.

I stepped back out of the bathroom, my hands behind my back, let Rose and Jason move past me and down the hall to his bedroom, Rose pulling him along. He was wiping tears with his free hand. I followed a few feet behind, then stood outside the room as Jason climbed up into his bed.

Rose said, "Now you learn to mind me, okay? I need all the help I can get around here. You're my only hope, all right? You're the one I love, so don't pull stuff like that on Mommy. You have to help me, okay?"

Jason, taking quick breaths, his eyes still wet, said, "Okay."

He lay down then, and Rose pulled the blanket up to his chest. She kissed him. He had already stopped crying, and rolled over toward her.

"Sweet dreams," she said. She stood, moved for the door. I stepped back into the hall. I wasn't sure if I wanted her to know I'd been watching.

I went into the living room, got the bottle of wine and our two glasses from the kitchen, and sat on the sofa. Rose was in the bathroom cleaning up the water. She turned out the light, came down the hall. She stopped, looked at me there on the sofa. I had my shoes off, my feet up on the coffee table. I'd filled both glasses.

"Well," she said.

"Please, sit down," I said, and made this sweeping gesture with one hand.

We sat there the rest of the evening, the TV going, one sitcom after another. We finished off the bottle, and then Rose got up, found another bottle in the refrigerator, opened it up.

The only words between us all evening were little cracks

about the programs we were watching, but all this time there was that feeling in me, the feeling something was going to happen. Each small movement Rose made—bringing the wineglass to her lips, crossing her legs, pulling back a strand of hair—I felt was aimed at me, to tell me something.

Finally I lifted my arm up, set it down behind Rose, let it rest there on her shoulders. Then she moved closer to me, nestled into my shoulder, still without a word. She put her feet up next to mine on the coffee table, then sipped her wine. She hadn't looked at me. I knew this not looking, too, was aimed at me.

The eleven-o'clock news came on, and Rose turned to me.

I said, "Well?"

"Well?" she said.

I stood, took her hands and pulled her up, and then we were holding each other, her face against my chest. We stood like that for what seemed a long time, and then she pulled away, went to the set and turned it off.

In her room we held each other again, and kissed this time. It was a strange feeling, this woman's lips on mine, her hair in my hand, my arm around her. And of course I thought of Paige, and of our making love the last time, up there in the hills above Colrain. I tried to put Paige out of my mind, replacing her with this woman now with me. I began undressing Rose then, both hands pulling up her sweater while we were still kissing.

Rose stopped, said, "No."

I wondered what I had done this time, if that feeling I'd had that something would happen had been wrong all along, but then she went to the lamp next to the bed, turned it out, and I heard her undressing there in the dark.

I took off my clothes, put my hands out in front of me and felt my way through the dark to the bed. I climbed in and under the covers. Rose was already there.

Our two bodies were awkward there in the bed, and neither of us could get comfortably situated against the other. Rose laughed a little, and I did, too, until I finally lay on my back, and Rose, on her side, moved next to me. I could smell her hair, could feel her cheek against my bare chest. I felt as if I'd never had a woman before, as if this were the very first time I'd ever made love.

I touched her. I touched first her shoulder, then ran my hand along the smooth line of her body to her hip, where I let it rest. She seemed to stiffen when I stopped moving my hand, and I raised up on an elbow, moved my face down in the dark to find her lips.

She moved her face from mine, leaned her head back, a signal for me to kiss her neck. Her movement, though, had been quick, jerky, as though she were obliged to let me have her. But this was a new woman, I thought, and this might be how she loved.

I kissed her neck, her shoulder, moved toward her breasts, and then my mouth was on her breast, drawing out the nipple hard. Her breasts were softer than I had imagined, the skin almost loose. This was another woman, I thought. A different woman. Not Paige.

I moved the hand that had been resting on her hip to her breasts, caressed them while I kissed her, and then I moved my hand down to her abdomen. I slowly stroked her stomach—the skin there, too, was soft and fleshy. I'd expected other things, expected her breasts to be firm, her stomach taut, but I'd known so few women in my life, and I knew so little about them, that I just accepted it.

Rose gave a small, quiet moan then, my mouth on her breast, my hand on her stomach. Paige and I had found what we wanted and needed from each other over the years, and small moans and movements of the hands and legs and head had become a language of its own, each move signaling that some next move was desired. And so I took her moan to mean she wanted more from me.

I moved my hand lower until my fingers touched her pubic hair, and she gave a shorter, quieter sound. Then her hand was on mine. She lifted it, said, "No."

I stopped. I lifted my head from her breasts, tried to see her face in the dark, but couldn't.

She gently pushed me away from her, both hands on my chest. She pushed me away.

She sat up in bed. "This isn't," she said, then stopped. She took a breath. "This isn't a good idea," she said.

I was quiet a moment, then rolled over onto my back. "What is?" I said. "What is a good idea? You tell me," but I knew what she had said was true. I put my hands behind my head, looked at the black ceiling somewhere above me.

"Too soon," she said. "If this is ever going to happen anyway."

"Why won't it?" I said.

She didn't move. "If you don't know by now, I'm not telling."

I could see the outline of her body as she leaned toward the lamp on the nightstand. She turned it on, and I closed my eyes for a few seconds. When I opened them, she was sitting up, her back against the headboard.

I looked at her. Her breasts were limp, and sat against her ribcage, the nipples now soft and flat. The skin on her abdomen was loose, too, marked along the sides with small purple striations.

I looked away.

But she had seen me take her in. "Stretch marks," she said. Her voice had taken on some quiet anger. "That's Jason you're looking at. I don't think they're ugly, but maybe you do." She paused. "They're a part of me. They're that kid there in the other room."

I was looking at the ceiling again. I said, "Is he the reason you think this is the wrong idea?"

"I love him. I do. But that's not the reason."

I turned, sat with my feet off the side of the bed. My back was to her.

I said, "It was a miscarriage. She had a miscarriage at a roadside stop on the Merritt Parkway, and it was my fault. I caused it. I even flushed the thing down the toilet."

I stood, went to my pile of clothes on the floor, and started dressing. I didn't look at her, but heard her take a quick breath. She said, "I'm sorry."

I said, "Me too." I had my clothes on, wanted to leave. I

wanted to take off without ever looking at her again, but I turned to her. She had the sheets up around her now.

I moved back to the bed, sat down. I leaned over, put my head in my hands. I wanted to cry, but couldn't, and then I felt Rose's hand on my back, the same gentle touch she'd given me the night we'd met, when we'd stood washing dishes. Consolation.

I sat up, my back still to her. I said, "I'm going to tell you one last story. And then I'm gone."

She said nothing.

"About a month after the miscarriage, which had been back in May." I stopped. I looked at my hands. Rose was quiet. I was on my own.

About a month afterward, we went up to a friend of ours' house in Colrain. That was the last time we made love. We spent the weekend up there with them, and then we came home, went back to work and started up again as if nothing had ever happened. Then a couple of weeks later, on a Sunday afternoon, Paige told me she wanted to go for a ride.

"Like we used to," she said. Before she miscarried we'd gone driving around just about every afternoon, looking for a bigger place to live, but mainly just driving through neighborhoods we knew we could never afford to live in. And there had been this one house in particular, a huge brown clapboard Garrison for sale up in Whately we must have driven past thirty or forty times, just staring at it. And so we got in the car and started driving, and ended up on Route 10 to Whately, and toward that home.

When we got there we saw that the place hadn't sold yet, and that there was an open house going on. Day-Glo orange flags were planted along the road and up the driveway.

"Stop the car," Paige said. "Stop."

We had nowhere to go, nowhere at all. I stopped the car.

We got out. I tucked the tail of my shirt in. Paige was looking at the house, one hand up over her eyes to protect them from the setting sun. I came around the car to her and held her hand, and we started up the flagstone path to the door. I couldn't tell what was going to happen, whether we'd be kicked out, ignored, or what. I was just a salesman. She was only a secretary. We'd never been to an open house.

The front door was open, and we walked in. We stopped in the foyer, Paige a little behind me.

"Hello," I called out.

The realtor came in from the room directly in front of us. He was wearing a loose-cut wool blazer, corduroy pants, and a plaid shirt.

"How are you?" he said. He put out his hand, and I shook it. Then he looked behind me at Paige, and offered her his hand. She smiled and shook his hand.

"My name is Robert," he said. He was all smiles. "This is just a gorgeous home, isn't it?"

"I'm Rick," I said, "and this is my wife Paige. Yes, it's a nice place. That's why we stopped." I laughed a little, and Robert laughed, too, though a bit loud for what I'd said.

About this time a woman came into the foyer. She was a good-looking woman, in her mid-forties, with gray hair to her shoulders and wearing a denim skirt and yellow jersey.

"This is the owner," Robert said, "Sarah Barton. Sarah, this is Rick and Paige." He stopped, then said, "I don't think I got your last name."

This is when I started telling lies. I think I wanted more than anything to impress them, impress the realtor, the owner. And Paige. We could not afford this house. We could never afford this house. I lied to them, and told them our last name was Seavers. It was a name that just came into my head.

"Rick and Paige Seavers," Robert said. "Great. Let's take a look around the place."

I looked at Paige. I was not sure what I was looking for, maybe a wince, a little frown, but I found nothing. She only smiled back at me and said, "Yes, let's look around."

Robert led us out of the foyer into the living room. The room had oak paneling waist-high on the walls, oil paintings above the wood, overstuffed furniture. The fireplace had a large hearth and mantel, an oil painting of the Barton family hanging above it. They had three kids.

Sarah Barton hung back from the three of us. Robert opened the drapes to show us the lawn and swimming pool, and Sarah said, "I've seen you somewhere. I know you from someplace, don't I?"

We turned around. Sarah's eyes moved from Paige to me and back to Paige.

Paige said, "Longmeadow Country Club? Do you get out there?" She smiled and put her hands together. I didn't say anything.

Sarah said, "No, no I don't get out there very often. I think it's your car. Your car is what I recognize. I saw you drive up, and thought I recognized your car."

"Oh," Paige laughed. "Actually, you've probably seen us driving around here. We've been scouting out homes for quite a while. Truth be known, we've had our eye on your place in particular for a long time." She turned to me. "Haven't we, dear?"

I had been watching Paige while she spoke, watched her making subtle gestures and little movements I had never seen her make before: a toss of the head as she laughed, her hands moving gracefully as she explained about the driving, her turning to me and calling me Dear.

I said, "Yes. A few years now, really." I turned to Sarah. I smiled.

Robert jumped in. "Longmeadow? You're from Longmeadow? I take it, then, you might be selling your home down there. That's a wonderful area down there." He put his hands in his back pockets and started rocking back and forth on his heels.

"That's the truth," I said.

Robert led us through the living room into the den, or library, as Sarah wanted to call it. She told me her husband was a lawyer. I told her I was an executive for a supermarket chain.

We went through the kitchen, down into the recreation room in the basement, where the Bartons had a pool table, Ping-Pong table, and a color television console set up. Then we headed to the second story, and the kids' rooms. All this time Paige was talking to Sarah. She talked about the grand piano she could see fitting perfectly into the living room, about the library being used as a studio for her painting. Robert was talking to me the whole time, and I kept nodding my head as though I were answering him, but I was listening to Paige. She surprised me. She told her lies very well. There was no hint of overacting. She was selling them. She was doing the best sales job I'd ever seen anyone do. Better than I would ever do. If I hadn't known her, I would have believed she could paint, play the piano.

We ended up in the master bedroom. It was as large as the living room, and had a dressing room, walk-in closet, two sinks, a shower, toilet, and a sunken tub.

I went to the window and looked out at the backyard. The sun was down, the sky purple and blue. Tall oak and maple trees lined the yard, the tips of the trees now black in the dusk. I could see the silhouette of their barn. There was a swing set down there, and a sandbox.

Robert came up next to me. "Beautiful," he said.

I turned from the window. Sarah and Paige were still talking. I looked at Paige, and said, "Let's talk price."

"Well, sir," Robert said. He smiled and put his hands in his back pockets again. "I was hoping you might say that."

Paige stopped talking. Slowly Sarah started moving out of the room.

"There's no need for me to go on any more about this house," Robert said. "You've watched it for years. You've had your eye on it. You know how valuable a home like this is, what an asset." He took a breath, looked down at his feet, then back at me. "Two nineteen nine. We can let you have it for that. And we're firm."

Paige and I didn't move. We were cool. I smiled first.

"You're firm," I said.

"Yes," Robert said. He tilted his head a little, and stopped smiling.

"Tell you what," I said. "You leave us alone in here for a minute to talk things over, Paige and me. We've got to talk."

"Fine," Robert said. "No problem." He quickly pulled his hands from his pockets and went out into the hall. He pulled the door closed behind him.

But we didn't say a word to each other. I went over to the king-size bed and sat down, ran my hand across the bedspread. Paige went over to the other side, her back to me. We sat that way for five minutes. I counted off the minutes on the clock on the nightstand.

Then Paige stood up and went toward the bathroom. "Paige?" I said, turning to her.

She went into the bathroom. I got up and followed her. I looked in the door, and she was sitting in the bathtub, staring at the faucet, an arm on either edge of the tub. I turned to leave, and saw my reflection in the mirror. I could see myself shaving in this mirror, or tying a tie, or combing my hair. I looked in the mirror a moment longer, then I went back into the bedroom.

Paige came out a few minutes later, and then I opened the bedroom door, started down the hall. I hadn't even looked at her.

Robert and Sarah were down in the kitchen drinking coffee. "Coffee?" Sarah said.

"No," I said, "but we've talked." I turned to Paige. She was smiling up at me, the same smile she had been giving while touring the house.

"Yes, we have," Paige said.

I said, "And I think we could offer you one eighty-nine."

Robert crossed his arms, leaned back against the butcher block counter. "One eighty-nine. That's thirty under what we want, you know." He had tilted his head again.

"We know," Paige said.

"We'll have to think on that," Robert said.

"You do that," I said, "and then you get in contact with me." I gave him a phone number, just seven numbers that came into my head.

Robert gave me his card, and then we shook hands with him and Sarah.

From inside the car we could see the master bedroom light still on. Paige was turned away from me, looking at the house.

She said something then, something I couldn't quite make out. The only word I'd heard clearly was the word Sorrow.

I was quiet a moment, then said, "Sorrow is a big word. Sorrow is not a word you throw around when you are talking about a house."

She turned from her window, and looked at me. Though it was dark, I could see tears welling up, her mouth a thin line, and I knew it was sorrow she felt. I was sorry I'd told her it was the wrong word. I thought about it. *Sorrow*, I figured, was just about the best word anyone could use.

She looked out the windshield.

"What do you want to do?" I said.

"Drive. Just drive," she said. She put her hands over her face. "Surprise me," she said.

I couldn't hear anything behind me, couldn't hear Rose moving, breathing. She could have been asleep.

"End of story," I said. We sat there for a long time, neither one of us moving. There was no clock here for me to count off how long we sat that way.

Finally I stood. Rose said, "You still don't know why we can't make love?"

"No," I said. "I don't."

"You're lying," she said, and this, too, was true.

I said, "You're right." I said, "I love her."

I stood there in her bedroom. I saw my shadow cast from the lamp behind me. I was big. I was huge, darkening most of one whole wall, but you could see right through the shadow, see that there was nothing on that wall that wasn't always there: paint, a dresser with a mirror. But for now my shadow was right there.

Rose said, "You and Cal are a lot alike."

I turned my head toward her, but didn't look at her. I could see from the corner of my eye my shadow shifting.

"You both still love your wives," she said. "And you're both trying to figure out what happened. What went wrong. But he destroyed his marriage. I don't know how or why—maybe he's told you—and neither does Carla. The fact is that he'll be spending the rest of his life trying to figure out what happened. But you." She paused. "You're not too late. You just think you are. I don't know if you're in the wrong or not. I don't know the situation, and I don't care to. You just think you're too late."

"Be quiet," I said, astounded at my voice.

"Listen," she said.

I said, "I'm going, I'm gone," and I left her there.

SIX

I got home. I sat at the front-room window, that same window I'd sat at months before, the window I'd eaten sandwiches and drunk milk at while I watched the night outside. The night I'd had the cold.

I wondered if that ghost would come down here to haunt me now, while I sat at the window. I wondered if it would come down here and dance for me out there on the lawn. It was my ghost, I reasoned. It was part of me. It could go with me wherever I went. Maybe that was what had happened to my marriage, to my wife, to me. Maybe that ghost had come back with us from Colrain that weekend, and had holed up in this apartment with us, and had haunted the two of us from that day on so that, some three weeks ago, this marriage had finally fallen apart like the skeleton of some dead animal out in the woods. And now it'd started in on me, started eating me to pieces.

I watched from the window for the ghost.

The phone rang, shattered the apartment. I turned from the window, looked at my watch. I couldn't read it in the dark of the apartment. I held it closer to the window for the light from streetlamps.

Three thirty.

Of course I thought of Paige having been killed somewhere, and then I thought of Rose calling. Calling for what? And then here was Paige again, dead somewhere. I didn't want to answer it.

It rang again, then again. I picked it up in the middle of the fourth ring.

"Hello?" I said.

"Jesus Christ, buddy," came the voice.

It was Lonny.

"Hey, Lonny," I said. I was smiling, my eyes closed for what felt like the first time all night.

"Where the hell have you been? I called you last night until just after midnight. Shoot, that's when I gave up, turned in so's I could get some sleep before heading out."

"Heading out?" I said. "Where?"

"What do you think? Come on, Rick, use your noggin."

I said, "Hunting."

"You ready?"

"When?"

"Now. I'm heading out the door. I've got a couple of worthless nephews who usually go with me. They informed me, though, that this was just too damned early to get up. This after we've been deer hunting every year for the last ten. So you're kind of second string, but I know you won't mind. I've got guns. I've got food. I've got some prime land up around North New Salem."

I said, "Get me out of here. You know where I live."

"Twenty minutes."

"The sooner the better," I said, then before I even thought about it I said, "And do you have an extra gun? Enough for three."

He was quiet a moment, then said, "Well, sure. You got somebody there with you? Somebody who can hunt, that is."

"Nobody here," I said. "But I know someone who'll go. A hunter. At least I think he is. Cal Riley. He's an assistant—"

"I know that boy," he cut in. "I know him. Fixed quite a few problems in his store."

"He knows you and I are going sometime, and I know he wants to go with us."

"Hell, bring him along," Lonny said. "We'll fit in the cab. And I got three tree stands up there. Things'll work out. Twenty minutes."

"Twenty."

"What?" Cal answered on the seventh ring.

"Get your ass out of bed. We're going hunting."

"Rick," he said. He moved the phone around. I imagined him sitting up in the bed that folded up into the wall.

I said, "Are you ready?"

"Listen," he said. "Work. What about work?" He was still half asleep, his voice quiet and cracked.

"Work," I said. I was standing at the window looking out, and felt the cold outside seeping through the panes of glass. That cold air hadn't been anything to me all night long. I hadn't even felt it. But now I did, and I stepped back from the window, sat down on the sofa.

"Rick?"

"Still here," I said. I thought about it, about work. I had to ride with Andros today. Go back to Cal's manager and make that sale cold turkey. Go to my independents, show Andros what I could do. Saturation. Goodwill. Help stab Mitchell in the back. Help kill him. Take his place. Hope someone didn't kill me later. I said, "Look. You said yesterday that you didn't care about work. About your market. And I don't care either. I have to get out of here. I have to get out of this place today so I won't go nuts. You come too. You go with us, with Lonny and me. He's expecting you." I was quiet, waiting for him to say something, then I said, "I don't care about sales. That's not what I care about. I'll miss a day. I won't die. Neither will you."

The line was silent a moment, then Cal said, "Let's go."

I was sitting on the front steps when Lonny pulled up. I had my hands in fists at my face, blew into them. I stood, trotted down the sidewalk to the street. Lonny popped the door open from the inside.

I climbed in. Here was that smell again, the cigarettes and burnt wood. I took it in, filled my lungs. The cab was warm; I could feel hot air blowing on my boots. The dome light hadn't lit up when I opened the door, and so all I could see of Lonny were his hands on the wheel, a cigarette burning between two fingers on his right hand, and his profile: the bill of his hunting cap, those old glasses he wore.

He put the car in gear. "Hell, buddy," he said. "What you been doing with yourself lately?"

"Working," I said.

"Ain't we all," he said, and gave a small laugh. He turned down the hill toward the Dunkin' Donuts at the intersection.

I said, "I ought to be working today, too, but I couldn't pass this up. I couldn't say no to this." I had my arms crossed.

He took a drag off the cigarette, held the smoke. He turned into the Dunkin' Donuts parking lot. "Some things just take precedence, you know?" he said. "One day out of the year. Hell. Not too much to ask of anybody." He parked the truck, then reached down under the front seat, felt around. He pulled a battered silver thermos out from under there, and then we got out, went to the door of the place.

All the women behind the counter knew him. I stood back from him a few feet, watched the three or four women walk past him, say, "Hi, Lonny," smiling and looking at him. Then the old guy back there turning donuts in the deep-fat fryer came to the glass wall separating the counter from the bakery. He tapped on the glass. Lonny turned, waved at the guy. The baker waved, a long wooden stick in each hand. He turned, went back to the fryer and the donuts.

A woman about Lonny's age stopped behind the counter. "What'll you have today, Lonny?" she said.

"Polly," Lonny said, "I want you to fill this with the blackest godamned coffee you can find." He put the thermos on the counter. "And my buddy here'll . . ." He turned, motioned to me with one hand to move closer. "Aw hell, buddy, why you standing out there in the cold?"

I moved next to him at the counter.

"My buddy Rick here," he said to Polly, "will do the choosing of the donuts. I don't know what donuts are good or what ones aren't."

Polly smiled. "Everything we have is good."

"I can tell that just by looking at you, sweetheart," Lonny said.

"That's a tired line," she said.

"So, I'm a tired man."

She laughed, and then Lonny laughed. I smiled. I ordered a dozen assorted donuts, then got out my wallet.

"No, no," he said. He pulled a wad of dollar bills from his pocket, paid for the donuts and coffee. I noticed then what he was wearing: that same down vest, the red and black plaid wool shirt, those same gray work pants.

He said good-bye to all the women. I smiled and nodded at Polly.

I gave him directions to Cal's apartment. When we got there, sky still black, streets empty, Cal was waiting on the sidewalk in front of his building. In the light from the headlights I could see he had on a complete camouflage fatigue outfit and a hunter orange cap and vest. The legs of his pants were tucked into his boots.

Lonny was laughing before he even stopped the truck. "I seen it all," he laughed. I opened my door, then moved over next to Lonny. Cal climbed in, Lonny still laughing.

"What?" he said. "What's funny, you old fart?"

"I seen it all now." He leaned over, pushed in the cigarette lighter in the dashboard. "Look at you, Mr. Hunter. All we're going to do is head out to some private, fenced-off land, sit in a tree and wait for some buck to walk up. You look so spit-polish. You look like you're heading out to bag a rhino. All you need is a cap and vest, but you got the whole goddamned camo outfit."

We all laughed. Cal shook his head. I could tell he didn't know what to say. He just laughed, shook his head.

The lighter popped. Lonny pulled it out, put it to the new cigarette he'd pulled out of his shirt pocket. He put the lighter back in, said, "Let's get out of here."

I hadn't been hunting since I was fifteen, when my uncle, my father's brother, took me. We'd gone with a few of his friends and his two sons, my cousins. They lived over in Pittsfield, and I'd met them only once or twice before.

We'd gone south and west of Pittsfield, almost to the Connecticut border, and had tried to drive deer up a ravine, me and a cousin, a boy a year younger than me, moving up one side, the other cousin, sixteen and with a thin mustache, moving up the other. We had nothing to say to each other. They'd hunted for years, and this was my first time. My uncle and his friends were somewhere else, working a hollow a couple miles away. The three of us hadn't gotten anything there in the ravine, hadn't, in fact, even gotten off a shot. But I wasn't going to tell any of this to Lonny. Or to Cal.

By the time we were on Pelham Road outside of Amherst, Cal had fallen asleep, his head against the window. He hadn't said anything after we'd laughed about his getup, only turned toward the door, crossed his arms, and started snoring.

We passed dark houses set farther and farther back from the road as we headed toward Pelham and Route 202. Lonny smoked another cigarette.

I wasn't planning to get off a shot today, either. All I wanted was to be out of the apartment, and off work. I wondered what would happen when Andros pulled up at the office, went inside and waited for me. I looked at my watch. Four thirty. I wouldn't be able to call in until six or so. By that time we would be out in the woods somewhere.

Forget it.

"So," Lonny said. "I'll bet you're trying to figure why we're heading out on second day."

I didn't even know the dates for hunting season. Today could have been the first. It could have been the last, for all I knew. Still, I nodded.

"I got this piece of property up here," he started. "Got it, jeez, some thirty-odd years ago. Real early on I found out that first day wasn't the day to go. There's so damned many hunters out that day you can't tell what's going on, who's shooting what. I knew a guy got shot by his own brother one time while they were out hunting. Shot him right through the head. The brother swore up and down he'd thought he was an eight-pointer." He stopped. We were at the end of Pelham Road. He leaned forward over the wheel, looked to his left down 202, then to the right. I tried to lean back to get out of his line of sight. It didn't matter, though; there wasn't anyone out on the road.

"So anyways," he went on after he'd turned left onto the road, "there's everybody shooting at everything. You'd think there was some kind of war going on. It took me three years of not taking home a damned thing other than a headache before I decided to try second day. And then I came up here, found myself a nice tree. I sat down against it, started waiting. And then I was just looking up, giving my neck a stretch, and happened to see what a gorgeous stand this tree would make. Perfect forks, view. So I climbed right up in the damned thing, sat down. I sat there and waited and waited, and I'll be damned if I didn't see three deer that day. First two doe, and then here comes a good-sized buck, a six-pointer, and I got him. He just walks right up to me sitting in this big old oak tree, and starts to grazing there, chomping on the mast there under the tree. He was only about twelve yards away when I plugged him. He went about forty yards and fell. Easiest hit I'd ever had. So since that day it's been second day, and it's up in the tree. Always has been."

"So why are they there?" I asked. "On your land."

"Aw, hell, I've got my ideas on this thing. I'm no natural biologist or anything like that, but I've seen enough things to get a good idea, hazard a guess." He tilted his head back a little, both hands on the steering wheel. "Hell, I think it's because the things are scared, that's what I think. My land's kind of funny-shaped.

One end of it lies real low, almost down near a stream. Then the other end of it—it's a thirty-two-acre parcel—sits way up high on a ridge. The other two ends are up high, too, sort of like a big bowl with the one side cut off where the stream sits. I've been up there all times of the year. I've been up there in snow to my waist, in thunderstorms, you name it, just to look around, see what it is these dumb animals are up to."

We'd come to a curve in the road. Lonny slowed down, turned left onto a dirt road I couldn't see until the headlights shone square on it. The road was a hard, rocky one only wide enough for the truck. Leafless branches scratched at the sides and roof. He turned off the headlights, leaving the parking lights on. We drove through empty woods with only that amber light to lead us.

"I was up here once when there was this terrible storm going on," he said, almost in a whisper. "Terrible. It was crazy. Hell, *I'm* crazy, crazy for having come up in it. It started snowing on me. This was a second day about fifteen years ago. All these clouds boil up on me, and then it starts snowing. The fastest snow I'd seen as best as I could remember. By about nine there's a couple three inches on the ground, and here I am still sitting in my tree. It's not that cold, I figure, so I'll sit and wait and see what happens. And I'm sitting and sitting, when here comes a big racker, making his way up through the snow, pawing here and there, just looking for something to eat. So I raise up my gun, I've got him in my sights, and *wham* comes this sound. It's thunder. Lightning had hit not fifty yards away. My eyes are all whited out as if I'd just stared into a flashbulb, and then I hear this creaking sound, and this tree over there just falls over, dead. Here I was in a tree holding a gun. Hell, I might as well be holding a lightning rod. Scared the holy shit out of me. I jumped out of my tree, eighteen feet right down to the snow. I ran back to the truck, climbed in, and backed down this old road right out onto 202. I never saw that damned deer take off. Hell, he was probably in Montana by the time I'd made it to the truck." We were still driving back into the woods, farther and farther, Cal still asleep, Lonny still leaning back in his seat. He had one hand on the wheel now.

It was quiet, the only sound the drum of the engine, the groan of the shocks as we dipped and rose on the rocks and hard mud. "But the queer thing of it is," Lonny whispered, "is the quiet of the whole thing. Lightning and thunder in the snow. I never saw that before. The sound was weird, like somebody banging the hell out of a bass drum that had been stuffed full with cotton or something. There wasn't any kind of echo, like comes with regular thunder. There was just the crash, and it was gone. It was just that real sound, no echoes to make it seem bigger or longer than it actually was. Just pure sound. And then that tree falling like it was in slow motion, down through branches of other trees. That sound, too. That was more a series of cracks than anything else, and when it hit the ground, there wasn't anything left. No sound at all." He paused. "Now I think about it, I'll bet you it was that sound that scared me more than anything." He straightened up in his seat now, put the other hand on the wheel again. He seemed to have started squinting. "That sound. I never heard anything like it. Probably never will. Just that one moment when it feels like you're going to die and everybody else out there in the world don't really give a damn about you and your worries."

I started squinting, too, looking for something out there in the amber light. Lonny slowed down, and then there was an old chain-link gate ahead, a cleared area before it. Lonny pulled into the area, cut the engine.

He opened his door, and cold air filled the cab. Cal woke up, put his hands on the dash. He looked around, his eyes open wide.

"Hunting," I said. "With Lonny. You remember."

Lonny was already around the truck and at Cal's door. He pulled open the door, Cal nearly falling out. "Come on, safari man," he laughed. "Let's find some wood, build a little fire to warm our bones."

Cal got out, rubbed his eyes. "This is too goddamned early for anything," he said.

"That's what my nephews said."

I'd begun to think the sun was never coming up, like this night was a year long. I was out in the woods, gathering pieces of wood, my hands numb, fingers slow as I picked up piece after piece, held them under my arm. This long night. Had I had dinner with Rose last night? Or was it the night before? And when had Andros ridden with me, and how many cases had I sold of some bogus product with no ads to back it up? And when had I tried to make love to Rose? I picked up a long branch, something I would have to break up back at the truck.

I dragged that piece behind me as I moved toward the truck; stepped over old logs, new trees, bare branches and evergreens all touching me everywhere. It was dark, and this night wasn't going to end. It had been a year ago, maybe, that I'd touched Rose, held her, felt that loose, soft flesh that meant she had given birth to something, another human being. That boy Jason, who ate a donut with two hands, and who'd thrown a frisbee out into the brush at the Quabbin.

The long branch caught on something behind me. I stopped, yanked it a couple of times. A few sticks snapped off it before the branch broke loose from whatever it was hung up on back there.

And it'd been three years, maybe five, since I'd spoken to Paige.

Through the trees I could see flashes of orange light ahead. They had already started the fire. The branch caught again. I dropped it.

Ten years since I'd seen her.

"Jesus, buddy," Lonny said. He and Cal were squatting next to the fire. They'd built it a few yards from the truck in the cleared area. The gate to what I figured must be Lonny's land was on the other side of the truck. "I didn't want you to bring back half a cord. I just wanted some kindling and crap." He had the thermos cup in his hands, steam coming up off it.

I couldn't tell how long it had been since that wedding, and since Paige had come home with the news. I didn't know when or how far back any of that was. Maybe that was somebody else. Maybe that was another person, someone I had known once. I was the one here in cold woods, a small fire in front of me, two other men down near it, both sipping at coffee, one with a thermos cup, the other with a styrofoam cup, a box of donuts on the ground between them.

"There should be a cup in under the seat," Lonny said. "Don't worry. It's not dirty. I keep extras under there."

I put the wood down, moved to the cab. I got a cup, then picked up the thermos from next to Lonny, poured myself some. I put the thermos down, then squatted next to Lonny. He and Cal were talking about something, and then Cal laughed. I laughed, too, though I hadn't even heard what Lonny had said.

I stared into the fire, both hands around the cup. I looked at that flame, looked and looked. I couldn't remember how old I was, where I lived. I tried to remember anything, anything, and then there was that toilet before me, and red water, and a piece of some small flesh of Paige and me in there, and then it swirled and swirled around in the water, more water down into it now, that flesh brushing sides of the toilet, then funneling itself down and away, and I remembered everything. Paige and that moment had been only a second ago, an instant. Paige had left me a minute ago, we'd made love at Larry and Wendy's up in Colrain only an hour ago.

I'd thought that that view from their kitchen, those hills out there, that forest almost in Vermont, had been the center of things, but it wasn't. It was that fetus in that toilet. That was the thing from which everything else had come—all pain, all grief, all sorrow.

I stood. I swallowed the coffee down hard. I said, "Let's go. It's getting late." I looked away from the fire, to the east. The bare trees stood out more now, black against a sky lighter, almost gray.

Lonny stood, said, "Head 'em up, boys." He started kicking dirt over the fire, one hand in his pocket, the other still holding the cup.

Cal had a half-eaten powdered-sugar donut in his hand. "The donuts," he said. "Slow down. I'm still eating."

I started kicking dirt over the fire then, too. Cal was watching for some answer from Lonny, but none came. He quickly finished the donut, closed the box and picked it up, then started in on the fire.

When it was out, Lonny went to the cab, pulled an old black flashlight from the glove compartment, then pulled the seat-back forward. He turned the flashlight on, shined it behind the seat. There, mounted on the cab wall behind the seat, was a gun rack with three shotguns.

"That top one's mine," he said. "You two can fight over the other ones. They're both twelve-gauge pump Winchesters. Mine's a twelve-gauge Browning. I don't know. I just like it more for some reason." He reached in, pulled off our two guns and handed them to us. The steel was cold in my hand, felt as if my skin might stick to it. Then he reached back under the seat, pulled out a box of shells. "These are slugs," he said. "I don't shoot buckshot. Too messy. Here's five apiece." He gave us the slugs. We started loading our guns, but Lonny said, "Wait. Hold on to them until we get up in the stand." He stopped, looked at us. I couldn't see the look on his face, but knew what he was thinking. He was quiet, then said, "I just don't want to get plugged on the trail is all."

I put the slugs in my coat pocket, then turned. I wanted to get out of there. I went around the front end of the truck to the gate, moved to open it.

"Whoa, buddy," Lonny said. "What are you doing?"

"Going. This is it, right?"

"Hell no, son. What do you think? You think I'm going to pull up here in my truck, build a fire and jabber all morning so deer can figure exactly where we are? You think then we'll just walk over a few feet, wait for deer? My land's another mile back in here."

His gun was crooked in his arms now.

"And I've got a few instructions for you two," he said. "First thing is, I don't know you two boys from Adam. I know you, Calvin, as a glorified stockboy. And you, Rick, you've got problems with your wife and your toilet. That's all I know about you two.

So if you've never hunted before, don't let me know. Just don't do anything stupid like point your gun at me. And think a second before you shoot at anything. Don't be a fool."

He went to the hood, leaned against it. The fire was out, but I could see his silhouette there, Cal a few feet off from him, his gun crooked just as Lonny's was. I held mine the same way: arms crossed, gun pointing at the ground in front of me.

Cal cleared his throat then, said, "Don't worry about me, boss. I've been hunting. Plenty of times, believe me. I've hunted for—"

"Oh knock off that shit," Lonny cut in. "I'll believe you're a regular big-game hunter so long as you don't shoot me."

I thought I could see Cal look down there in the dark. He moved the tip of his boot in a small circle on the ground.

"My land up there's all fenced off and posted no trespassing. There shouldn't be anyone waltzing in on us. We'll be coming up the back of the ridge that sits at the top of the parcel. Then we'll go through an old gate, and then we'll hit the top of the ridge, and there'll be two big old oak trees I'll show you two. Two oaks. One of us will sit in one tree, the other two in the other. There's some two-by-fours nailed into the trunks to help us into the trees, and then up in it you'll find a chair of sorts. Not really a chair, but more a piece of plywood with a cushion and a little swatch of carpeting nailed to it."

He stopped, uncrossed one arm and fished a cigarette out of his shirt pocket, then a lighter from his pants pocket. He lit the cigarette, dragged long on it. The tip seemed as bright as anything I'd seen in days.

"I'm telling you all of this stuff," he said, "because once we get away from the truck here there won't be any talking. Nothing. Understand?"

"Yes," I said.

Cal said, "Sure."

"These two trees we'll be sitting in aren't too far apart, but each of the chairs is facing in a different direction. Each of them is facing down into the bowl, so as to get the deer as he comes up from the stream at the bottom, but the way each stand is situated no one will be shooting at the same deer. You just keep your eyes open on what's in front of you, and watch for what comes up through the trees. No trick shots. If he's in front of you, take him. Nobody shoot for something that's not in front of you. I can tell you that one of us will get something here today. I'm doing this just for the sport, the fun. So it don't have to be me, but there's only been four times in the last thirty years I didn't bring something home."

He hadn't been speaking straight at us, but to the air around and above us. He knew what he was talking about. He knew what had to be done here. From the steady tone of his voice and how he held his head, that cigarette still in his mouth and burned down to the filter, I could see this was more important to him than plumbing would ever be.

He went back to the cab, shined the flashlight behind the seat again, brought out an old knapsack. He pushed the seat back, put the knapsack on the floor, then put his gun on the seat. He untied the knapsack, pulled out two hunter orange caps and vests.

He turned to me. "Here, Rick. Buddy. You put on this hat and vest, and try your best to look like Captain Deerhunter here." He nodded at Cal, and I could see him smiling there in the gray before dawn, the flashlight in his hand pointing at the ground. He turned it off, and the night seemed lighter. He said, "But just don't plug me later on."

I took the cap, put it on. It was too big, and sat flat on my head, the lining inside coming down below my ears and onto my neck. Then I pulled on the vest.

Lonny looked at me. "Only a kid," he said, and shook his head.

Cal, next to me, laughed.

Lonny looked at him. "Don't you laugh. It's you I'm worrying about. You and your camo duds. I'm surprised you didn't just go ahead and put on the warpaint."

Cal looked down, quiet, and Lonny put on his hat and vest, then picked up the knapsack.

"I've got the knife in here we'll use to dress whatever it is we get. You dress what you get. Don't expect me to do the dirty work for you. I've got a piece of rope in this old day pack, and some paper towels, too. We'll break for lunch probably around eleven thirty or so, if we haven't already got something. Let's grab a donut, eat it, then get out of here."

Cal turned, picked up the box. He opened it, and we each took one. Lonny said, "I came up here just the day before yesterday, looked around. You boys follow close on me. We should be there and waiting before it gets light. Overcast this morning, that gives us a few extra minutes." He took the last bite of his donut, finished off his coffee, then got his gun from the cab. Cal and I still held our guns, tried to eat the donut and drink our coffee with one hand.

Lonny said, "That's it."

The trail was not a difficult one. You could tell by the trees and brush growing alongside it that the trail had been used for years: the ground was hard, dry dirt except for dead leaves. Lonny was first, then me, then Cal. I wondered what Cal was thinking about; it seemed obvious to me he'd never been hunting before: his clothes, his eagerness to let us know he knew what was going on. That last fact scared me, that he thought he knew what he was doing. I imagined us side-by-side in the tree, guns loaded, Cal holding his in some strange way so that he accidentally popped the trigger, shooting me. We came to a low branch, and I pulled it back, held it for him behind me. I looked at him, wondered if I even knew this man.

I wondered what Lonny was thinking, too, what he thought of these two greenhorns accompanying him to what I knew he must have regarded as sacred ground. He'd called me and asked me to go. That was something. I'd been the one to invite Cal along. Anything that would happen because of Cal would be my fault.

The trail weaved between larger and larger trees now, fewer

low branches, more open ground. It took on height, too, heading up the back of the ridge at an angle, cutting across the hill. We were moving slowly, Lonny taking measured, soft steps, his head moving from side to side, looking. I kept my eyes on him, though. I didn't want to see anything. I wanted to walk, and to be here in this cold with these two men who didn't, really, know me, and who expected nothing from me.

As we neared the crest I could hear Cal breathing hard behind me, and when we got to the top he was puffing. I looked back at him. He had put his gun on the ground, had both hands on his knees. Lonny turned then, too, saw him. We stopped.

"Just a few seconds," Cal puffed.

"Be quiet," Lonny whispered. He stood a few feet ahead of me, still looking around. Down below, in the direction we had come, were gray and black folds of land. Nothing else.

Cal leaned over, picked up his gun. "I'm okay," he whispered.

I turned. Lonny was already gone.

I moved quickly to catch up with him, but by the time I was behind him he had stopped, turned toward me. I looked past him, saw a gray wooden gate behind him. A three-strand barbed wire fence went off in both directions from the gate, and I could make out orange and black No Trespassing signs nailed to a couple of trees.

Cal caught up with us a minute later. He was still breathing hard.

"You didn't tell me we were going mountain climbing," he whispered between breaths.

"Cal, you take the tree with the single stand," Lonny whispered as if Cal had said nothing. "I'll point it out to you, you climb it and sit back and wait. Rick, you come with me." He turned to the gate, lifted a wooden latch that made no noise, pulled the gate open. He signaled for Cal and me to go through, then closed the gate behind us. He looked around again, Cal and I looking at him, and then he led us over the crest along the same trail. On the other side of the ridge the growth had become heavier, the trail less worn.

We came to a big oak, maybe six or eight feet around. "Cal," Lonny whispered, "this is yours."

Cal came around me, went to the tree.

"Give me your gun," Lonny whispered. Cal gave it to him. Foot-long two-by-fours had been nailed to the trunk, just as Lonny had said. Cal put his foot on the first board, said, "Happy hunting, boys." He grinned.

I smiled, looked at Lonny. He only held Cal's gun, looked up into the tree, waiting.

Cal slowly mounted the tree. The two-by-fours stopped about eight feet off the ground, where the tree branched into three sections. Cal got to the fork, sat in the crotch. Lonny handed up the gun. Cal took it, then disappeared around the other side.

With his hand Lonny motioned to our left, and I followed him some thirty yards over to another tree, this one even bigger. I gave him my gun, then started up the tree.

The boards went up about fifteen feet. I hadn't thought of how to get the guns from Lonny until I'd reached the top and had moved out onto a thick branch perpendicular to the trunk. I looked down then, and here came Lonny, both guns in hand. I couldn't see how he was moving from one rung to the next with only one hand, but he was doing it. His movement was quick, silent, and then he was at the top two-by-four. He handed me my gun.

"You're on the right, I'm on the left," he said. He stepped up onto the branch I sat on, then leaned around the trunk to the left, disappeared.

I moved closer to the trunk, then stood, stepped to the right to a fork off the trunk. There at the crotch was mounted a square carpeted seat. The gun in one hand, I leaned toward the fork, and then I brought my left leg over, straddled the branch. I was sitting on the cushion, then leaned back. I felt around with my feet for something to rest them on, found another board nailed crosswise onto a branch below. I put my feet there.

It was a comfortable place to be. I wasn't cold; the walk up had warmed me without making me sweat. I looked around. I could make out more detail than before. The sky was still overcast, but lighter now, gray all the way across. No sunrise in the east, only light above that illuminated the cloud sheet from horizon to horizon.

A few feet in front of me, the limb I sat on forked into two branches heading straight up. Beyond that, through the fork and on either side, lay the forest, a short, cleared area a few yards out, the ground sloping down and away from me. Everything—the bare trees, the evergreens, the dead leaves on the forest floor— was gray there in the twilight. No color. This night was ending.

I loaded the gun, then put it across my lap and crossed my arms over it, settled back against the tree.

In my dream someone was whispering to me, and I was falling from somewhere, my feet and legs tucked up, close to my chest. I was falling, and then I woke up, shot both eyes open as I hit whatever it was I had been falling toward in my dream.

I was there in the tree, straddling that branch.

"Rick," Lonny whispered again.

I blinked, turned to his voice. I couldn't see him, and so brought my leg over the branch, leaned closer to his side of the tree.

He was sitting on the branch at the top of the ladder, the thermos in his hand. He was unscrewing the cap. "Want some?"

"Won't they smell it?" I whispered.

He shook his head. "We're up too high," he whispered. He poured coffee into the lid, handed it to me. "The wind's always up from the stream anyways."

I sipped at it. I whispered, "You know, somebody told me we couldn't talk."

"If we whisper loud enough they'll hear us. If we whisper quiet, they won't. It's been an hour up here. I need a break, you need a break." He put out his hand for the cup. I took another sip, gave it to him.

He took a drink, winced at the heat. "Calvin over there scares me. He's greener than cowshit. That scares me." He nodded his chin to the other tree. I turned, looked over there. I could see only one of Cal's legs, the foot tapping on the branch it rested on. "He does that tapping stuff any harder and the deer'll think there's somebody up here sending Morse code."

"I'm sorry I invited him," I whispered. "I just thought—"

"No, no. Don't worry about it. Besides, he'll never nail me from where I'm sitting. You're the one closest to his line of fire." He smiled, took another sip.

I said, "You never told me why it is the deer come up here. You said they were scared. But why come up here?"

Lonny still smiled. He looked at me, shook his head. "You're just as green as he is."

"I am," I said, and I thought of what Rose had said about Cal and me. "I'll tell you. I've been hunting once. Down around Pittsfield. I was a driver, up a ravine. Didn't see anything."

"That's what driving'll do for you up here. Forest you either stalk or sit. I'll sit any day." He handed me the cup. "What happens," he whispered and pointed down the hill, "is that the deer hang out down there near that stream. That's their turf, their home. All their regular trails are down there."

I listened to him, both my hands around the cup.

"So first day comes, what happens?" he whispered. You could see in his eyes this joy, this clear joy in talking of woods, deer, sky. "All these hunters start banging away, scares the hell out of Mr. Buck and company, and they go tearing off into the hills. Right up into my land." He put his hands together. "My land which, of course, is fenced off and posted." He reached for the cup. I gave it to him, and he poured more coffee into it. "Every once in a while I'll come out here on first day with my gun, but not to shoot deer. I like to keep my eye on the property here. One time I was here, down there at the bottom property line. I'm just sitting there next to a tree, figured I'd be quiet, give a listen and see if anyone would try anything. Lo and behold up stalks this boy, some fifteen-year-old punk with hair down on his shoulders and into his face. He doesn't even have his orange on. Quiet as you please he comes up to my fence, then leans a little on the wire, puts his gun to his shoulder, then fires right into my land. I'm getting so old it takes me longer to get up from where I'm squatting next to the tree than it does for this little punk to climb over the barbed wire. So he hops down, and then he sees me. He stops in his tracks, and I say, 'Leave it.' Then this punk, this little kid maybe one-fourth my age, tells me to go fuck myself. Can you imagine that? Can you see that?" He shook his head.

I put out my hand for the cup. He gave it to me. I said, "They're dangerous these days. Kids."

"Everybody is, buddy," he whispered. "Everybody's dangerous these days. I told him he was on private property, posted No Trespassing no less. And then he tells me that it's his, he shot it, he'd been watching it for over half an hour. And then he turned and just headed on up to where his deer lay. That was when I took my gun, fired it off into the air. He stops, turns to me ever-so-slowly. Know what I said?" He looked up at me, that same grin he'd given me telling me about the ceiling falling in.

I shook my head. "What?"

" 'Go fuck yourself, son,' I says, and he takes off. I watched him climb over the fence and take off running. I guess you just have to use their own lingo on them. The deer he'd dropped was just a little guy, little spikes. Made good eating, though." He silently chuckled, then stopped, looked down the hill. "But why they're scared," he whispered more quietly now, "is that that stream down there, that drainage is their home. They take off into my land, and it's usually on some old escape trails. Though they're up here during the year, this area just isn't as familiar to them. All that shooting going on down there runs them right up here. That fear in them, that's the death of them." He paused, moved his head from side to side. I looked down the slope, tried to find what it was he saw. I saw nothing. "They're a lot like humans in that regard. They get scared, they go running off somewheres where they don't know the ground as well, don't know the smells. Then they just run smack into their deaths, in a deer's case a mess of tasty acorns sitting beneath a couple of big oak trees. These dumb animals are just like humans. They get spooked, leave for parts unknown, and that's the death of them. That taking out for no other good reason than they're scared of what's behind them." He paused, his eyes on something out there. "Of course with deer there's guns and bullets and smoke involved here, so their running makes a lot more sense."

He froze then, his eyes still on something down the slope. "That's it," he whispered, "no more talk." He finished off the coffee, put the lid on.

He moved back to his seat, and then I stood on the branch, made my way back to mine. The seat was cold again, but I had the coffee in me.

By ten thirty I hadn't seen anything. Cal's foot kept tapping, but no stronger than when Lonny had pointed him out to me. A couple of times he had leaned over to where he could see me, given a little wave. I waved, and then he sat back. Once I had seen the barrel of his gun rise. I tensed up, ready for the crack of sound through these woods, but a minute or so later the gun was lowered. Cal leaned forward, waved again.

The warmth from the coffee had gone a long time ago; the air around me was colder than when we had settled in. The sky hadn't gotten any lighter, either, the thick cloud layer holding out light and warmth.

I wondered if I'd lost my job yet or not, if, when Andros had waited until, say, seven, then called my apartment to find no one there, he'd fired me on the spot, or if he were waiting to hear from me. I would have to sell him, I knew. There was some story I could tell him, some lie about going to the hospital or someone I knew dying. Whether he bought it or not depended on how well I could lie to him. He was a salesmen, and would watch for small gestures: the blink of an eye, the hand in the pocket. No small move would go unnoticed, unaccounted for. I could try and sell Andros some lie. And that would be the best I could do, I knew. To try.

I thought of Paige then, and that story, that true story I had told Rose only last night. Eleven hours ago. I thought of those gestures Paige had made and what she had said as we moved through the house, about the piano, and our living in some palace in Longmeadow. So maybe I wasn't a salesman, not being able to spot her lies. Or maybe she hadn't been lying, maybe she really was that person she was pretending to be, and then I thought I didn't know her. I didn't even know who she was any more. And, I thought, who *could* I know?

My feet were numb now, the temperature dropping even more. The clouds seemed even darker. I wondered when we would break for lunch, head back to the truck and build another fire. That was what I wanted.

My gun was across my lap, my arms crossed with my hands in my armpits, when I saw some movement ahead of me, off in the trees below.

At first it'd seemed like only some small push of wind on the slope below. The trees were thick down there, evergreen and hardwood mixed all through. But there was no wind, and then there was the movement again, the soft scratch of dead leaves. I sat up slowly, leaned forward. I glanced at Cal. He was sitting back, his foot still tapping. I turned toward Lonny. I couldn't see him for the tree.

The sound came from straight in front of me, one small break of leaves at a time, this deer measuring its steps, meting them out.

It would be for me, I knew.

From behind a tree some forty yards away came the deer. I could only see its body and legs, the head lost in the foliage. It wasn't a big one, as far as I could tell. It took its small steps, went behind another tree and out again, slowly making its way back and forth up the slope. It seemed to take hours between each step it made, waiting, waiting. Then I glimpsed its head through the branches as it dipped, took in the smell, slowly bobbed its head. It had gotten a few yards closer.

I brought my gun up, though I'd not wanted to. It was what was expected of me here in these woods.

I put the butt to my shoulder, closed one eye and looked down the barrel. I pointed the gun to where I'd seen the deer last, but it had gone.

I looked for it, the gun still at my shoulder, found it moving straight at me, a few yards to the right. I couldn't get a clear shot at it with all the branches between us. It was still moving toward me, and I watched it with that one eye. I would let it come as close as I could, and hope something might let it catch on to us up here. But still it came.

I had my finger ready on the trigger, anticipated the recoil. I closed and opened my eye once, twice, three times.

The deer cleared the foliage then, was only twenty-five yards away and nosing up to the acorns there on the ground.

I blinked one last time, resolved to firing not because I wanted to, but because I had to. Because I had to prove something here, and I saw I was no different from Cal after all, that Rose had been right all along.

I started squeezing down the trigger, ready for the blast that would break everything.

"Don't," I thought I heard from my left. It was Lonny, barely whispering. "Don't shoot her," he breathed. "A doe."

I closed both eyes, brought down the gun. I thought I felt sweat trickle down the small of my back. I took a shallow breath, turned.

Lonny was crouched on the branch at the top of the ladder. He wasn't looking at me, but was watching the deer, his eyes squinted behind his glasses.

I looked back down. The deer started in on the acorns, its black nose pushing a few around, then taking them up with its tongue. I saw for the first time that there were no antlers, no spikes. And I saw it was a beautiful animal, harmless and hungry. It took in the acorns, then slowly raised its head, turned as though to some sound or smell, the acorns moving around in its mouth like so many marbles. I could see its eye then, large and brown, just the touch of white at the outside corner.

A gunshot sounded then, the deer hit. The side of its head

and that eye I'd watched exploded, pink bursting like a firecracker, pieces of skull and hide sent up into the air.

The deer stood a moment, its legs wavering, then buckling beneath it. Before it had hit the ground, though, another shot was fired, hitting the ground a few yards beyond the deer. Dead leaves and dirt flew into the air.

"Son of a bitch," Lonny whispered, then said, "Son of a bitch. Son of a bitch." The gun in one hand, he took hold of the branch he crouched on, then let himself down. He hung there in the air a moment, then dropped to the ground, a good fifteen feet. He hit, then stood up. "Son of a bitch," he said.

I turned to the other tree. Cal still had the gun up to his shoulder, ready to fire again. He was lying out on a branch, his legs hanging down on either side. He was smiling. Lonny was already moving across the clearing between us. He was limping.

Cal shouted, "Thought you clowns were never going to shoot. Why didn't you?"

Lonny said nothing. Halfway to Cal's tree he let his gun drop to the ground.

I watched. I hadn't moved.

The smile left Cal's face as Lonny neared the tree. Cal brought his gun down, sat up on the branch, his eyes on Lonny. Finally Lonny made it to the base of the tree. He had his hands in fists at his side.

"Come down here, you son of a bitch. You goddamn son-of-a-bitch idiot. Come down here."

"Look, Lonny, if—" Cal started.

"Come down here," Lonny said.

Cal brought one leg over the branch, started down the ladder. He handed his gun down to Lonny, who took it, leaned it against the tree.

Cal got to the bottom, dusted off his hands. "If I took some-body's deer, I'm sorry. Really. It's just that it looked like nobody was going to—"

"Shut up," Lonny said, and Cal went quiet. I could see the look on his face: his mouth slack, his eyes open wide. He had no idea what was going on. "What does that deer look like to you, huh? What do you think that fucking animal is over there? Is it a buck or is it a doe? Which, you son of a bitch? Buck or doe?"

Cal didn't say anything, looked past Lonny to where the deer lay.

"It's a doe, you idiot," Lonny said. "A doe. Good-sized, no antlers. Is that a clue? You don't shoot does. Anybody ever tell you that? You ever heard of that?"

Cal looked at the ground, put his hands together. "I've read before where you can—"

"I don't give a shit what you read. I don't give a good goddamn what you read anywhere. You just don't shoot a doe, whether it's against the law or not. You don't shoot a doe." He moved closer, his face a foot or so from Cal's. "And what the hell you think's going to happen once you blow away the fucking skull of the animal? You think he's going to trot away, go lick his wounds somewhere else? What's the idea of firing twice at the thing? Couldn't you see you destroyed the damn thing the first time? I feel like hitting you," Lonny said then. He clenched his fists tighter. "I feel like punching you one right in the nose."

Cal looked up at him. His mouth was closed now, his jaw set. He moved his hands to Lonny's chest, gave him a quick shove back. "Listen, you old shit," he said. "I didn't know. All right? You can forget that shit about hitting me. Just forget it, old man."

Lonny raised his fist, held it in the air a moment.

"Knock it off," I shouted down at them. "Just knock it off. He didn't know, Lonny. He didn't know." I heard my voice in those woods. It was quieter than I thought it would have been. "Just knock it off," I shouted again, louder.

Lonny turned around. "You," he shouted up at me, his fist in the air. "You. You would have shot the damn thing if I hadn't told you not to. I brought a couple jerks with me. A couple fools."

I climbed down from the tree, the gun in my hand. I leaned back from the last few rungs, dropped to the ground. I propped my gun against the tree.

Lonny was over at the deer. He stood with his hands in his

pockets, his shoulders hunched. He was staring at the deer. I went over next to him, stood there. I said, "It's my fault. The whole thing."

He said nothing, only turned, walked around to the other side of the deer, stood there.

Cal was next to me now. We three stood looking at the deer, the air around us growing colder, the sky darker.

The deer lay on its side, and looked as if it were asleep, unharmed; the gaping hole in its head lay against the ground. Its right eye was still open, though clouded. A stain of red deepening to brown gathered on the ground around the head. Its legs were bent at the joints, as if in motion, running yet flat and still there on the ground.

Lonny, his hands still in his pockets, touched the deer's neck with his boot, then stepped back.

The deer's legs kicked then, first slowly, as if in water, then thrashing the air. Cal and I, startled, moved back a few feet, and then the deer's body rose in a great spasm, lifted itself off the ground a few inches as its muscles rolled from neck to flanks. The head stayed on the ground, barely moved, and then the legs kicked again, slower and slower, until it gave out.

I looked at Cal. He was sweating, hair on his forehead and neck matted down. I felt my legs shaking, my hands in fists in my pockets.

"She's gone," Lonny said. He hadn't looked up. "You shot her, Cal. Now you dress her. Show us what you learned in your books."

Cal leaned over the tailgate, let the gutted deer slip from his shoulders to the bed of Lonny's pickup. The sky, bruised over, had made his hunter orange vest even brighter. Blood dripped down the orange, brown yet still wet.

I had offered to help him.

Lonny had gone to the knapsack after he'd told Cal to dress it, pulled a length of gray nylon rope and a knife from inside. He'd dropped the rope next to the deer, handed the knife across to Cal without looking at him.

That was when I'd offered. I'd stooped down to pick up the rope, but Cal stepped on it. I looked up at him. He nodded his head for me to step back. I did.

Lonny had had both hands in his back pockets, watched while Cal dragged the deer over to his tree. He stopped, threw one end of the rope over a low, thick limb, then took the other end, tied it around the hind hoofs, hoisted the deer aloft. He tied the rope off around the trunk.

He took the knife from its sheath, went to the deer. He pulled back the head, then slit the throat where the jaw and neck met. Blood flowed freely from the deer; steam rose from the ground below where the blood formed a small puddle, then seeped into the dirt and leaves. Cal looked as if he knew what he was doing, and Lonny and I moved in closer, Lonny still with his hands in his back pockets, still silent.

Cal then untied the rope, let the deer fall to the ground. He untied the hind legs, put the loop around the deer's neck, then hoisted it up again. Cal looked at Lonny with this face I'd never seen before. He looked like some fat little boy proud of what he'd done. Just some kid.

He turned back to the deer and pushed the knifepoint into its belly. Slowly he moved the knife up and down, then stopped, turned to us. He was smiling.

Lonny took a step back. I turned, looked at him, wondered why. I stepped back, too.

Cal pushed the knife in deeper and started gently sawing up. He cut a few inches, and from the corner of my eye I saw Lonny look down, the bill of his cap point to the ground, when a gush of blood and shit and urine burst from inside the deer onto Cal's hands and forearms.

He quickly pulled the knife out, fell back onto the dirt. He looked at his hands. "Oh God," he said.

The smell was tremendous and awful, the warm blood and urine odor hanging there in the cold air like heat from a fire. I gagged, put my hand to my throat. Cal, the knife in one hand, got back to his knees, looked at the ground for a few minutes.

Lonny said, "Better hurry. She'll spoil quick now."

Things had gotten even messier after that, Cal cutting into organ after organ, shit and urine and blood pouring onto his hands. I'd watched him, wanting to help. I'd watched his eyes as he worked, couldn't tell if the glistening there was tears or sweat.

Lonny threw an old green tarp over the deer in the bed. "I'll be goddamned if I want anyone to spot us with this on our hood," he said to no one.

Cal said nothing, climbed into the bed, moved up to the wall against the cab, sat down. He crossed his arms. Though Lonny'd brought a roll of paper towels with him in the knapsack, Cal had refused, his white hands marbled now with dried blood. Lonny was at the cab. He put the guns back on the rack, then stuffed our hats and vests back in the knapsack.

I slammed the tailgate shut, stood there a moment. I said,

"You sure you want to ride back here?" I looked at the sky above the black tips of the trees. "Snow soon."

He turned his head from me, looked off into the woods. He said, "Positive." He rolled his sleeves down, crossed his arms again. He wouldn't look at me.

Lonny pushed the seat back into place, climbed into the cab.

I came around the bed, got into the cab. Lonny started the engine, and the truck coughed a couple of times. He put his arm on top of the seat, looked over his shoulder, then backed into some bushes. He put it in forward, the gears grinding as he shoved the stick, a black metal rod with no ball, into first, started down the road toward 202.

We got to the highway, and Lonny leaned forward again, looked both ways. There were no cars. He pulled out.

I glanced back through the cab window, saw Cal's hair flying around. It must have been thirty degrees out there.

I said, "You didn't have to ride him so hard." I looked at Lonny. "It was a mistake."

He reached into his shirt pocket, pulled out a cigarette. He leaned over, pushed in the lighter.

"Don't I know it," he said.

It wasn't until he'd finished his second cigarette, the warm cab dusted with smoke, that he spoke again. He said, "In regards to your question."

I turned to him. "What question?"

He put the blinker on, turned right onto Pelham Road. The cigarette hung from the corner of his mouth. "The one you really wanted to ask me. The question you followed me out into the hall of your apartment building to ask me." The cigarette bobbed up and down as he spoke, ash breaking off and scattering on the front of his vest.

I turned back to the windshield. "I asked if you hunted."

"You're right," he said. He seemed to soften then. He drove with one hand on the bottom of the steering wheel. He leaned his head to one side. "That's what you asked, but that's not all you were asking about. So, in regards to your question, I wouldn't know what to do, what to tell you. I never been married. I wouldn't know how to live with a woman, really. I came pretty close a couple times, awful damn close, but like they say, that's another story." He gave a kind of laugh then, not for me, but for himself.

We were coming closer and closer to town; those houses that had disappeared into the woods on our way out were moving back to the road now.

I said nothing, held my hands in my lap. The heat was on full blast, my feet sweating inside my boots.

"But that was something else you wanted, too, wasn't it," he went on. "You wanted me to tell you more stories. Fact of the matter is that, since I've never been married, I got no stories along those lines for you. No wisdom to impart, so to speak. But one thing. One thing." He reached into his shirt pocket again, felt around for another cigarette. He pulled out an empty pack, crumpled it and tossed it on the floorboard.

"In the glove box," he said. "Open it up."

I opened it. He had five or six packs of cigarettes in there. I took one, tore off the cellophane, peeled back the foil top. I gave it to him.

"Thanks, buddy," he said. He had the smallest trace of a grin on his face. He wasn't looking at me, but at the road.

"What?" I said. "What thing?"

He said, "One thing is, though, that you got to have the stories to tell. You have to. You have to share the stories you got, or you'll die." He paused, slowly leaned over and pushed in the lighter again. He waited for it to pop, then took it, lit the cigarette.

I looked at him, then at the road, at the homes. Traffic was picking up now. We rolled down into Amherst, stopped at the light. The streets were jammed with people all bundled up against the cold.

"They all have stories," he said, and I swallowed hard, looked at him. He was watching the people. Slowly I turned back to the crowd. "All of them," he said.

The light changed. We turned left, passed the commons, then turned right, back onto Route 9 and down the hill into Hadley.

"Cal, too, no doubt you know. I give him an hour, maybe less, before he turns what happened today into some grand story about ⌐ ⌐erior hunting skills. Either that or some sob story about ⌐ow ⌐ ⌐ Lonny the plumber really is. I've dealt with him enough times to know about him and his stories."

I turned to him. "What about you? What about today, the story of what happened back there?"

"I don't think I'll tell it too soon," he said quickly, and I knew he'd already thought over my question a long time before I'd ever asked it. I imagined he'd thought about the story of what happened from the very moment that deer had fallen.

We drove past the mall, the parking lot packed.

"Christmas shoppers," he said. "Already piling into the stores. I remember when this was all fields. Not long ago."

He turned to me, grinned. "But ⌐at's another story, right, Rick?"

I looked at him, smiled. "Right."

We were quiet until we were in Northampton and under the railroad bridge, waiting for the light. Lonny said, "So, you're coming back to my place and help carve this up, aren't you?"

I said, "No," surprised at how quickly I answered, and I wondered if I hadn't already answered his question in my mind, decided long before what exactly it was I wanted to do. "You just take me home, if you don't mind. You could drop me off on King, if you wanted."

"Taking you home's no chore," he said.

I looked back through the window. Cal hadn't moved.

We pulled up in front of the apartment. Lonny put his arm up on the back of the seat. His other hand was on top of the steering wheel, smoke drifting up off the cigarette he held in that hand. "You sure you don't want to come over? Maybe watch Cal try his hand at butchering?"

"Thanks," I said, "but there's something that has to be done." I climbed out of the cab. The cold air hit me then, cut into my neck and face and hands. I leaned back into the cab. I said, "I hope it'll make a good story someday."

He grinned again, then laughed out loud. He flicked the filter with his thumb, sent ashes to the floor. "You tell 'em," he said. "You tell 'em, buddy."

I closed the door, then turned, put my hands on the cold steel of the bed.

Cal looked at me, his jaw clenched in the cold.

I said, "It's warm in the cab."

He smiled, the muscles in his face relaxing. "But I smell like shit and piss and blood."

"He's smelled worse."

He glanced back into the cab, then slowly stood. There were spots of blood everywhere: on his face, his fatigues, his vest, but I knew him. This was Cal.

He hopped out of the bed, opened the door. He stood there a moment, looking at me. "See you at work?"

"Maybe," I said.

He looked at me a moment longer, then raised a bloody hand, gave a sort of salute. He grinned, climbed into the cab.

Lonny gave it the gas, and they were gone.

I turned to the apartment building, looked up to my black window, but there was nothing for me there now. There never had been, not without Paige.

I had the car keys in my pocket. I looked up to the sky, at that even shade of ash gray. I closed my eyes, took in a huge breath of cold air, and felt pinpoints of ice on my nose, my cheeks, my eyelids. Snow.

I opened my eyes. Nothing was different. Nothing around me had changed. Only now I knew what to do. I'd walked the Quabbin, lived there in those dead towns. Now I'd surfaced for air.

I went over to the car, got in. I started it up, drove off without letting the engine warm up so that it stalled twice before I made it to the corner. At the bottom of the hill I pulled into the Dunkin' Donuts, got a large coffee. I looked for the women Lonny and I had seen this morning, but they were all gone. This was a whole new crew, all young girls, teenagers. None smiled, said anything.

I got into the car, put the coffee between my thighs.

I headed south on the interstate, snow falling steadily now. I passed through Springfield, the river flat, black. Freeway lamps were already on, the sky had grown so dark. Snow continued, had started collecting on the road by the time I'd crossed the Connecticut border. Tractor trailers followed by huge whirlwinds of snow led me through Hartford, and then I was on the Merritt, a moment later at the roadside stop where everything had happened.

I slowed, pulled into the stop. An attendant came out.

I got out of the car, said, "Fill it."

He nodded, the hood of his green parka drawn tight around his face. He put the nozzle into the tank.

I walked over to the brick building. I went to the door of the women's room, stood at it a moment. Then I walked to the end of the sidewalk where the grassy area had been last summer. Where I'd watched a man in cut-offs play with his dog while my wife miscarried.

The area was covered now with the thinnest sheet of new snow, as white as it would ever be. I watched that small field, and waited for that ghost, my ghost, to appear.

But nothing happened. Snow only fell from the sky to the ground before me, filled the woods, covered rooftops.

I left the wipers on through the tunnel at New Haven. A helicopter lifted off at the Sikorsky plant as I passed, the dark green machine rising up into the snow-filled sky as if it ruled the world. Traffic thickened at White Plains, stopped on the Tappan Zee. It seemed there were twice as many tolls as there had ever been on the parkway south, traffic slow until I was over the Raritan.

I got off the parkway, wound toward her parents' house along a road that could have been in Massachusetts, and then I was there, moving up the driveway, freshly plowed as if they'd known I was coming.

It was dark now, snow still falling. I got out of the car, left the engine running in case she would have none of me.

I went up the driveway to the porch, past wood stacked under the eaves. Light shone through curtains onto the porch, quickly covering over with more snow. I smelled chimney smoke.

I knocked on the glass storm door. I waited, heard nothing, rang the doorbell.

The door opened then. Light spilled out onto me, the snow, this world outside, and Paige stood before me.

I had my hands in my pockets. I looked down, then back at her. She had on a white turtleneck wool sweater, a sweater I'd seen her in a thousand times before. She had on an old pair of jeans and wool socks.

She looked at me, one hand on the door, the other at her side. I looked at her through the glass of the storm door, looked at her eyes, and I could see she was waiting for me.

I could begin with a ghost. Or with Vermont. Or with a bath-room on the Merritt. A plumber. An open house. But I had to start. Now.

I spoke.

About the Author

BRET LOTT's short fiction has appeared in a variety of publications, among them the anthology of important young writing, *20 Under 30*. The recipient of several awards, including the PEN Syndicated Award, Bret Lott was born in Los Angeles and lives in Mount Pleasant, South Carolina, with his wife, Melanie, and their two sons, Zebulun and Jacob. He is writer-in-residence and assistant professor of English at the College of Charleston. His second novel will be published next year.